A TRUE STORY

A BOLD GAMBLE
AT LAKE TAHOE

DORESA BANNING

Published by Houdini Publishing

Cover Design by Shay Swetech, WoundUp Studio

Edited by Darlena Kellogg
Kathy Berry
Barbara Hunt
Marti Benjamin

ISBN: 978-1-7336021-1-2 (paperback, 2019)
ISBN: 978-1-7336021-2-9 (e-book, 2019)

ACKNOWLEDGEMENTS

My wholehearted thanks goes to Larry Dardick, my beloved constant and incurable solver, whose enduring support means always giving me free rein to pursue my ambitions and ideas and talking me away from the cliff when necessary.

To the gracious, generous and "Get It Done" Geno Munari, my business role model, whose enthusiasm for writing and life are contagious, and to his company, Houdini Publishing, for magically transforming my words into a tangible form.

To the bevy of editor friends whose comments and critiques only improved the final product and whose genuine encouragement motivated me. They are Darlena Kellogg, my compassionate and silently strong sister, blessed with literary genes; the inspiring Kathy Berry, a published author and fellow First Class Girl Scout; the delightful Barbara Hunt, a like-minded spirit and grammar obsessive; and the wise Marti Benjamin, a deep thinker with refreshing perspectives.

To Shay Swetech of WoundUp Studio, the design genius behind my book covers and websites, who amazingly captures my artistic preferences.

You all rock.

CONTENTS

CONTENTS (CONT'D)

CHAPTER 1

DIP INTO THE UNDERWORLD

<u>1964</u>

With Jimmy Hoffa and the fund's co-trustees waiting inside their headquarters to meet him and seal the deal, California businessman Bill Swigert told the broker his company now was refusing the proffered loan.

"You are finished with the Teamsters, and you better get out of Chicago," Norman Tyrone said while dragging a thumb across his own throat.[1]

"We got the hell out of there," said Swigert, referring to himself and his attorney.[2]

Desperation for financing is what had spurred William "Bill" G. Swigert, Jr. to the Windy City that autumn. He and his two partners — collectively Pacific Bridge Company & Associates (PBC&A) — recently had built and opened The Sierra Tahoe, the premier hotel in a new, sparsely inhabited, developing community on the north shore of Lake Tahoe* in Nevada, U.S.A. Four months later, they still needed money to cover the construction and other

---

* Often called the "Jewel of the Sierra" or "Big Blue," Lake Tahoe straddles the California-Nevada border. With a surface area of 191 square miles, it's North America's largest alpine lake.

incurred expenses and to fund the project's next phase, adding a casino and more guestrooms.

A few months before, Swigert had received a telephone call from Norman B. Tyrone, who'd introduced himself as a financier and had asserted he could arrange a Teamsters Pension Fund (TPF) loan for PBC&A for The Sierra Tahoe.

By that time, the TPF had underwritten more than $20 million in loans ($163 million)[†] in Nevada, for hotel-casinos, including the Riverside in Reno, and the Dunes and the Desert Inn in Las Vegas, as well as other facilities.

The TPF — formally the Central States, Southeast, Southwest Areas Pension Fund of the International Brotherhood of Teamsters — collected and managed employer contributions for retirement, disability and death benefits for its unionized truck drivers and warehouse workers in about 20 states.

One of the fund's eight trustees was James "Jimmy" R. Hoffa, who, as the Teamsters union president, allegedly had ordered bombings, arsons, beatings and murders and had aligned himself with Mobsters nationwide.

Tyrone had arranged for PBC&A to receive $2.6 million ($21.2 million) in financing from the TPF. The loan was PBC&A's last resort, as Swigert had exhausted all other potential options over the prior 2.5 years. Swigert and his counsel, Frank E. Farella, had flown to Chicago to finalize the transaction.

On Friday, September 25, the two men convened with Tyrone in the new riverfront, 36-story, downtown Executive House hotel,

---

[†] With most of the dated dollar figures throughout this book, a corresponding current value is provided in parentheses immediately after. These amounts are based on 2019 United States government consumer price index data and adjusted for inflation.

about seven blocks from the TPF's building. Tall but portly, the man wore expensive apparel.

"Tyrone just looked dishonest," Swigert said. "He looked like a big, tall gangster, like Al Capone[‡] on steroids."

In Tyrone's suite, piles of papers lay strewn across the furniture. The loan liaison darted around and made and answered several calls supposedly to and from Elliott Roosevelt, who was said to be waiting in the TPF's boardroom to meet Tyrone and his loan applicants from the West Coast. Tyrone had indicated this son of Franklin D. and Eleanor Roosevelt, former United States president and first lady, was his business partner.

"God, it was almost like a show," Swigert said about Tyrone's behavior.[3]

Swigert and Farella reviewed the loan papers. As a condition of the financing, PBC&A previously had agreed to pay 1 point, or 1 percent of the loan amount, which equaled $26,000 ($212,000), to the TPF for appraisals, estimates and other costs. It also had agreed to pay 2 points, which was $52,000 ($424,000), to Tyrone as commission for brokering the deal.

However, among the documents, Swigert spotted a letter that committed PBC&A to giving an additional $208,000 ($1.7 million), or 8 points, as a subsidiary loan to the International Mortgage and Statistical Corporation, supposedly Tyrone and Roosevelt's company in the Bahamas.

"What's this? What's it all about?" Farella asked.

"To Swigert and Farella ... the Bahamas loan had an immediate and unmistakable stench," reported the *Oakland Tribune*.

[‡] Alphonse "Scarface" Capone was the American Mobster who allegedly murdered his way to becoming Chicago's organized crime boss during the U.S.' Prohibition Era.

The additional $208,000 meant PBC&A would pay 11 versus 3 points on the loan. Tyrone defended it as "a hell of a good deal"[4] and said all TPF financings were transacted at a 10 point-minimum.[§]

Frank Sheeran, who once had been Hoffa's right-hand man, explained to author Charles Brandt how the TPF loans worked: "Jimmy's cut was to get a finder's fee off the books. He took points under the table for approving the loans. Mob bosses would bring customers. The bosses would charge the customers 10 percent of the loan and split that percentage with Jimmy."[5]

If this were to have been the case with the loan to PBC&A, then $104,000 of that $208,000 would have gone to Hoffa, the rest to Tyrone. (Tyrone wasn't a Mob boss, but like one, he connected loan candidates and the TPF.)

When Swigert asked him what his corporation did, Tyrone explained that it was somewhat of a startup, aiming to computerize global information about potential loan sources. Farella requested the business' latest financial reports, but Tyrone said they weren't and wouldn't be available. He admitted that no paper trail documenting the $208,000 disbursement would exist.

"We said that if this was a legitimate loan [to Tyrone's firm], then there was a legitimate business reason for doing it," Swigert recalled. "Otherwise, this clearly would be immoral and illegal."[6]

About then, it was time for Swigert and Farella to rendezvous with the TPF's trustees at their 29 E. Madison Street offices. Swigert told Tyrone he and Farella would catch up with him there with a final decision on the loan. First, Swigert had to discuss with his partners the surprise term just thrust upon PBC&A, by phone. He did so.

[§] That was true, but it was a high rate, as traditional lenders typically charged borrowers 1 to 4 origination points.

"It didn't take us long to decide we wanted no part of any deal like that," Swigert said.[7]

CHAPTER 2

HAIR-BRAINED SCHEME

<u>1959</u>

Five years earlier, George Whittell, Jr. gambled on nearly one-quarter of his 40,000 Lake Tahoe acres with a prospective buyer of that land, Arthur "Art" L. Wood, according to rumor.

If Wood could come up with $1 million in cash ($8.6 million) within 30 days, then Whittell would sell him the property for $5 million ($43.4 million). This was a cheap price, as the same parcel would sell the next year for five times as much.

Wood, 49, was a certified public accountant with decades of experience and co-founder and partner of Billups, Wood & Champlin in Oklahoma City.

In contrast, Whittell,[*] age 77, was a wealthy, eccentric owner of land along the lake's Nevada side, which amounted to a bit more than the acreage of New York's Staten Island. Known for playing games of chance, along with womanizing, drinking and activities involving high speeds, the former U.S. Army Captain reportedly had accrued a $70,000 ($1.2 million) debt, all in one night, at the

---

[*] George Whittell, Jr.'s Lake Tahoe residence at the time, the Thunderbird Lodge, today is a national historic site, open to the public.

Riverside Buffet casino in Reno, Nevada in 1937 and hadn't paid it, ever.

Wood corralled some businessmen from Oklahoma, Hawaii and Kansas to acquire, collectively as an investment, Whittell's wagered land. To do so, they formed a conglomerate called the Nevada Lake Tahoe Investment Company (NLTIC).

Wood and several NLTIC members sold another of their jointly owned enterprises, 19 movie theaters in Hawaii, and used the funds from that deal for this new one.

On behalf of the NLTIC, Wood delivered not just the required money to Whittell by the deadline but also the remainder of the $5 million purchase price, all in cash. Whittell kept up his side of the agreement.

The NLTIC-Whittell transaction at the time constituted the largest single-property purchase of land for development in the history of The Silver State, if not the country's entire western region.

Now, in the mostly forested, Northern Nevada locale, the NLTIC owned 9,000 acres of undeveloped property, about one-third the size of today's City of San Francisco. Roughly 2.5 miles of it were Lake Tahoe shoreline, and another three miles extended away from the coast, into the Carson Mountain Range. It was "one of the most attractive pieces of property overlooking Lake Tahoe," noted a local newspaper.[1]

1960

After moving with his family to Crystal Bay, Nevada from Oklahoma, Wood, with some investors, established and headed the Crystal Bay Development Company (CBDC) as president.[†] Harold B. Tiller, 39, a friend of Wood and previously an accountant at his firm, was vice president. Raymond M. Smith, former director of Washoe County's[‡] Regional Planning Commission, served as vice president of planning.

In June, the CBDC acquired from the NLTIC that same 9,000-acre woodsy parcel for $25 million ($213.5 million), a 400 percent higher price than what the NLTIC had paid for it the year before.

For the virgin land, the CBDC's owners envisioned a master-planned vacation resort for about 25,000 people,[§] complete with apartments, houses, schools, churches, a shopping center, restaurant, golf course and more.[**] It would be called Incline Village. Development was to be approached and accomplished such that it capitalized on but also protected the region's natural beauty and pristine, azure body of water, Lake Tahoe. Wood estimated that by 1965, the township would boast about 1,000 additional homes and multiple new businesses.

"Art was a wheeler dealer and very smart," said Mr. Sherrill Broudy, who would become one of the Pacific Bridge Company & Associates (PBC&A) partners. "He was just the right guy for [developing the area]. He just plowed ahead."[2]

This new Incline Village would differ from its historic roots. The original, simply named Incline and with about 1,000 residents,

---

[†] The company was given this name as it was located in Crystal Bay, which is adjacent to Incline Village, on Lake Tahoe's North Shore in Northern Nevada.
[‡] Washoe County, located in the State of Nevada along the eastern slopes of the Sierra Nevada range, covered 6,600 square miles and encompassed Incline Village along with the cities Reno and Sparks.
[§] This population would fill about a third of the stadium of the National Football League's Broncos team in Colorado.
[**] Incline Village eventually would become a tax haven, especially for wealthy Californians and businesses, due to Nevada's favorable tax structure that today, for one, excludes levies on personal income.

had prospered nearly a century before. During that earlier period, logging companies had commoditized the region's abundant, 110,000-plus acres of timber (an expanse at least twice the State of Utah's total area today), which miners in nearby Virginia City had needed to build and support the square-set frames they'd used and to fuel steam engines.

In Incline, workers had milled hewn trees, and a tram had transported the logs about 1,400 feet, or the length of 3.5 football fields, up a mountain in the Sierra Nevada. From this steep gradient the original town derived its name, Incline.

A water flume then had propelled the timber to Lakeview, just north of Carson City, Nevada's capital. From there, the logs had been shipped on the Virginia & Truckee Railroad to the Comstock mines, most of which had been closed by 1890.

In Incline Village in late 1960, Wood requested the Board of Commissioners, charged with managing Washoe County, rezone seven CBDC-owned acres along Lake Tahoe's shore so a hotel could be built there.

The commissioners declined. They claimed that they wanted to keep the beach free for recreational purposes and pointed out that sewer and water utility plans for the area hadn't been solidified and approved yet. Additionally, they stated Wood's application was premature in that it diverged from the development timeline outlined in the area's master plan.

Consequently, the accountant-turned-developer tabled his idea … temporarily.

1961

Following the Recession of 1960-1961, when construction of the Incline Village golf course was underway, Wood met with three professionals to negotiate the construction of an inn in his advancing master-planned community.

The men were Bill Swigert, 39, president of the Pacific Bridge Company (PBC), an Alameda, California-based commercial builder known for having constructed major bridges in the western U.S., including the Golden Gate and Bay; Sherrill Broudy, 38, an architect with an office in PBC's building; and Jack A. Ferguson, 31, a local businessman.

Ferguson and Swigert recently had collaborated on Incline Village's first gas station, named Orbit, with Ferguson as the owner, Swigert/PBC as the designer and builder. Wood had donated the land for that project to Ferguson in exchange for him seeing it through.

Similarly, Wood offered to give the trio 20 acres of CBDC-owned, Incline Village property — 5 acres on the beach and 15 acres across the street that snaked along the lake's perimeter — if they'd agree to erect a 100-room hotel on the land within a year. The lakeside parcel alone, at the then average sale price, would've cost a buyer about $200,000 ($1.7 million).[††]

The men agreed to Wood's deal, either unaware of the county's initial refusal to rezone the lakefront area or confident they'd obtain approval because a year had passed since the commissioners' denial.

"We thought, geez, we could really put a hotel together," Broudy said. "Fortunately, it was an opportune time."[3]

The only hotel-casinos in the vicinity stood in the adjacent community, Crystal Bay, which was roughly about a 10-minute drive away, to the northwest, and closer to the Nevada-California

---

[††] At the time, the price of residential lots on the beach started at $25,000 ($212,000) and further up the hillside, at $6,000 ($51,000).

state line. Those enterprises were the Cal-Vada Lodge Hotel, the Cal-Neva Lodge, the Nevada Lodge and the Crystal Bay Club.

Swigert, Broudy and Ferguson, operating as Pacific Bridge Company & Associates (PBC&A) — an entity separate from Pacific Bridge Company (PBC) but with Swigert as the common element — dreamed up for the land an estimated $15 million ($127 million), 40-acre recreational and cultural complex called Tahoe Forum.

It was to feature a major hotel, casino, convention hall, swimming pool, ice skating rink, and tennis and badminton courts and, ultimately, showcase events such as art exhibits, symphonies, lectures and films. To be part of Wood's master-planned Incline Village, Tahoe Forum also was to blend into the natural setting.

Broudy conceived of the architecture, from which freelance artist Mario Valenzuela prepared concept sketches. Using those as a visual aid, PBC&A proposed the project to the CBDC, the press and others. Wood endorsed it.

Fruition of the concept in physical form, however, would prove much more difficult to attain.

CHAPTER 3

SEEKING ELUSIVE MONEY

<u>1963</u>

T wo years later in May, Bill Swigert's primary business, Pacific Bridge Company (PBC), with the required permit from Washoe County, began constructing the Tahoe Forum's main, three-story, 54-guestroom building, using redwood, native rock and concrete.

The location, on the northwest corner of then State Route 28 at Country Club Drive, was adjacent to the new Robert Trent Jones, Sr.-designed, 18-hole Incline Village Golf Course (today, the Championship Course).

After PBC completed the first structure, the county commissioners granted the builder a special use permit to build lodging across the street on Lake Tahoe's shore, an area with an R-3, or urban residential, zoning designation.

There, the developer erected six chalet-type buildings, each containing an octet of units. PBC also built a pentagonal pavilion to house a restaurant and bar, whose floor-to-ceiling glass windows afforded lake views, with a landscaped terrace for outdoor dining and dancing.

Finally, to create access for pedestrians between the two properties that didn't require crossing the thoroughfare, PBC designed and installed a covered, 81-foot-long, 25-ton, redwood and cedar pedestrian bridge.

Charles Warren Callister[*] of the Belvedere-Tiburon, California area had designed the buildings' architecture, yet Don Sandy of San Francisco had prepared the final blueprints.

In the lakefront bungalow units, natural wood cabinetry ensconced the amenities, including a refrigerator, bar sink, cooktop and television. Ceramic tiles in mottled earth tones adorned the fireplace hearth and floors in the hall, bathroom and bedroom. Carpet in shades of ochre and sienna harmonized with the color scheme.

Though Tahoe Forum's first phase was finished, it'd taken longer than anticipated. The delay had been due to Swigert doggedly, but unsuccessfully, looking for a willing lender from which to borrow $6 million ($51 million) for that initial development.

"We spent an awful lot of time looking for people who would finance the hotel, which ordinarily wouldn't be too big a job," he said. "Those days, you couldn't finance anything up in the sticks. There was absolutely nothing up there then."[1]

Instead, Swigert contributed more than $1 million ($8.3 million) to complete what PBC had built so far.

Also, Pacific Bridge Company & Associates — Swigert, Sherrill Broudy and Jack Ferguson — had planned to add a fourth partner, specifically a hotel operator, because the three lacked

---

[*] Charles Warren Callister's most notable Northern California projects include the First Church of Christ Scientist in Mill Valley (1955), the Duncan House (1959) in San Francisco, Rossmoor Leisure World (1963) in Walnut Creek and the Mills College Chapel in Oakland (1968).

experience with running a hospitality business. The trio had lined up a Reno, Nevada man who was a perfect fit, but he reportedly had died in an airplane crash before The Sierra Tahoe opened.

"[Art Wood] assumed I would put up enough money to build something, which is actually what happened," said Swigert. "It was a lot of money for a small company to invest in a project they didn't want to own. We were left with nobody to run it and no connection to finance it."

1964

In late spring, The Sierra Tahoe was nearly primed for its debut, only the furniture on the grass needed moving inside and arranging. Just then, a surprise snowstorm hit, perhaps an omen of what was to come.

With two water-loving, white Saint Bernards named Sierra and Tahoe as its mascots, PBC&A opened its long time coming lodging on Friday, May 29 and celebrated with a week of ill-attended performances by the Frisco Banjo Boys in the lakeside pavilion. An advertising pamphlet billed The Sierra Tahoe as "a luxury resort hotel on the beach."

Simultaneously, Swigert kept trying to procure financing, but now mostly for Tahoe Forum's second phase, the addition of a casino and more guestrooms.

"I was desperate, flailing around, looking for money," he said.[2]

Meanwhile, the U.S. government, after two years of Federal Bureau of Investigation and grand jury inquiries, charged union head Jimmy Hoffa, 51, and seven other people with fraudulently securing $20 million in loans ($163 million) from the Teamsters Pension Fund (TPF) over 4.5 years to finance companies or construction of hotels, shopping centers and other entities in six states — California, Florida, Louisiana, Alabama, Missouri and New Jersey.

During the ensuing trial, prosecutors claimed the defendants had provided false and misleading information to get loans approved. They'd fabricated and embellished relevant details such as the purpose of a loan; the construction costs to be financed; the amount the borrower would invest; the borrower's assets, net worth and ability to repay a loan; and the value of the collateral offered as security.

The defendants also had been charged with pocketing in kickbacks $1.7 million ($13.5 million) of the $20 million of proceeds — in the form of fees, padded accounts, and stock options and interest — for their personal use. They'd used those monies to fund their enterprises and to pay debts, other entities and individuals (including other defendants) and expenses, both personal and business.

In June, after 13 weeks of testimony involving 140 witnesses, the sequestered jury found Hoffa guilty on four counts — three of fraud and one of conspiracy. The judge sentenced him to five years in federal prison with the possibility of parole and fined him $10,000 ($82,000).[†]

"We didn't know that was going on," Swigert said about Hoffa's indictment and trial.[3]

Hoffa co-defendant, Calvin Kovens, also was convicted and sentenced, to three years' prison and a $5,000 ($41,000) fine. He was a Florida commercial real estate developer who later would become involved in The Sierra Tahoe.

[†] In the prior year, 1963, Hoffa had been found guilty of jury tampering, attempted bribery and fraud, for which he'd been sentenced to eight years in prison. That decision was under appeal at the time of this subsequent trial in 1964. Hoffa, who still had to serve his time for the 1963 sentence, would remain free on appeal bonds for years.

It was three months after this latest conviction of Hoffa, in September, that Swigert declined the TPF loan in person in Chicago after broker Norman Tyrone insisted PBC&A pay his and Elliott Roosevelt's firm $208,000 in the guise of a loan.‡ Subsequently, Tyrone avowed that the West Coast three had ruined their chances of ever getting TPF financing.

"What [Wood] didn't understand and what I didn't understand was that we were never going to borrow any money for anything like a casino-hotel any place but from the Teamsters," Swigert said.[4]

That, in large part, was because a loan for that type of business involved too much risk.

"What life insurance company is going to lend money to expand a gambling joint when the loan must be for a term of years and the gambling house would become an abandoned ruin if the state law should change?" Wallace Turner wrote in *Gambler's Money*. "What bank has the resources to risk in such loans? Individuals with that kind of money to commit would want to buy into the ownership, and the gamblers§ could never agree to that."

In Incline Village, with no capital to fund further development, Swigert, Broudy and Ferguson had to scrap not just the plan to add a casino and rooms to The Sierra Tahoe but, also, the larger project, Tahoe Forum. Managing and operating The Sierra Tahoe hotel in the black posed a great enough challenge.

---

‡ It later was learned that a former representative of Swigert's firm, Pacific Bridge Company, had talked preliminarily with Tyrone about a possible PBC&A loan of $160,000 ($1.3 million) to the Nassau firm but in exchange for common stock.

§ Whereas the term "gamblers" connotes individuals who play games of chance, it also refers to, as it does here, casino and gambling house owners, operators and licensees.

"When it got down to brass tacks, [the Tahoe Forum] idea was pretty farfetched," Broudy reflected.[5]

Within a week of his encounter with Tyrone in Chicago, Swigert received a letter, signed by the TPF's executive secretary Francis J. Murtha, which indicated the trustees had approved the Tyrone-arranged loan to PBC&A.

But since the partners of The Sierra Tahoe had refused that financing offer only days earlier, who ended up with the money?

CHAPTER 4

CHANGE OF HANDS

1965

Early in the year, a Los Angeles real estate broker telephoned Bill Swigert out of the blue and said he had two clients in Southern California who unintentionally had driven by The Sierra Tahoe and now wanted to buy it, using already-secured capital from a Texas lender.

One of the interested parties was Roy G. Lewis of Playa del Rey, who owned one of the U.S.' two exclusive Mercedes-Benz dealerships, the West Coast one, and was the building and safety commissioner for the City of Los Angeles.

The other prospective buyer, Harold K. Riel of Studio City, was the president of Allied Appliance Company, which designed and built auto parts and accessories.

"To my knowledge, they were gangsters," Sherrill Broudy recalled.[1]

With the broker, Pacific Bridge Company & Associates (PBC&A) negotiated the sale of its two Sierra Tahoe buildings for an undisclosed price and agreed to lease the land underneath.

When the deal was about to close, the partners learned that Norman Tyrone, the menacing loan intermediary from the past, was a buyer, too, along with Lewis and Riel.

The PBC&A trio hadn't known that Tyrone, Lewis and Riel all were acquainted with one another, Swigert said.

Further, the hotel proprietors hadn't been aware that the same day in Chicago in 1964, when Tyrone had requested a loan from the Teamsters Pension Fund (TPF) for PBC&A, he also supposedly had asked for a $7.5 million ($61.1 million) loan for Lewis, Riel and a third person to fund their purchase of Pacific Plaza, an apartment complex in the Southern California beach city, Santa Monica.

With the information it did have, PBC&A refused to sell to Tyrone and closed the transaction with Lewis and Riel only.

Then Swigert, Broudy and Ferguson learned that Riel and Lewis hadn't funded the acquisition of The Sierra Tahoe with monies from a Texas financier but, rather, with the very $2.6 million TPF loan that PBC&A had turned down in the Windy City the previous fall!

Right after the acquisition went through, in February, Riel and Lewis assumed operation of the Incline Village establishment and announced their plan to expand it, to add about 100 rooms, to the hotel only (not the bungalows), and introduce gambling in the standalone, lakeside building.

That structure, or annex, however, was in an area zoned for private homes, not commercial use. As such, the Washoe County Board of Commissioners granted Lewis and Riel a temporary special use permit, allowing them to establish a casino there on the condition that within a year they move it across the street to the main hotel property, which was zoned for business entities.

Late in the prior year, 1964, Lewis, Riel and Tyrone — yes, Tyrone, too — had requested approval from the Nevada Gaming Commission (NGC)[*] to open a year-round casino at The Sierra Tahoe and had applied for gambling licenses, which the state required of all gaming enterprise owners and operators.

The three had proposed to the regulators that Tyrone would invest $150,000 ($1.2 million) in and own 50 percent of the gambling operation, and Lewis and Riel each would contribute $75,000 ($611,000) for a 25 percent interest.

Upon learning about their application, a handful of Incline Village and Reno residents and Sierra Club members had objected to it on several grounds. At an NGC meeting, they argued a casino would ruin the area's stunning aesthetics and granting a gambling license would set a negative precedent. They'd purported also that license approval would lead to numerous other large, gaming establishments being erected on Lake Tahoe's North Shore, similar to what protestors believed had happened on its South Shore, where, they'd said, the people had been and were "too numerous, too commercial and too lustful after the tourist dollar," reported the *Nevada State Journal*.[2]

Art Wood, however, had presented an opposing view to the gambling authorities.

"We are developing the finest resort area in the world, and when you get the right kind of a gambling area, at least you have a pretty good percentage organization going for you," he'd said, according to May 18, 1965 NGC meeting minutes.

---

[*] Created in 1959, the Nevada Gaming Commission is the state gambling regulatory agency that denies or grants gambling licenses, administers regulations and manages disciplinary actions. It's comprised of five members appointed by the governor to four-year terms, with one serving as chairman.

As was its usual practice, the Nevada Gaming Control Board (NGCB)[†] had investigated Riel, Lewis and Tyrone, obtaining background checks, personal histories, fingerprints and head shots, then had made its recommendation to the NGC.

In agreement with the NGCB and after a unanimous vote, the NGC granted individual gambling licenses in May 1965 but only to Lewis and Riel. Tyrone at some point had withdrawn from the process. It's unknown whether the NGCB had encouraged him to back out or whether he'd done so on his own.

Thus, instead of the original ownership arrangement, Riel and Lewis each invested $125,000 ($1 million) for a 50 percent stake. This was for five table games (21,[‡] craps[§] and roulette) and 50 slot machines.

With those games, the casino's total gambling taxes — federal slot machine, state gross receipt, state table game, county table game and city licensing — amounted to about $27,500 ($221,000) per year plus 3 percent of the gross table game earnings.

F.E. Walters, NGC member, expressed concern about a casino of that breadth carrying the entire Sierra Tahoe enterprise.

"It's too small to be economically possible or feasible for any lengthy period," he said.

Why did Riel, Lewis and Tyrone want a casino at The Sierra Tahoe? Was it perhaps Hoffa and/or one or more of his gangster friends who desired such an enterprise there? Or was it a combination of those parties who did at the time?

[†] Founded before the NGC, in 1955, the Nevada Gaming Control Board is the investigative and enforcement arm of the state's gambling regulatory division. The three governor-appointed people who comprise the board serve four-year terms.

[‡] In Nevada, 21 is another name for the game blackjack.

[§] Craps is a table game in which players bet on the numbers they anticipate, or hope, will show on the two dice when the shooter rolls them.

It's well documented that various National Crime Syndicate factions then had ties to and influence over many Silver State casinos, particularly those in Las Vegas.

"There is no question in the minds of the best investigators that the criminal underworld still has a big equity in the Nevada gambling industry, no matter how well the gaming officials keep the surface polished clean," wrote *Chicago Daily News* reporter Edwin Lahey.[3]

One reason for racketeers and others' casino involvement was that these operations could be huge money makers. For instance, in 1961, Harrah's Lake Club on Lake Tahoe's South Shore raked in $20 million ($169 million) in reported gross winnings, and Harolds Club in Reno yielded $13 million ($110 million).

Those numbers surpassed the gross revenues that year of the U.S.' three largest corporations, General Motors, Exxon Chemical and Ford Motor companies — $12.7 million, $8 million and $5.2 million ($107.4 million, $68 million and $44 million), respectively.

Casinos also afforded their owners, visible or hidden, the opportunity to skim, or take cash tax free, from the operation's incoming revenue. This practice, common among organized crime figures, entailed secretly sequestering money then distributing it to the various hidden investors, or points holders.

"These [federal] investigators know beyond reasonable doubt that persons on the edge of gangland come in and out of Las Vegas on Mob business, and that when they leave they carry attaché cases full of currency," Lahey wrote. "This money goes to Florida, Chicago, New York and New Jersey. Some of it finds its way into Latin America under cover of diplomatic passports. The money can make the return trip as a loan from a foreign bank not subject to scrutiny by U.S. officials.

"These investigators also feel certain that underworld leaders control equity in some casinos through the use of 'fronts' who appear as owners of record. Some of these fronts are legitimate businessmen who act as transmission belts for the Mobs in different cities."[4]

Mobsters sometimes used this "black money" for contributions to political campaigns, for payoffs to various people and government officials at any and all levels and for illegal activities or enterprises.

In 1965, as planned and approved by the gambling regulators, Lewis and Riel opened a casino in The Sierra Tahoe's lakefront building.

Also, as promised, over the ensuing few months, the duo had 146 additional guestrooms built onto The Sierra Tahoe's three-story hotel to accommodate a potential increase in patronage. This took the total unit count, including those in the chalets, to 200 from 54.

While these advancements were happening, Lewis and Riel each repeatedly withdrew from the corporate account $10,000 or $20,000 ($80,700 or $161,400) at a time and didn't spend them for legitimate Sierra Tahoe purposes.

Was this a skimming attempt by amateurs? Were Lewis and Riel giving the money to Hoffa for approving the loan? Were they giving a portion to Tyrone, too, and/or keeping some or all of it for themselves?

"The two were making a mess of it, losing money," Broudy said, referring to Riel and Lewis.[5]

Quickly, the hotel-casino plummeted into debt. By fall 1965, the account's balance had plunged by $180,000 ($1.5 million), for a year-to-date net loss of $231,000 ($1.8 million).

Consequently, Riel and Lewis defaulted on their land lease with PBC&A and owed vendors $158,780 ($1.3 million). Creditors complained to the Northern Nevada Board of Trade about the two hotel-casino proprietors being in arrears and having skirted payment when they'd tried to collect.

"The [Sierra Tahoe] licensees have apparently lapsed, and they certainly [are] not running the place," NGCB Chairman Edward "Ed" A. Olsen said at an October 1965 meeting.

Riel and Lewis' days as the operators and owners of the Lake Tahoe business would be numbered.

CHAPTER 5

TO THE RESCUE?

<u>1965</u>

Alvin B. Kroll, 39, appeared at The Sierra Tahoe in July, only five months after Roy Lewis and Harold Riel had purchased it. Likely sent by the Teamsters Pension Fund (TPF), his mission was to resuscitate the failing business.

He was the president of the Miami, Florida-based construction company Home Additions, Inc. and the brother-in-law of Calvin Kovens, the Jimmy Hoffa crony who'd been a co-defendant and had been convicted with the Teamsters union leader in the 1964 loan fraud trial.

Despite a lack of hospitality industry experience, Kroll began running the hotel. He applied with the Nevada Gaming Commission (NGC) for a gambling license, telling the regulators he wanted full control of the casino and hotel.

"I do not want [Lewis and Riel] in this operation," he said, October 1965 board meeting minutes noted. "For the past two months, it has been my operation. I have come out [from Florida] because they haven't been there. There no planning or foresight in this operation."

Kroll explained that he already had started to cut costs, reducing payroll expenses by 60 percent, to $9,518 from $27,000 (to $76,810 from $160,500). He was optimistic about The Sierra Tahoe's future and said he'd move to Nevada and manage the full enterprise on site, full time, if he received a gambling license.

"If I use the same figures that I've seen from auditing and only the normal increases that I think would be met in the hotel and food and beverage and in the casino ... this hotel can do very well," he said. "It can not only exist, but it can make money. And this is what I'm banking on."

In considering Kroll's application, the Nevada Gaming Control Board (NGCB) members contemplated various factors, meeting minutes showed. They were concerned that he lacked a contract with Riel and Lewis detailing his management takeover. They wanted to help avoid a potential involuntary bankruptcy action against the Southern California co-owners, which could've resulted if creditors weren't paid. They wanted to prevent the TPF from assuming control of the hotel-casino.

"I just don't think it is a proper function for a lending institution, which is what they are," NGCB Chairman Ed Olsen said, referring to the pension fund.

Consequently, the NGCB recommended the NGC approve a six-month license for Kroll with three stipulations.

One, within three weeks, Kroll was to deliver to the NGCB a partnership agreement between him and the current owners of The Sierra Tahoe.

Two, Kroll was to infuse the business with $120,000 ($963,000), earning him a 45 percent share of The Sierra Tahoe casino; Lewis and Riel's interest in it would drop to 27.5 percent from 50 percent each.

Three, Kroll was to use his capital injection to pay the business' creditors.

The NGC concurred and granted Kroll a probationary gambling license that would expire in March 1966.

It's unknown whether Kroll moved to Incline Village or even Nevada or California. Regardless, The Sierra Tahoe's financial footing continued to wane.

In late fall, the newest trio — Kroll as operator, Riel and Lewis as the owners — closed the business for reorganization. Signs on the buildings indicated it was to reopen the next year, in February.

Subsequently, on November 30, PBC&A — Bill Swigert, Sherrill Broudy and Jack Ferguson — terminated their lease on the Sierra Tahoe land with Riel and Lewis, which required the two men to vacate the hotel-casino's premises in 23 days' time. They did.

As The Sierra Tahoe struggled, Incline Village development burgeoned, with journalists touting 1965 as the most successful year in its history. About $20 million ($160 million) worth of construction was completed during the period, expanding infrastructure to more than 400 single-family homes, 510 multiple dwelling units and 35 commercial buildings.

New recreational facilities included a golf course, tennis courts, bowling alley and beach. Ski slopes were nearby at Mt. Rose and Slide Mountain and, a bit further away, at California's Squaw Valley, which had hosted the 1960 Winter Olympics. These snowsport resorts helped extend Incline Village's tourist season to year-round from only spring and summer.

In 1965, the Incline Village-Crystal Bay area drew about 75,000 bus travelers and more than 4,500 airline passengers. Completion of the segment of Interstate 80 between the Nevada-

California line and the town of Verdi in Nevada, which improved auto access to Lake Tahoe, led to a greater influx of visitors.

Development and construction indicators projected that 1966 likely would outpace the preceding year. Already, $10 million ($81 million) worth of projects was underway.

One was Incline Village developer Art Wood's $3 million Ski Incline, a complex with 300 acres of trails, a mountaintop restaurant and cocktail lounge, a day lodge and motel at the base, which was slated to open in the fall.

1966

Early in the year, another supposed savior appeared at The Sierra Tahoe to resurrect it. He was Calvin "Cal" Kovens, 39, Kroll's brother-in-law, and "a long-time Teamster courtier,"* as described by the *Oakland Tribune*.[1]

Kovens had been found guilty, along with Hoffa in their 1964 trial, on six counts — five of mail fraud and one of wire fraud — and had been sentenced to three years in prison with possible parole and a $5,000 ($41,000) fine. Like Hoffa, he hadn't started serving that time yet. Kovens also, in 1963, had been fined $12,000 ($99,000) and placed on probation when convicted in a Federal Housing Administration loan fraud case in Miami.

A self-described expediter for the TPF, Kovens traveled cross-county to Incline Village intending to acquire The Sierra Tahoe's buildings and acreage. To purchase both, he needed to refinance the existing loan with the TPF, the original $2.6 million given to Roy Lewis and Harold Riel after Pacific Bridge Company & Associates had turned it down.

---

* A courtier is one who gains favor through flattery or other ingratiating behavior.

Kovens and certain TPF trustees wanted the pension fund to issue a second loan for the property for $1.65 million ($12.9 million). They wanted it to be large, for more than PBC&A's asking price for the land, to cover future additions and enhancements to the resort.

This amount would take the sum of the mortgages on The Sierra Tahoe to $4.25 million ($33.1 million).

However, PBC&A insisted the TPF loan not exceed 6 percent of what the total mortgaged amount would be, or $700,000 ($5.5 million). Were it to surpass that 6 percent amount, an additional mortgage would be required, which the original owners wanted to avoid.

The difference was $950,000 ($7.4 million) between the loan amount Kovens and his financiers wanted, $1.65 million, and the loan amount PBC&A would agree to, $700,000.

Kovens and the TPF demanded that PBC&A waive the 6 percent loan cap.

"They said, 'You better take it, or you're in trouble,'" Broudy recalled.[2]

After being threatened, the trio accepted it, said Broudy, unsure of what "it" even was.

However, Broudy added, once he was back home in Santa Barbara and reflected upon it, "I thought, this is crazy, us getting pushed around like this."

With his partners' consent, he informed Kovens they'd changed their minds, the deal was off.

Despite PBC&A's stance, though, Kovens continued to press the issue, at times even insisting that Broudy, Swigert and Ferguson cover the $950,000.

"We went through weeks of negotiations and threats until 5 p.m. on the date [for us] to come up with the money to close the deal," Broudy added. "Kovens told us, 'Either you come through or you'll own the hotel.' Kovens told Bill [Swigert], 'When this deal is complete, we're going to take care of that Broudy.'"

Remaining steadfast, PBC&A neither paid the $950,000 nor waived its 6 percent loan max requirement.

"I said, 'I guess we own the hotel,'" Broudy recalled.

Roughly a month later, in February, despite his statements to the contrary, Kovens produced the $950,000, thereby assuming ownership of the entire resort and the two land parcels on which it sat.

With the acquisition, Kovens officially removed Lewis[†] and Riel from the picture and released PBC&A from its ties to The Sierra Tahoe for good.

Regarding PBC&A's hotel-casino pursuit, Swigert commented, "It started off as a good deal, but from then on, we just totally botched it. We had already built part of it, and that was obviously not the part that was going to pay off."[3]

Broudy reflected on the undertaking more fondly.

"It was like being involved in an exciting adventure, like in the Old West," he said. "You dream up an idea and do it. It's the type of story that couldn't occur today. Those were exciting days."[4]

[†] Lewis would be charged with felony drunk driving the following year.

CHAPTER 6

A FRESH START

1966

Still running The Sierra Tahoe and with his six-month gambling license about to expire, Alvin Kroll, in March, applied for a 100 percent interest in the property's casino and to become its sole licensee. This meant he'd assume Roy Lewis and Harold Riel's combined 55 percent share. He also asked to scale back the club's offerings to three table games and 15 slot machines, from five and 50, respectively.

The Nevada Gaming Control Board (NGCB) recommended approval.

Soon after, though, both state gambling agencies learned that Cal Kovens not only had become involved in the resort, against their wishes, but had acquired it, too. They previously had deemed him unsuitable as the landlord of a casino-containing entity due to his criminal record and looming prison sentence.

"I am mainly concerned that Kovens moved into this," said James W. Hotchkiss, Nevada Gaming Commission (NGC) member.[1] "There is a certain amount of arrogance in his move. Kovens had been warned that his record could threaten the operation, and his association with the hotel-casino was not in Nevada's best interests. He moved in in spite of it."

Consequently, the NGC extended Kroll's license for 30 days, during which time Kovens was to sell The Sierra Tahoe to an outside party who would meet the state's standards. Kovens and Kroll agreed to the plan.

Shortly thereafter, however, gaming officials discovered that Kovens had arranged to transfer The Sierra Tahoe asset into a trust for his children, which was not what they'd directed. Thus, they revoked Kroll's gambling license and shuttered the casino.

By this time, per Washoe County officials, the casino was to have been relocated to the hotel property on the opposite side of State Route 28, but that hadn't been done. Consequently, the commissioners extended the original special use permit for two years to give the new owner, whomever it would be, ample time to move the gaming enterprise.

At the time, Art Wood, Incline Village's visionary and developer, had his eye on The Sierra Tahoe as a possible venture for himself. He wanted to purchase it entirely but lacked sufficient capital to do so. Instead, he chose to go after a part of it — the casino, restaurant and bar, all of which were housed together in the lakefront building. To initiate the process, he applied for the requisite gambling license.

Again, Northern Nevadans, primarily local environmental activists intent on preserving Lake Tahoe's beauty, protested. They argued three points in opposition:

One, a commercial establishment on the beach would mar the area aesthetically. Mrs. Richard G. Miller, an objecting Carson City resident, wrote in an April 18, 1966 letter to the NGCB:

I find that a great measure of responsible world consideration on Lake Tahoe believes Nevada gambling at the lake to be a ruinous travesty of a great national asset. I find that that opinion, which along with that of many Nevadans may be perfectly willing to suffer gambling elsewhere, wonders now what kind of tiger's tail we have hold of that we cannot control its proliferation and its destruction of the beauty of this spot.

Two, because the casino already should've been moved, a license to operate it in its current place contradicted the special use permit's provisions. Further, it incentivized the owner to keep the gambling setup where it was, further delaying the mandated relocation of it.

Wood, however, reassured the NGCB at an April 1966 meeting: "The hotel is already booking 600 and 700 and 800 [person] groups for conventions for 1967 and 1968, so in all probability, unless the money market is absolutely crazy and the [Vietnam] war psychology continues, to where it would be difficult to get financing, then all of this [the casino, restaurant and bar] will be back over on the C-2 [general/tourist commercially zoned] property [across the street] by next spring, by this time next year. And the casino as such as it is now will become a little convention room, just a little recreation room."

The third argument against granting the gambling license was that the casino, restaurant and bar business couldn't be separated from that of the hotel, and as such, would remain linked to Kovens.

"Mr. Kovens is still there, and he still has everything to do with it," Oliver Custer, attorney, told the NGC members. Custer represented Rene Gaubert, who owned some property near the casino.

Wood countered that he could run the three components wholly independently of Kovens.

"It is important that the place start operating," he added. "It was such a flop last summer."

Wood won the battle. In April, the NGC issued him a gambling license with the caveat that the casino had to be transplanted in accordance with the county-issued permit, within two years.

For $725,000 ($5.6 million), he purchased, through his corporation, A.L.W., Inc., The Sierra Tahoe's casino, restaurant and bar and the land on which they sat.

After bankrolling 10 table games and 54 slot machines with $150,000 ($1.2 million), Wood reopened the gambling house as the Incline Village Casino.

The six lakeside guestroom buildings, their land and the high rise across the street remained under Kovens' ownership, with the NGC's blessing. Kovens chose that time to change the name to the Lake Tahoe Hotel from The Sierra Tahoe, as the latter moniker was confused often with the Sahara-Tahoe,[*] a hotel-casino that had opened on Lake Tahoe's South Shore the previous year.

"There is a faint ersatz sniff of half-timbered house about the Lake Tahoe Hotel where the design is officially called 'modern western,'" reported the *Los Angeles Times*. "Still there is a whiff of the frontier about the hotel."[2]

Certainly, the odor of the underworld would continue to waft throughout the property.

---

[*] Today, it is the Hard Rock Lake Tahoe hotel-casino.

CHAPTER 7

CATCHING THE CASINO BUG

<u>1966</u>

While the Lake Tahoe Hotel and the Incline Village Casino struggled for sustainability, a hotel-casino of a much grander scale — Caesars Palace — debuted on Southern Nevada's Las Vegas Strip, a stretch of South Las Vegas Boulevard that contained many such resorts. It was the first, new, major resort built there in a decade.

The Teamsters Pension Fund (TPF) had floated Jay J. Sarno, 44, the developer, designer and vice president, a $10.5 million loan ($82 million) for the $25 million ($195 million), luxurious destination in the desert. Sarno had recruited one of his brother's wealthy friends, Nathan "Nate" S. Jacobson, 51, to help raise additional capital and serve as president.

Jacobson was a Maryland-based insurance brokerage owner who specialized in corporate and estate planning and who'd established insurance and profit sharing plans for a number of hotel clients in Las Vegas. They included Morris Lansburgh, a Miami hotelier, reputed underworld figure and co-owner of the Flamingo hotel-casino in Las Vegas since 1960.

For the Baltimorean, Sin City held the allure of being "the last vestige of creativity and individual expression," reported the *Nevada State Journal*.[1]

"I had no gambling or hotel background," Jacobson said. "I picked it up by trial and error. I had to scratch. I didn't know."[2]

Jacobson, in turn, had called on a buddy of his, Irvin S. Kovens, 48, also in Maryland, for assistance. He was the brother of Calvin Kovens, current owner of the Lake Tahoe Hotel in Northern Nevada. Irvin Kovens' reputation was of a fundraiser extraordinaire, having amassed campaign war chests for several politicians, from a former City of Baltimore mayor to four former Maryland governors, including Spiro Agnew.

"Few political figures enter a campaign without first consulting [Irvin] Kovens, so powerful is his influence," wrote *The Daily Mail*.[3]

Jacobson and Irvin Kovens had engaged about 50 licensees to back Caesars' casino, including several Miami businessmen whose names Hoffa had provided, their combined investments totaling roughly $5 million ($39 million).

Sarno held the largest casino interest, at 10 percent; Jacobson had a 4.6 percent share. Irvin Kovens[*] was an initial investor, too, with a 0.7 percent piece.

The Nevada Gaming Control Board's (NGCB's) routine background checks of the many potential licensees required the use of in-state and out-of-state investigators and took six months to

---

[*] In 1977, Irvin Kovens would serve six months of a three-year prison term for 15 counts of mail fraud and one count of racketeering for allegedly having Maryland Governor Marvin Mandell influence race track legislation in return for $380,000 ($1.6 million) in bribes.

complete, costing the investors more than $15,000 in fees ($117,000).[†]

Sarno — who would later create Circus in Las Vegas — designed the 700-room Caesars Palace to reflect an opulent, ancient Roman ambiance, outside and in, as he wanted guests, men primarily, to be doted on as though they were a Roman emperor. In the Bacchanal Room, the theater restaurant, for instance, waitresses who were dressed like Roman goddesses poured wine and delivered back massages to the male patrons. The showgirls were Italian beauties.

Marble columns ringed the oval-shaped casino called Caesars Forum, the name perhaps taken from the proposed Tahoe Forum project that hadn't come to fruition in Incline Village. Along with the largest crystal chandelier in the world, the ornate room boasted 27 table games and 208 slot machines.

"Most agree that Caesars set the stage for the theme resorts of today," *Los Angeles Times* staff writer Diane Haithman would write 33 years later.[4]

Jacobson estimated the gross earnings from Caesars Palace's hotel and casino to be about $23 million ($180,453 million) in its first year of operations. The Nevada Gaming Commission (NGC), however, calculated a lower figure of $18 million ($141,220 million) gross.

"Nate Jacobson ... is determined to make the hotel show a profit even without the casino, and he just may do that," wrote columnist Mel Heimer.[5]

That was, if he could keep Sarno from spending money extravagantly.

[†] The gambling license application fee then was $50 ($390), and the investigation cost was $250 ($1,950), per individual. Applicants also paid the expenses the Nevada Gaming Control Board incurred during its inquiries.

"Jacobson infuriated Sarno with his penny-pinching; Sarno's disregard for the bottom line drove Jacobson nuts. ... Fundamentally, they just didn't like each other," wrote David G. Schwartz in *Grandissimo: The First Emperor of Las Vegas: How Jay Sarno Won a Casino Empire, Lost It, and Inspired Modern Las Vegas*.

The Caesars Palace opening proved to be a star-studded bash attended by major celebrities, high rollers and well-known casino operators, many of whom the hotel-casino management flew in on chartered planes.

Jimmy Hoffa[‡] and Nevada Governor Grant Sawyer were present.

Actresses Rhonda Fleming, Ann Baxter and Maureen O'Hara and actors Adam West, David Janssen and Robert Cummings showed.

Other notables present included Ed Sullivan, television host; Bobby Morse, actor and singer; Joe Louis, World Heavyweight Champion in boxing and Sidney Skolsky, Hollywood columnist.

Singer Andy Williams performed at the event, crooning favorites such as *Who Can I Turn To*, *Call Me* and *What Now My Love*.

"What Caesar's [sic] Palace is trying to tell everyone, in spades, is that the steady flow of gamblers who stream into Las Vegas at the rate of 16 million a year — 55 percent of them from California — make a $25-million hotel a most solid investment," Jane Wilson would write in an June 18, 1967 *Los Angeles Times* article.

"After real estate tax, table tax, annual state and federal tax of $550 for each individual slot machine, and after an estimated running cost of $40,000 a day, the owners of Caesar's [sic] Palace

---

[‡] Jimmy Hoffa would begin his federal prison sentences in March 1967.

still expect to recoup the whole of their original investment within 10 years."

CHAPTER 8

MORE GAMBLING DRAMA

1966

Back at Art Wood's Incline Village Casino, trouble brewed. One of the people working there was Edward "Marty" A. Buccieri, although in an official or unofficial capacity and for how long are unknown.

Previously, in his hometown of Steubenville, Ohio, a Cincinnati suburb, he'd been the president of Associated Credits, Inc., which collected gambling debts for North Kentucky operators.

The Cleveland Syndicate had run illegal gaming freely in that state in the City of Newport located just across the Ohio River from Cincinnati — for decades.

In that town, Buccieri also had co-owned and co-operated the Tropicana Club casino inside the Glenn Hotel until he'd run afoul of the law in 1961.

Supposedly at the behest of the Cleveland Syndicate, Buccieri, then 39; his business partner Tito Carinci; the Newport police chief and two detectives had set up George Ratterman so he'd get arrested, convicted and imprisoned.

Ratterman, 35, a former National Football League Cleveland Browns football player and father of eight, had been running at the time for sheriff of Campbell County, Kentucky on a platform to eradicate gambling and vice in Newport.

Buccieri and his co-conspirators allegedly had knocked out Ratterman with chloral hydrate, posed him salaciously with a stripper in a hotel room bed at the Glenn and photographed the two. The involved officers had arrested and charged the candidate for sheriff with solicitation of prostitution.

The charges against Ratterman had been dropped once it was proven definitively he'd been drugged. Subsequently, he'd won the election in November.

For his reported role in the setup, Buccieri had been convicted of conspiring with others to commit an offense against the laws of the U.S., specifically violating someone's "right not to be deprived of liberty without due process of law, the right to be free from arrest by an officer acting without legal justification and the right not to be denied the equal protection of the law." In August 1963, he'd been sentenced to a year in prison, pending appeal.

Seven weeks before Buccieri would learn the outcome of his final appeal, the Incline Village Casino was robbed late on a Wednesday night. Three individuals, all of whom somehow allegedly hid their faces with toilet paper, pried open the cashier's cage, and the change and counting rooms.

"What are you doing here?" asked the custodian, Dominic E. Pagan, upon seeing them.[1]

"You keep quiet and say nothing," ordered the man wielding the revolver. "We aren't going to hurt you."

The thugs forced Pagan to the ground and bound and gagged him with torn strips from a bar rag. They stole several sacks of money but the exact amount taken hadn't been disclosed publicly.

A *Nevada State Journal* reporter interviewed Buccieri about the crime for an article and in it, identified him as the casino's proprietor.

Had Buccieri posed as such or had the journalist gotten the title wrong? Had Buccieri unofficially been in charge? Why had he even been there? Was the robbery perhaps an inside job? Was it a one-time skim maybe? Or was it truly a random event committed by unknown perpetrators?

In July, the U.S. Court of Appeals for the Sixth Circuit upheld the lower court's ruling regarding Buccieri's alleged 1961 crime.

He'd go to federal prison in March 1967 to serve a year-long sentence but would be back at this very Lake Tahoe casino in the 1970s.

1967

Perhaps in anticipation of Buccieri soon becoming unavailable, or perhaps not, Benjamin "Benny" Lassoff applied in late January 1967 for a gambling license and a 50 percent stake in the Incline Village Casino. He'd been the manager of the adjacent bar since Wood had taken over those facilities.

Lassoff may have even known or had a history with Buccieri, as Lassoff hailed from Cincinnati, and the two allegedly had Mob connections.

In 1963, the FBI had charged Benny, along with his brother, Robert Lassoff, and 11 other individuals, with using illegal, long distance telephone hookups between 1952 and 1959 to conceal a nationwide horse race betting system in Ohio. Described as some of the biggest names in lay-off horse race gambling operations, these men allegedly had bribed telephone company employees to fix switchboards so that wagering calls went through unauthorized, toll free and untraceable by U.S. agents.

The Lassoffs, though, had been acquitted.

Nevada's gambling regulators approved Lassoff in April for a gambling license and a lower-than-requested casino share, 10 percent. He invested $25,000 ($189,000) in the enterprise.

The Incline Village Casino continued for months without problems and seemed as though it finally could succeed.

That prospect changed, however, in the fall. While on the job there as a craps stickman,[*] Clayton P. Gatterdam pulled misspot dice[†] — ones missing certain numbers — from a hidden pocket in his apron and swapped them for those in play. One die of his, for instance, bore two ones, two fours and two fives.

Two Nevada Gaming Control Board (NGCB) investigators, who at the time happened to be conducting a random, undercover cheating check at the casino, witnessed Gatterdam in flagrante delicto.

The cunning employee had arranged in advance with an acquaintance to collude in the swindling and split the winnings. The accomplice was to bet at his craps table, and to ensure he won, Gatterdam was to insert the misspot dice.

"[We was] going to try to put the dice in and take the place off, shoot the bankroll. We was going to try to beat the house," Gatterdam said in his statement to Wood's attorney. He also admitted to having been a crossroader,[‡] or swindler, for the past 20 years.

---

[*] A stickman is a casino employee who's responsible for calling dice rolls and moving around the dice with a stick, especially in a game of craps.

[†] Misspot dice have numbers missing, say a two, a four and a six or other combinations.

[‡] A crossroader is a casino cheater; the term, which originated in the Old West, denoted someone who practiced their trickery at saloons located at crossroads.

Gatterdam[§] originally was from Louisville, Kentucky, but most recently had been living in Fort Worth, Texas. *Had he known Buccieri and/or Lassoff? Had one of them put him up to cheating the casino? Or were only Gatterdam and his co-conspirator behind the plot?*

Consequently, the NGCB closed the Incline Village Casino on October 15, 1967 — standard procedure — and filed a formal complaint against Wood and Lassoff despite neither having been on the premises when the chicanery had occurred. The board recommended the Nevada Gaming Commission (NGC) revoke both men's gambling license.

Per Nevada law at that time, once the NGCB registered a house cheating complaint, the named gaming operator or operators had 15 days to surrender their license or appeal the charge(s), and they were entitled to a hearing before the agency. Should a licensee disagree with that proceeding's outcome, they could fight it via the courts.

Any time the NGC witnessed insider cheating at any gambling joint, it could suspend or revoke the owner or operator's gambling license or, due to a state law passed only months earlier, fine the licensee — regardless of whether or not the licensee had known the fraud had been occurring.

With a suspension, the operator could reapply for and possibly obtain a license any time afterward. With a revocation, a harsher penalty, the operator had to wait until a period of time set by the NGC had elapsed before trying for a new license.

[§] About 1.5 years later, Gatterdam again would be caught using misspot dice, this time in London, England, to swindle unsuspecting Americans, on an overseas gambling trip, out of their cash. He'd be sentenced to three years in prison there.

"These procedures were established for two purposes, to protect players against cheating and to protect the reputation of the state," stated an editorial published in the *Las Vegas Sun*.[2] "Should it ever become established that the state allowed a cheating operation to continue one minute after irregularities are detected or even strongly suspicioned, the fat's in the fire for sure and there'll be a field day for the ever-ready critics of our major industry."

To keep the casino running and to clear his name, Wood requested the NGC permit him to reopen the Incline Village Casino under his personal supervision.

In exchange, he'd, one, pay a fine of whatever amount the NGCB determined; two, abide by whatever the NGCB's ruling would be with respect to Lassoff; and three, ensure the shift boss present at the time of the cheating stayed off of the premises.

Though the regulators acknowledged Wood likely hadn't known about the cheating, the NGC rejected his plea and invalidated his license for a year.

"I think this thing was handled unfairly, but [the NGC] is the boss," Wood said.[3]

Lassoff took a different tack in addressing the NGCB's complaint. Through his attorney, he publicly questioned NGC Chairman George M. Dickerson's right to participate in Lassoff's disciplinary proceeding due to a supposed conflict of interest. Dickerson was the brother of Nevada Attorney General Harvey Dickerson, whose office served as the legal counsel for the gaming commission.

Chairman Dickerson refused to recuse himself, and the NGC honored his decision. Lassoff then filed a lawsuit to recuse Dickerson from the hearing. As a result, the NGCB postponed the formal inquiry until after a court decision. In the meantime, Lassoff's gambling license, too, would remain null and void.

Unable to run the casino, Wood sought to lease or sell his 90 percent interest in it and if necessary, even unload, as a bundled asset, the connected restaurant and bar components he also owned.

That task would prove to be easier imagined than achieved.

CHAPTER 9

A TENTACLED REACH

<u>1967</u>

With Caesars Palace open and his relationship with Jay Sarno now combative, Nate Jacobson looked to other casino opportunities.

"Sarno, meanwhile, had come to detest being Nathan Jacobson's partner," wrote Pete Earley in *Super Casino*. "Both of them were quick-tempered and had massive egos. Sarno complained that Jacobson was taking credit for Caesars Palace. 'They acted like a bunch of children running around, fighting all the time,' [Sarno's wife Joyce] said."

Jacobson, a graduate of the University of Baltimore, had excelled in business at an early age. At 24, he'd become the youngest chartered life underwriter of insurance in the U.S. while working at his father's Maryland insurance firm. By age 30, he'd achieved lifetime member status of the prestigious Million Dollar Round Table by having sold a million dollars' worth of insurance annually for many consecutive years. He'd established his own insurance agency at age 36 and by that time was married with two sons.

At 5 feet, 4 inches in height, the "truculent hotelman" was "trim and fit," with "hair carefully sprayed and arranged," and he moved "like a tornado within a tornado," reporter Foster Church would describe later.[1]

"He was a fiery little man, but he knew what he wanted, and he was a good executive. The only thing is he had trouble getting along with a lot of people," said Arthur "Artie" Selman, who'd met Jacobson in 1966 and would become a close friend and business partner.[2]

Jacobson, though, had a softer side as well.

"He actually was a really sweet guy and had a great sense of humor," recalled Pamela Picard, an Eastern Airlines flight attendant who would have a brief relationship with Jacobson in 1972. "He had a great heart and was a lot of fun to be around. He was dynamic, just a live wire, so colorful and so out there."[3]

With his business acumen and experience with the Caesars Palace project, the "tiger in business" pursued additional deals and expanded the number of casinos he was involved in, as an investor, owner and/or operator, not only in Southern Nevada but also in the state's northern counterpart.[4] At times, he juggled responsibilities for two or more gambling properties.

A rumor persisted that Jacobson was affiliated with the "Jewish Mafia," which he denied vigorously and which couldn't be substantiated. The "Jewish Mafia," an unofficial name, collectively referred to Jewish-American alleged organized crime figures, such as Arnold Rothstein, Meyer Lansky, Benjamin Siegel and Mickey Cohen.

Jacobson's next business arrangement was with Frank Sinatra, to whom he supposedly broached the idea of Sinatra ending his relationship with the Sands hotel-casino in Las Vegas where he'd put on concerts for 16 years. Jacobson offered him a performance contract with Caesars Palace, one that would allow Sinatra to own a share of the gaming corporation.

Shortly after, in September, at the Sands, a drunken Sinatra reportedly provoked a fight with the 250-pound casino manager Carl Cohen, yelling obscenities and upending a table that spilled hot coffee on him.

With one punch, Cohen knocked out two of Sinatra's front teeth, or maybe just some caps, and sent him to the floor. Sinatra tore up the hotel switchboard, drove a golf cart through a glass window and tried to call and complain to Howard Hughes, who'd just purchased the Sands.

The media cited the reason for the dispute as Cohen stanching Sinatra's $200,000 credit line ($1.5 million) at the Sands and "Ol' Blue Eyes" refusing to sign a marker, or I.O.U., for what he owed.

Jacobson, however, said the cause was the more lucrative contract he'd offered Sinatra, and noted that the singer hadn't been concerned about credit because Caesars would've advanced him all that he'd wanted.

After the brawl, Sinatra signed a three-year agreement in September with Caesars Palace to perform there biannually for the next three years. As part of the arrangement, Caesars' owners, Desert Palace, Inc. — Jacobson, Sarno and others — acquired the Cal-Neva Lodge in Crystal Bay from Sinatra's[*] gaming corporation Park Lake Enterprises for a reported $2.5 million ($19 million).[†]

---

[*] Although the Nevada Gaming Commission had revoked Frank Sinatra's gambling license in 1963 allegedly for allowing Momo "Sam" Salvatore Giancana, boss of the Chicago Outfit, to stay at Lake Tahoe's Cal-Neva Lodge in Crystal Bay, Sinatra had retained ownership of the property. Giancana was one of a list of personas non gratas in Nevada's casinos, as determined by the state's gambling regulators. This compilation was dubbed the "Black Book"

"We may reopen it as Caesars Cal-Neva Palace," Jacobson said.[5]

Jacobson subsequently sought a gambling license to operate the casino there — 10 games and 170 slot machines. When the license application came before them in November, the Nevada Gaming Commission (NGC) members expressed their reluctance to approve it. This was due to a recent *LIFE* magazine article that had alleged that Mobsters were connected to Caesars Palace — a valid claim.[‡]

After the exposé published, however, Jacobson wrote a letter to *LIFE*, a copy of which he mailed to the NGC. In it, he demanded a retraction and to be told the basis of the publication's assertion about the Las Vegas resort.

"To me, for this commission at this point to consider this application without at least some exhaustive search back into the records that may have been made available to the board and the comFmission before passing upon the suitability of this applicant for multiple licensing would be doing a discredit to the state of Nevada," said NGC Chairman George Dickerson.

The NGC referred the application back to the NGCB for further investigation, which it conducted. After, it recommended giving Jacobson a six-month gambling license, which the NGC granted the following month.

The question of Jacobson being a Mobster or him and his properties having ties to organized crime syndicates would arise again.

---

because it occupied pages in a black-covered, lined notebook; today it's called the Excluded Person List.

† This sale price couldn't be verified.

‡ It later would be confirmed that Jerome Zarowitz was the front man and casino manager at Caesars Palace for Miami Mobsters and that they and others were skimming from the casino's revenue.

CHAPTER 10

WANTING STABILITY

<u>1968</u>

For nearly the year's first half, Art Wood's challenges with the Incline Village Casino persisted. In January, it looked as though he'd sell it for $70,000 ($508,000) to a local, Newell F. Hancock.

A CPA like Wood, Hancock, 49, was familiar with the business and industry inasmuch as he'd provided services to various casinos and was a maiden Nevada Gaming Control Board (NGCB) member, in 1955. Also, he'd represented Alvin Kroll in his dealings with Nevada's gambling regulators regarding The Sierra Tahoe in previous years.

Hancock applied for a gambling license, proposing to operate only 64 slot machines initially. Yet seven days later, he reversed course, opting not to acquire the casino.

"I was trying to do something to allow the casino to reopen, but I have an accounting business to think of," Hancock said.[1]

What the impasse was remains unknown. *Had someone from the underworld convinced him to renege?*

In that same period, the county commissioners expressed their dissatisfaction that Wood and the previous casino owners — Cal

Kovens, Harold Riel and Roy Lewis — hadn't moved the gambling operation to the Lake Tahoe Hotel property across the street as mandated and hadn't made any efforts in that regard.

Officials already twice had extended the special use permit that let the commercial enterprise temporarily remain lakeside, and the most recent allowance was due to expire in May.

Wood explained to them he'd wanted to move the casino, but doing so hadn't been feasible financially. He cited his not having enough capital, the Incline Village area having experienced only minimal economic development in the past two years — both symptoms of Northern Nevada's equally long recession — and the general inability to finance gaming projects. He requested more time.

A conservationist group, the Lake Tahoe Area Council, urged the county in a letter to revoke the casino's special use permit.

The group's president, Marden D. Simms, argued that the permit amounted to spot zoning and conflicted with the goals already set in the regional plan for the Lake Tahoe Basin. He also stressed that the presence of gaming facilities along the lakeshore was impractical and inappropriate aesthetically.

Attorney Oliver Custer, who represented some other area residents in the matter, added that the casino drew many cars and traffic, which created a noise nuisance for neighbors.

The county's Zoning Board recommended the permit be withdrawn, but the commissioners, the ultimate arbiters, were mixed in their opinions. Three of the five felt Wood should be given some leeway because his previous, extensive Incline Village commercial real estate development had benefitted Washoe County. Chairman Howard McKissick, Sr., for one, however, was less forgiving.

"I think they're kind of laughing at these boards and coming in with excuses," he said.[2]

Ultimately, the commissioners added another six months to the deadline, noting the special use permit unequivocally would be rescinded when that time elapsed, which would be October 31.

"Rather than work a hardship on the man, we thought we'd help him out a little, and it'd be up to him to play ball," said Lou Berrum, the Zoning Board chairman. "You take the difficulty he ran into in losing his license. We figured a man who had come in, spending a million dollars and so on for the good of Nevada, we figured that ought to have a little consideration."[3]

In late spring, another potential buyer of the Incline Village Casino came forward — Robert "Bob" J. Peccole, 53.

He was a Las Vegan with an extensive gambling industry background that had begun in his hometown in 1934 at the Big Four casino. More recently, he'd leased and had run nearby Cal-Neva Lodge's gambling operation, in 1965 and 1966, before Nate Jacobson, Jay Sarno, et al. acquired the property from Frank Sinatra.

The Nevada Gaming Commission (NGC) issued Peccole a new gambling license in May, and Wood and Lassoff[*] sold him their interests in the Incline Village Casino.

The new owner invested $125,000 ($908,000) for 10 table games, 71 slot machines and a keno counter. For that assortment and accounting for the on average 20 percent increase in gambling taxes in 1967, the annual amount due for the casino totaled about $65,000 ($472,000) plus a percentage of gross gaming revenue.

---

[*] In November 1968, Chairman George Dickerson resigned from the Nevada Gaming Commission. Subsequently, Lassoff aborted his lawsuit challenging Dickerson's right to preside over Lassoff's penalty hearing, and the Nevada Gaming Control Board dropped the cheating charges against Lassoff.

Peccole opened the casino on June 1, in time for summer, the busiest season thanks to tourists.

He eventually also took over as the general manager of the Lake Tahoe Hotel, which Cal Kovens still owned. The hotel was doing well, Peccole said, particularly due to small convention business and local attractions.

The Ponderosa Ranch,[†] for instance, a theme park based on the 1960s television western *Bonanza*, which had been launched in Incline Village the previous year, drew tourists. Another popular destination was Ski Incline, which had been open since late 1966. Also, the Greater Reno Chamber had initiated three-day, Reno-Tahoe adventure packages for visitors; the $49.50 Western Scenic Tour included lunch at the Lake Tahoe Hotel and a tour of the Squaw Valley ski resort.

"Families like it because it's quiet here, away from the crowds and the neon [of downtown Reno and Las Vegas]," added Peccole. "We run bus trips for the ladies to places such as Virginia City[‡] and almost babysit the kids at Ponderosa Ranch."[4]

He also commented that about six firms, including two major chains, had expressed an interest in buying or leasing the Lake Tahoe Hotel.

"I don't know who is going to buy it or when, but the price is $6.5 million [$47.2 million]," he said.

After about nine months of disruption, business at the Lake Tahoe Hotel and the Incline Village Casino appeared to be under control and stable.

[†] The Ponderosa Ranch was the fictional setting of the Cartwright family ranch for the TV series *Bonanza*. Parts of the show's last five seasons and three TV movies were filmed at the Incline Village location.

[‡] Virginia City, an inhabited mining ghost town, was a popular spot. During the 1800s, it had been the destination for much of the timber logged in Incline.

The status quo though for Bill Swigert, an original owner and developer of these enterprises' predecessor, The Sierra Tahoe, was disrupted with a lawsuit. Years after that Pacific Bridge Company & Associates (PBC&A) business venture concluded, Norman Tyrone, the financier with connections to the Teamsters Pension Fund (TPF), sued Swigert.

Tyrone claimed Swigert still owed him a $58,200 finder's fee ($425,130) for the $2.6 million TPF loan he and his partners had turned down in 1964 and thus, never received!

"These provocative transactions show what has happened to some legitimate developers who have tried to borrow money from the huge pension fund," reported the *Oakland Tribune*.[5]

The case would drag on for three years. Swigert would file a countersuit, arguing that Tyrone, Harold Riel and Roy Lewis[§] fraudulently and successfully had represented themselves as agents of PBC&A to receive the $2.6 million loan in PBC&A's name, and then they'd used it to buy The Sierra Tahoe from PBC&A's trio of owners.

Eventually, Tyrone would drop the finder's fee issue, but in the meantime, that very loan again would come to the fore for him. In 1970, the U.S. government would investigate how Tyrone had handled the brokering of it.

"The feds were looking into it. They interviewed [attorney Frank Farella and me] several times," Swigert said.[6]

During the federal grand jury hearing on the matter, Tyrone allegedly would lie about the loan.

[§] In early 1973, Roy Lewis would be sentenced to six months in jail for lying to a federal grand jury that was investigating the financial transactions ($13 million from the Teamsters Pension Fund) related to development of Beverly Ridge Estates, a residential community in Santa Monica, California — in which Cal Kovens also had been involved.

He'd claim he hadn't, one, demanded an 11 percent commission on it; two, conditioned PBC&A getting the TPF loan on the company paying $200,000 to his and Elliot Roosevelt's Bahamas corporation; and, three, presented to Swigert and Farella, in the final TPF loan documents to be signed, a prepared agreement to pay that $200,000.

Ultimately, the grand jury would indict Tyrone on three counts of perjury.

The self-described broker would fail to appear for the setting of a trial date, but in 1971, a jury-less proceeding would occur in federal district court. Swigert and Farella would testify. Tyrone, on the stand, would refute the allegations.

U.S. District Judge Bruce R. Thompson would deliberate for under an hour and find Tyrone guilty of perjury. He'd sentence him to three years of probation and a $4,000 fine ($25,000).

Later that year, an appeals court would affirm Thompson's ruling.

CHAPTER 11

WHEELING AND DEALING

<u>1968</u>

Nate Jacobson continued his frenetic business maneuvers and became one of the few Nevada casino owner-operators to have held multiple gambling licenses simultaneously.

In the fall, still with a gambling license for the Cal-Neva Lodge in Crystal Bay, the former insurance man applied to Washoe County for a permit to turn the one-floor, 40-room inn into a 10-story, 240-room hotel.

About 25 local residents, along with attorneys representing other nearby property owners, objected to the proposed high rise, insisting it would spoil the beauty of the northern Lake Tahoe region. The Help Protect Lake Tahoe Association placed a roughly three-quarter-page ad in the local *Nevada State Journal* and *Reno Evening Gazette*, urging concerned citizens to share their disapproval of the project with any of the county commissioners.

The Committee for the Planned Development of Lake Tahoe published an Open Letter, pleading for denial of a permit.

In the end, the Zoning Board members and county commissioners allowed the high rise. The green light to expand had been the final criterion needed to be met before Jacobson and his co-owners could sell the property.

The owners of the Club Cal-Neva in nearby Reno — the Sierra Development Company — acquired the Cal-Neva Lodge for $3 million ($22 million).

1969

Early in the year, Jacobson teamed up with the Levin-Townsend Computer Corporation, a New York-based computer leasing firm owned by Howard S. Levin, president, and James Townsend, executive vice president.

Together, the parties planned to acquire and reopen the closed Bonanza hotel-casino in Las Vegas; take over the Lake Tahoe Hotel in Incline Village; and build a new 1,500-room resort on the Las Vegas Strip.

First, Levin-Townsend and Jacobson purchased the bankrupt 160-room Bonanza for $10 million ($69 million) from Nevada financier, Kirk Kerkorian, early in the year. Levin-Townsend held an 85 percent interest and Jacobson, 15 percent.

They then acquired the Lake Tahoe Hotel from Cal Kovens,[*] whom Jacobson knew, and the Incline Village Casino from Bob Peccole. Jacobson owned 80 percent and Levin-Townsend, 20 percent, of the combined entities.

For the transaction and anticipated revamping of the facilities, Jacobson refinanced the existing mortgage with the Teamsters

---

[*] In February 1971, Cal Kovens would begin his three-year prison sentence resulting from his conviction in the 1964 trial with Jimmy Hoffa. He'd be released on parole early in January 1972, allegedly to help then presidential nominee, Richard Nixon, garner Florida's Jewish vote.

Pension Fund (TPF) and borrowed another $6.5 million from it ($45 million) for a total $15 million loan ($103 million).

He planned to remodel and expand the existing Lake Tahoe Hotel tower and the lakefront annex, which would render, inside and out, the appearance and feel of his new name for the whole resort: Kings Castle.

The casino corporation would remain A.L.W., Inc., originally formed by Art Wood. Jacobson would form a corporation for the hotel, Kings Castle, Ltd.

In May, after Jacobson resigned his post as Caesars Palace's president, the Nevada Gaming Commission (NGC), in a 3-to-2 vote, approved him for a temporary gambling license to run the Bonanza casino. He and Levin agreed Jacobson was to run the casino as the president, paying Levin-Townsend $300,000 ($2 million) in rent per month to do so, and was to carry this out only until Levin found a suitable replacement.

The businessmen moved forward quickly so the gambling house could begin generating revenue. In short order, Jacobson opened and was operating it.

However, his relationship with Levin then soured, and Levin sought to oust him from the casino presidency and all involvement with the Bonanza. Jacobson, though, successfully sued Levin to remain put. He also obtained a court order that prevented Levin-Townsend from interfering with his running of the casino until the court could review Levin's complaint against him.

While the Bonanza drama unfolded, Jacobson received a second gambling license in June, this one for the Kings Castle casino, formerly the Incline Village Casino, for 20 games and 303 slot machines. It was only for four months, through October 31, at which time the special use permit, temporarily allowing the casino on the lakefront, would expire.

At the June 1969 Nevada Gaming Control Board (NGCB) meeting, when his application was discussed, Jacobson said he believed he could make money with the casino, funds which he then could use to offset some of the operating losses at the Kings Castle hotel. He added that he expected to construct a new casino across the street, and therefore close the lakeshore one, by July 1, 1970, the grand opening date for the entire, renovated Kings Castle resort.

"I'll be very candid with you. I could never vote for [license approval] if I thought, through one way or another, you'd keep that [casino] running on that side of the lake, or try to," Frank Johnson, NGCB chairman, said in the meeting.

"I'm committed to the Variance Committee, and we are committed to you," Jacobson responded. I will give it to you in a signed statement or any other document that would make you feel at ease with us."

In July, trees were felled and earth was moved for the Kings Castle hotel expansion. The work had to be rushed to beat the expected winter snowfall.

One day during this time, Jacobson and Arthur "Artie" Selman, 35, were sitting and talking in Kings Castle's lakefront restaurant. Selman was Jacobson's partner and second in command at Kings Castle, with the title of vice-president of food and beverage; all employees worked under him.

Nevada Senator Coe Swobe entered and ate lunch, Selman recollected. After, he approached and confronted the duo about having cut down an extra 150 to 200 trees on the hotel property across the street, which they'd done but with approval from the various pertinent regulatory bodies.

Incensed, Jacobson stood and, yelling, asked the senator where he'd been when the Crystal Bay Development Company,[†] the original developer of the Incline Village master-planned community, had decimated 10,000 trees.

"I said to [Nate], 'The handwriting is on the wall. I'd stop this right now,'" Selman recalled, referring to the entire Kings Castle project, "but we were in too deep with the financing."[1]

The two forged ahead with Kings Castle as planned, opening the casino, still on the lake, which Richard "Dick" Piper, who had years of gambling industry experience, ran for him.

"The casino resembles a great hall of an ancient palace, with huge wooden beams supporting the ceiling and torches (electric, naturally) lighting the walls," reported the *Los Angeles Times*. Crests and coats of arms adorn the lighting fixtures, and shields are done in stained glass."[2]

There, in the Lakeside Lounge, The Kirby Stone Four, a vocal ensemble, provided nightly entertainment and dancing. The subsequent act would be Deacon Jones, former defensive end for the Los Angeles Rams turned singer, backed by Ray Frazier and the Continentals. The Carpenters would follow.

Ads for the casino began to appear in local newspapers. One read:

> Welcome to Lake Tahoe's new realm of fun. For 'round the clock action in the bawdy tradition of Old England, it's the Kings Castle Hotel and Casino. Where nitehood is in flower.[3]

[†] Art Wood sold the Crystal Bay Development Company and its assets to the Boise Cascade Corporation in mid-1968.

Meanwhile, in Las Vegas, the Levin-Townsend Computer Corporation applied for a gambling license[‡] of its own to remove Jacobson from the Bonanza for good. The NGCB, however, recommended denial because of "unsuitable financial arrangement[s] and misrepresentation made to the board at the time of the original licensing" by both Bonanza owners, board member Wayne Pearson said, according to the July 1969 NGCB meeting minutes.

"While the parties told us this was a happy marriage, in fact there was an argument between the two parties, and one or both failed to live up to the commitments which they had told the board would be carried out," Johnson said.

Before ruling, the NGC requested more information about the Jacobson-Levin spat, which had been about money. Jacobson had wanted Levin to pay him for Jacobson's stock interest in the Bonanza's operating company, but Levin had said Jacobson wasn't entitled to any money. Levin, however, had offered $475,000 ($3.3 million) to settle the issue, but Jacobson had refused it, insisting the amount was too little. Then the two had refused to speak to each other.

It's unknown how, but Levin and Jacobson finally reached an agreement.

Levin bought Jacobson's 15 percent interest in the Bonanza, making Levin-Townsend the single owner of that property. Levin

---

[‡] The Corporate Gaming Law that Nevada legislators had passed in 1967 allowed publicly traded corporations to own casinos without requiring all of their numerous shareholders to be investigated for a gambling license. The entities, however, were subjected to rigorous review and regulation. The intent of the law was to help clean up and legitimize the state's gambling industry by making it harder for individuals to conceal disallowed ownership in gambling clubs.

also turned over to Jacobson Levin-Townsend's 20 percent ownership in Kings Castle, leaving Jacobson as its only proprietor.

Jacobson quit as president of the Bonanza, and Levin assumed the position after the NGC approved his corporation for a gambling license.

Around the same time, the original partners of Caesars Palace hotel-casino sold it to Lum's, Inc., a nationwide family restaurant chain, for $58 million ($400 million). It was their only move if they wanted to avoid charges of being complicit in the skim taking place there because federal agents had Caesars Forum, the casino, in their sights for shutdown.

In the fall, with the expiration of the Kings Castle casino's gambling license and special use permit looming, Jacobson sought extensions of both.

He told the NGCB he intended to remove any public areas from the lakefront. In fact, he said, he was considering turning the existing casino facility into a club for teenagers, those living in the area and staying at the hotel, where they could have ping-pong tables, a soda fountain and a dance floor. He again reiterated his promise to move the casino by July 1, 1970.

"When we granted you that temporary license, I was pretty adamant that on October 31 it went and that was it. But the more I see of some of those condominiums and the junk that's getting put up there with the blessings, apparently, of Washoe County, I think your place has got twice the class of those, and I'm personally in favor of extending it," Johnson said in an October 1969 NGCB meeting. "I'm all for going along, trying to save things, but I think the local people ought to think a little bit about it, too, now and then."

Despite previously committing to pulling the special use permit when it expired this time, the county Zoning Board agreed to extend it a fourth time, through July 15, 1970.

Now, no longer involved with the other hotel-casino ventures — the Cal-Neva Lodge,[§] the Bonanza and Caesars Palace — Jacobson would focus all of his attention and efforts on Kings Castle. He would be in for some surprises.

[§] Larry Ellison, co-founder, chairman and chief technology officer of Oracle Corporation would acquire the Cal-Neva Lodge for $35.8 million in January 2018. He'd express his intent to turn the property into a high-end resort.

CHAPTER 12

ONE-TWO PUNCH

1969

When, earlier in the year, Nate Jacobson had acquired the Northern Nevada properties he'd renamed Kings Castle, Incline Village's thoroughfare State Route 28 meandered along Lake Tahoe between his casino, restaurant, bar and bungalows (on the lakefront) and his hotel (on the landlocked side).

Yet, months after the resort expansion and renovation began, the State of Nevada moved further north a four-mile stretch of that road, including the segment that ran by Kings Castle, thereby bypassing it completely.

"Apparently, Jacobson, in his search for a choice location, selected a wooded paradise whose inhabitants wanted to keep the public out. ... The unsuspecting Jacobson went ahead with Kings Castle, in the meantime, unaware that he had picked the only spot on the lake so exclusive that the traffic was to be routed around it," wrote *Merry-Go-Round* columnist Jack Anderson.[1]

The hotelier became furious when he learned of it.

"They stole the highway from me," he said.[2]

He suspected the owners of the nearby Ponderosa Ranch, Bill and Joyce Anderson, had been behind the change as their tourist attraction was on the new route, Jacobson told the press. He believed Joyce unduly may have influenced Republican Nevada Governor Paul Laxalt's actions on the matter, as she'd been, at the time, head of the Nevada Federation of Republican Women.

In reality, the Andersons hadn't been involved. The county and state long before had approved moving that street portion as part of the region's master plan because surveys had projected that by 1987, traffic there would exceed 9,000 vehicles per day and would double or triple that during peak weekends.

"The [new] location of the highway will lessen the problem for people in the residential area," said William Engel of the Nevada Division of Highways. "It will take motorists to the heart of Incline Village, an obvious benefit to the community."[3]

In fact, the number of automobiles on that stretch already had hit 7,600 during a July 1968 count. That's about as many American-owned cars that were in the entire U.S. in 1900. Further, the Nevada Gaming Commission members had mentioned in a meeting as early as May 1965 that a move of SR 28 was likely.

1970

The next blow Jacobson perceived to his envisioned North Shore empire happened early in the year when construction on the Kings Castle hotel still was in process. He requested county approval of his plan to build another project on the lakefront near the Kings Castle bungalows. Kings Manor Condominiums was to consist of two, 10-floor towers with a swimming pool and tennis courts.

Local property owners and conservationists balked at his proposal, alleging it would lead to urbanization of Lake Tahoe, much like that of Miami Beach, they said. One Incline Village resident, T.R. York, expressed his dissent via an Open Letter to Coe Swobe, the Nevada senator who previously had boasted of his own environmentalism. It read:

> You are the protector of Lake Tahoe? Where were you on Tuesday, February 4, 1970, when Kings Castle applied to the Washoe County Regional Planning Commission to build twin-tower 10-story condominiums at Incline Village? Where were you on Tuesday, January 21, 1970, when the Crystal Bay Club won approval for their proposed 11-story hotel from the same planning commission?
>
> ... Aren't the high rises detrimental to Lake Tahoe in the areas of pollution, environment, and the newest phrase, ecology — or are hotels above all that? Are the gaming industry's building plans, regardless what area of Lake Tahoe, acceptable to you, but developers, who are building homes or subdivisions for individual families a more logical and easier opponent? You sure give reasons by your actions to believe so! ... Where was 'the protector of Lake Tahoe' when his objection was needed?[4]

To the protestors, Jacobson responded, "This is progress, not destruction," emphasizing that his plan satisfied all existing county ordinances and zoning requirements.[5]

With a 6-to-5 vote, the county's Planning Commission recommended that the final decision makers, the Board of Commissioners, disallow the project, suggesting it'd be better to wait to consider the issue until the congressionally created, bistate

(Nevada and California) Tahoe Regional Planning Agency (TRPA)[*] released its finalized development standards for Lake Tahoe, which were due out shortly.

The board then refused Jacobson a building permit for the condo development. The next day, the TRPA officially adopted the new building codes for the lake region. Among other regulations, they limited building height to 2.5 stories and population density to 15 living units per acre, both maximums that Kings Manor Condominiums would exceed.

Jacobson sued both commissions, claiming they'd acted "arbitrarily, capriciously and without just cause and in excess of their jurisdiction."[6] He requested the judge order the Board of Commissioners to approve his condominium plans.

In a subsequent hearing, the commissioners explained they'd rejected Jacobson's plan because it breached TRPA rules. Further, they accused Jacobson of trying to fast track his project through the permitting process before the planning agency released its relevant restrictions.

Reno Justice Judge John E. Gabrielli upheld the commissioners' decision, stating Jacobson lacked a "vested right, as against future zoning, merely by purchasing the property in reliance upon existing zoning."[7]

Gabrielli agreed the TRPA standards hadn't been in effect when the commissioners had ruled.

Yet, he said, Jacobson had been "fully aware of the impending limitations and regulations from the Tahoe agency and [had been] seeking to avoid the consequences of a lawful exercise of the

---

[*] The Tahoe Regional Planning Agency was created in 1968 to adopt rules, regulations, ordinances and policies to effectuate a regional plan for the Lake Tahoe area, setting minimum standards for water purity, zoning, shoreline development and more.

policy power of the county and the Tahoe agency by taking undue advantage of the time lapses inherent in governmental processes by 'rushing' this project through before the changes in the law could be final." It had been well publicized that the TRPA had been considering those very development controls for the area since 1968.

Gabrielli's decision was "unexpected and unfair," said Jacobson, who was "damned sore" at the local officials and opposing residents.[8] He threatened to appeal, which he did.

The case would wend its way to the Nevada Supreme Court over the next two years.

Ultimately, the high court would back Gabrielli's ruling, contending the pending regulations took precedence because they were based on standards the Nevada Legislature had established before Jacobson had purchased the Incline Village properties.

Though Jacobson had to scrap Kings Manor Condominiums, his vision for the hotel-casino's metamorphosis would be realized in the new year.

CHAPTER 13

ASSUMING THE THRONE

<u>1970</u>

It snowed and snowed heavily throughout June, rarely letting up. Consequently, much of what was needed to open the hotel-casino the following month — gaming equipment, food and the like — was stuck in Reno because delivery trucks couldn't make the treacherous climb up the Mt. Rose highway, or State Route 43, to the property.

"We all were sweating it out that month," Artie Selman said. "The snow almost put us out of business."[1]

Eventually, the precipitation stopped, the route was bulldozed and disaster was averted.

A swanky gala, much like Caesars Palace's unveiling, marked the grand opening of Kings Castle Hotel and Casino on July 1, 1970. Many Hollywood celebrities attended, such as actresses Barbara Stanwyck and Lana Turner and actors Chuck Connors, Pat O'Brien and Ross Martin. Comedians Bob Hope, and Groucho and Zeppo Marx and producer Sheldon Leonard were a few of the others.

Nevada Governor Paul Laxalt showed, as did Robert "Bob" Maheu, a former FBI and Central Intelligence Agency agent who'd become Howard Hughes' chief executive of Nevada operations, as well as Las Vegas hotel-casino industry bigwigs — Kirk Kerkorian, of International Hotel fame, and Del Webb, who'd built the Flamingo for Benjamin Siegel and the Sahara.

To start the evening, then Miss World USA Gail Renshaw snipped the ceremonial ribbon, and guests dined in the Camelot theatre restaurant. Teresa Graves, a singer and actress who regularly performed on TV's *Rowan & Martin's Laugh-In*, sang and danced for the audience.

During her act, comedian and Kings Castle headliner, Buddy Hackett, unexpectedly usurped the spotlight, entering the stage sporting only a G-string embellished with three identification medallions attendees had been asked to wear during the soirée. The stunt got the audience talking so much that Graves stopped mid-song and said, "I know I'm not the star here, but I'd like it if you would listen to me sing this song."[2]

During Hackett's show that followed, he introduced the notables in the audience and took several potshots (in jest, of course) at Laxalt, Hope, Don Rickles and the casino business. Known to gamble his earnings occasionally, Hackett said, "In Nevada, you don't work for take-home pay but for leave-there pay."[3]

Line Renaud, French songstress, actress and producer of the musical, *Irma La Douce*, debuted her new revue, *FLESH*, in the Jesters Court. The show featured topless beauties along with comedians, Patchett and Tarses, and the vocal quartet, The Sugar Train.

At midnight, Jacobson threw the first dice, rolling a seven (which, in craps, means game over), and Laxalt introduced and paid tribute to him.

Unexpectedly, during the evening, someone attempted to cheat the casino, but Jacobson, with the help of Nevada Gaming Control Board agents and Sheriff Bob Galli, thwarted it.

"Opening night was like a page out of a Las Vegas book," wrote columnist Perry Phillips.[4]

The festivities were to celebrate completion of the transformation of Kings Castle, formerly the Lake Tahoe Hotel and the Incline Village Casino, and before that, The Sierra Tahoe. Jacobson had conceived Kings Castle's theme and resort elements. Martin Stern, Jr.,[*] a renowned Beverly Hills, California-based architect, had translated those ideas into a design.

With the $12 million ($78 million) renovation, several floors were added to the three-story hotel to accommodate 264 new guestrooms (230 single rooms, 18 deluxe bedrooms and 16 suites). The revised unit total, including the 48 lakeside chalets, was 470.

The bevy of new amenities included the 960-seat Camelot theatre restaurant, in which paintings of costumed lords and ladies sitting in private boxes adorned the side walls, and the Jesters Court, a 250-person performance lounge that displayed an eye-catching, Bettina Rakita tapestry.

There also were the Excali-Bar casino bar, the Kings Table restaurant, the Royal Box gourmet eatery and a handful of shops — H.B. Burnett (ladies apparel), Mort Wallin (menswear), Faye's, Inc. (gifts) — along with a beauty salon and barber shop.

---

[*] Martin Stern, Jr., who'd designed numerous hotel-casinos in Las Vegas, was credited with the concept of combining spaces for various resort components — accommodations, gambling, entertainment, parking, convention rooms and shopping — in one facility.

Jacobson and Artie Selman had made over the hotel into a stately, 16th-century Tudor castle, outside and in. A burnt orange roof and pennant-embellished battlement topped the neutral-colored exterior. A nude, life-sized, horse-straddling Lady Godiva stood guard with two sentries at the property entrance. Two huge, plastic, silently roaring lions greeted guests at the main doors.

The building's interior showcased various regal color schemes (lots of golds, oranges and earth tones), furnishings and décor (medieval-looking chandeliers, trumpets, swords, stained glass shields, battle axes, coats of arms, crests and torches, for instance), which, together, aimed to evoke a royal, yet romantic, air. The 158 original rooms were refurbished to match the style of those in the new tower section.

Having drawn on his numerous years' experience as a maître d' and having outfitted the Sands' Regency Room and the Sahara's House of Lords — Las Vegas steakhouses — Selman had selected and installed all of the gaming and hotel equipment needed at the Lake Tahoe resort.

"It was a beautiful hotel," he said. "We opened up with a bang."[5]

Outside reactions to the fresh Kings Castle look were mixed. A *Los Angeles Times* article read, "It's one of the most picturesque resorts in the U.S. and built in an idyllic location between the awe-inspiring lake and the majestic High Sierra peaks."[6]

Yet, one critic described the architecture as King Arthur meets Robin Hood. Further, *Oakland Tribune* staffers wrote, "The gaudy high-rise ... bears no resemblance to the quality resort envisioned by the original developers of Sierra Tahoe."[7]

The kingly theme extended to the approximately 900 employees (even the telephone operators), all of whom wore costumes. For example, the maître d' was dressed as a prince, the dining room hostess as a princess and the doorman as a knight in armor. Michel Fresnay[†] designed the outfits, which he described as "mod-medieval." He chose crepes and French silk-cotton for the materials, heavily used the colors deep orange and Gainsborough blue and embellished the women's garb with pearls, brass and gold braid, the men's with leather and faux chain mail.

Even the way the Kings Castle staff paged guests maintained the royal fantasy. For instance, Lana Turner was called "Lady Lana of Turner" and Bob Hope, "Sir Bob of Hope."

As part of the property overhaul, Jacobson had the casino moved from the lakefront facility to the hotel and expanded it to 8,500 square feet. His doing so finally resolved the ongoing, years-long issue of the since-expired special use permit that only temporarily had permitted a casino on the beach. The new gambling area featured 303 slot machines and 23 table games (1 keno, 1 baccarat, 2 roulette, 4 craps and 15 blackjack/21).

The restaurant and bar facility on the beach also was updated to reflect the Kings Castle motif. Even with the absence of the casino, Jacobson had food and drink services continue there, despite the area's residential zoning designation.

"Jacobson ... is a modern day rarity. A dreamer who somehow always manages to make his dreams come true," Phillips wrote. "The idea of putting a multi-million dollar resort hotel in an area not exactly known for its accessibility had to be the wildest of dreams. Making it a reality is even wilder. ... If someone had told me five years ago I'd be someday sitting in a plush 900-seat showroom on the North Shore of Lake Tahoe and seeing Buddy Hackett headlining, I'd have laughed hilariously."[8]

[†] Michel Fresnay had gained notoriety for the gowns he'd hand made for Marlene Dietrich for her performance at the Olympia in Paris.

Behind the glitz, Jacobson would work diligently to make the resort, in its newest iteration, successful.

CHAPTER 14

BETTING ON BUSINESS

<u>1970</u>

The king of the castle publicized his belief that the tourist boom, convention business and an increasing permanent Incline Village population would sustain his hospitality-gaming business. The number of local residents had grown to about 4,200 by the hotel-casino's official launch, about a 33 percent increase over the previous year. That count typically doubled in the summer and peak winter months.

Nate Jacobson estimated Kings Castle would host about 3.5 million guests in the first year and with a 71 percent hotel room occupancy rate, the region's average, generate a comfortable profit.

Navigating the new hospitality and gambling venture, he executed strategies, some of which bucked the industry norms, to boost the bottom line.

One was accepting corporate shareholders. By the 1970s' end, 10 men would acquire and own shares. They would include fundraiser extraordinaire Irvin Kovens, the brother of Cal Kovens who, against the Nevada Gaming Commission's (NGC's) wishes, had bought the hotel-casino in 1966; Morris and Samuel Jacobson, Nate's brothers; and Artie Selman.

Jacobson also offered partial ownership to big-name entertainers like he'd done with Frank Sinatra at Caesars Palace and the Riviera had done with Dean Martin. Don Rickles (1.6 percent ownership) would become one such Kings Castle shareholder. Buddy Hackett applied for a partial interest as well, but the NGCB recommended denial without prejudice to the comedian.

"Stars are in such demand that the club bosses are willing to give away a piece of the business to the stars just to ensure they'll keep playing their clubs," said Marilyn Beck, *Hollywood Hotline* columnist.[1]

Contrary to regular practice, Jacobson avoided exclusive artist contracts. Instead, he booked up-and-comers as well as stars, even ones who'd just performed at Lake Tahoe's South Shore. He started with comics then expanded into musical attractions.

Those initially scheduled to appear were comedians Don Adams, Woody Allen and Rickles and comedienne Phyllis Diller.

Singers included Tony Bennett, Johnny Mathis, Sarah Vaughan, Della Reese, Thelma Huston, Pearl Bailey, Peggy Lee, Connie Stevens and Phyllis McGuire. Also on Kings Castle's entertainment calendar were The Platters vocal group, "The Hip Hypnotist" Pat Collins, singer-songwriter and guitarist B.B. King and many more.

Additionally, Jacobson refused to pay entertainers the salaries they were garnering in Las Vegas, which were steep. For example, four years earlier, in 1966, the Dunes had paid five times as much for lounge entertainment and 15 times as much to produce a show than it had a decade earlier. The costs for each were:

Costs	1956	1966
Lounge	$2,000–$3,000	$10,000–$20,000
Show	$50,000–$75,000	$1 million

Major Riddle, president of the Dunes in Southern Nevada, had cited competition with other properties as the reason for the escalating costs.

"Las Vegas pays the highest amount of money for entertainment," Jacobson said. "I don't know why. I don't accept it, and I don't see any reason for it."[2]

Jacobson advertised Kings Castle extensively. Two days before the grand opening, he ran a full-page, color enticement in the *Nevada State Journal* that read:

> It's a merry forest of fun and games on the status side of the lake — new Kings Castle at easy-to-reach Lake Tahoe. Surrounded by a babbling brook, a sandy beach and a forest of towering trees, it's Nevada's crowning jewel — and perhaps the world's most opulent hotel casino and vacation resort.
>
> Kings Castle returns thee to those deliciously decadent days of old when living and laughing and lavish love verily crackled in the air.
>
> Nearly 1000 loyal servants, knights of old and ladies-in-waiting, garbed in courtly costumes, will pamper thee with endless pleasures. Forsooth[*] — a king should have it so good!

---

[*] Forsooth is an archaic word meaning "indeed," "in truth" or "in fact," often used derisively or to express disbelief.

Golf, swimming, fishing, riding, hunting, tennis, dancing, dining or a regal romp in the woods — all are here in our 20-million dollar kingdom of pleasure.

Buddy Hackett, in the Camelot Theatre, will tickle thy fancy and thy funnybone as a feast of kingly proportions is laid upon thy table. And, in the Jesters Court, *FLESH*, a mad, mod, marvelous review — will raise thy spirits and thine eyebrows.

Thy room accommodations wilt feature tapestries, palace paintings and coats of arms to put thee in touch with the past; but touch the buttons on thy phone and thou wilt be in touch with thy Japanese masseuse, thy recreational director, thy hairdresser, or any of the thousands of regal services the Castle provideth.

Kingly pleasures for a pittance await thee at Kings Castle where thou wilt be the guest of the most laughable, lovable landlords ever: Sir Buddy of Hackett, Sir Don of Rickles, Sir Woody of Allen, Sir Don of Adams, Sir Nathan of Jacobson and the lovely Lady Line of Renaud. And soon Sir Tony of Bennett and Sir Shecky of Greene will add to the pleasure of the court.

Come ye for a day — a weekend or a week. The keys to the kingdom are all thine, even if thou dost not stay at the Castle.[3]

Other ads, like this one titled *Kings Castle-Ski Casino Tahoe*, which would appear in area newspapers in November 1970, would promote the area's winter sports and opportunities for fun:

> Nineteen ski areas only minutes away. Ski Incline is at our doorstep. Snowmobiling. Sleigh rides. Winter swimming. Kings Castle exclusive Royal Ski Club. Guide service. Junior Ski School and supervised youth center. Lavish accommodations. Exquisite dining. See Line Renaud's mad, mod, marvelous musical revue, *FLESH*. Fun and games in the snow at this magnificent 16th Century Ski Headquarters.

Like all of the proprietors before him, Jacobson was gambling boldly, in a big way, on this hotel-casino, albeit now transformed. He'd made sizable wagers before but on a much smaller scale in comparison.

Forsooth, he enjoyed high-stakes games of chance. On New Year's Eve in 1972, he would win $80,000 ($484,000) while playing blackjack at Caesars Palace then immediately lose that amount plus another $80,000, Pamela Picard, his companion that evening, would recall.

About his daring wager on Kings Castle, though, the *Los Angeles Times* wrote, "Nate Jacobson ... is betting that a swinging resort on Tahoe's North Shore will prosper. ... [He] has a beautiful area working for him as well as a picturesque resort facility."[4]

FROM JEWELS TO JUNKETS

<u>1970-1973</u>

During Kings Castle's first two years, Nate Jacobson tried in various ways to garner media attention for the resort and, thereby, attract guests. For instance, the hotel, for a period, displayed replicas of England's Crown Jewels, valued at $60,000 ($391,000). Antique British weaponry and 48 diamonds rounded out the exhibit.

"What is a castle without treasures and legends and intrigues and curses?" asked John Polando, the resort's publicist.[1]

Jacobson also expanded local athletic offerings, augmenting developer Art Wood's prior efforts to transform Incline Village into the world's best recreation area.

"We want to see this community take its place in the national field of winter sports," Jacobson said. "We have an area that is comparable to anything I've seen in Switzerland. We want to work with the people of Incline Village to let the world know it."[2]

He started the annual Kings Castle Snowmobile Grand Prix, which the local media touted as "the world's richest snowmobile race and the first race of its kind in the West."[3] The competitors drove at speeds of up to 100 miles per hour on a three-mile loop around the resort, and the winner received $50,000 ($326,000).

Before the event took place, however, area residents had complained that construction of one track segment had caused land depressions that had collected water and, in turn, had polluted Incline Creek.

In its first year, 1970, the series of contests drew the likes of Rodger Ward, a two-time winner of the Indianapolis 500; Duane Eck, the snowmobile speed record holder; Roger Jannson, the world's snowmobile champion; and Paula Murphy, who'd claimed the women's land speed record.

Celebrities who participated for fun or simply attended as spectators included: Woody Held, Major League Baseball player; Don Drysdale, former Los Angeles Dodgers pitcher; John Brodie, San Francisco 49ers quarterback; Deacon Jones, Los Angeles Rams defensive end; Joe Louis, former heavyweight boxing champion; Buddy Hackett, comedian; Ken Venturi and Bob Rosburg, golfers; and Mama Cass Elliott, singer with The Mamas & The Papas. Nevada Governor Paul Laxalt presented trophies to the winners.

The Grand Prix, which generated no income, cost Kings Castle $100,000 ($651,000 today) to stage, including the $50,000 prize, Jacobson said.

In 1971, turnout was equally, if not more, impressive.

Jacobson welcomed another sport in the North Shore township, too — boxing. At the time, major fights weren't broadcast to households. Instead, they were aired live via closed-circuit television only in two or three select Northern Nevada locations, and Kings Castle was one of them. The hotel sometimes even offered fight packages that included a ticket to watch the match on site, drinks and transportation to and from Reno.

Some of the bouts that aired at Kings Castle were:
• Jerry "Irish Jerry" Quarry v. Cassius Clay/Muhammad "The Greatest" Ali (October 26, 1970, Atlanta)
• Joe "Smokin' Joe" Frazier v. Bob "Blitzin' Bob" Foster (November 18, 1970, Detroit)
• George "Big George" Foreman v. Daniel "Boone" Victor Kirkman (November 18, 1970, New York City)
• Cassius Clay v. Oscar "Ringo" Bonavena (December. 7, 1970, New York City)

Jacobson, who loved playing tennis, wanted to make the nearby Incline Village tennis courts usable year-round. In late 1970, he commissioned the installation of a $40,000 ($261,000), three-story-high, vinyl, bubble-like cover over them. Inflating the 6,000 pounds of material required huge air blowers.[*]

"You can tell that Nate is a tennis lover when he spends $50,000 to build something that can keep guests away from the casino," Clyde Billman, Kings Castle's public relations director said, embellishing the cover's actual cost.[4]

Kings Castle hosted sports competitions and/or related awards banquets, such as the British Motors championship tennis tournament and the Kennett Sandbag Golf Open Invitational.

Among the many national magazines that praised Kings Castle for its sports offerings, *SKI* magazine, in its August 1971 issue, named the resort one of the "10 Great Lodges to Stay At," due to its "comfort, flamboyance and central location."

Other types of events took place on the property, such as the 1970 Miss World USA contest,[†] with Bob Hope as the emcee.

---

[*] Months later, someone intentionally would puncture the bubble with a 31-inch-long slash, but it wouldn't collapse entirely.
[†] Leanna Johnson, 20, of Las Vegas competed for Nevada, but Sandie A. Wolsfeld from Illinois won the title.

North Lake Tahoe's 11th Annual Snowball and Miss Sierra Snowflake beauty pageants followed a year later.

Numerous groups held conferences and conventions at the resort. Among them were the National Association of Attorneys, the Nevada State Dental Society and Creative Merchandise.

Also to boost revenue, Jacobson kept the showroom open during the winter whereas the other Lake Tahoe hotel-casinos didn't. *Love-In* was one show that ran at Kings Castle during such a period, from October to January.

Produced and directed by the resort's entertainment director Line Renaud, the musical revue at one time featured 30 dancers, the Matt Vernon III vocal group, the Trotter Brothers puppeteers and the Hereafter Band.

"Other clubs in the area may be watching Kings Castle to determine the feasibility of running year-round entertainment in their showrooms," reported the *Nevada State Journal*.[5]

Jacobson and Renaud maintained an impressive calendar of performances. Well-known groups that performed at the hotel-casino included the groups, The 5th Dimension, Joe Frazier (the boxer) & The Knockouts, and Brasil '66. Singers included Sergio Mendes, Hal Frazier, Lou Rawls, Robert Goulet, Jose Feliciano, Paul Anka and Tony Bennett.

Comedians, as well, remained a mainstay at Kings Castle, including the likes of Joan Rivers and Shecky Greene. Don Rickles, who appeared frequently, often poked fun at Jacobson during his act. One time, Rickles said about the chief executive officer: "I hear he slept out in the parking lot in a Brink's car, counting his money all night."[6]

Jacobson and Rickles, in 1971, held an "Insult Don Rickles" contest. The person who submitted the "nastiest, most venomous" statements about "Mr. Love and Warmth" would win an all-expense-paid, two-day vacation for two at the hotel-casino, including tickets to Rickles' act.[7]

"I am entering this contest in the hope of losing. I couldn't accept a prize that contained seeing Don Rickles perform," one contestant wrote. Another joked, "Rickles has never been in a crowd. Who would stand next to him?"[8]

The winning entry, however, was this barb from Susan Reynolds of Taos, New Mexico, who relayed it to Rickles on stage at Kings Castle: "Dear Don, I despise myself and have absolutely no regard for myself as a person. Marry me!"

"I'd really like to take you up on your offer to get married, but I have a low tolerance for boredom," Rickles retorted.

"Does that mean you never rehearse your act?" she quipped.

Kings Castle also hosted gambling junkets, organized groups of usually out-of-state residents with ample money, a good credit history and a desire to gamble. The resort covered the costs of transportation, meals and accommodations for these visitors with the hope they would spend and lose money — lots of it — in the casino.

This tactic, however, backfired, Artie Selman said, when Jacobson began accepting junketeers with questionable finances and an unsavory reputation. Selman disliked it and warned Jacobson it could lead to money problems for the resort.

Ultimately, their differing opinions on the junkets escalated into an unresolvable conflict between them in 1971. Selman consequently resigned his position, withdrew his investment in Kings Castle and returned to Las Vegas, he said.

Selman was yet another person in a long string with whom Jacobson fought ferociously to achieve an end.

Tahoe Forum, rendering by Mario Valenzuela

The Sierra Tahoe, photo by Thomas "Doc" Kaminski

The Sierra Tahoe's lakefront bungalows

The Sierra Tahoe's mascots

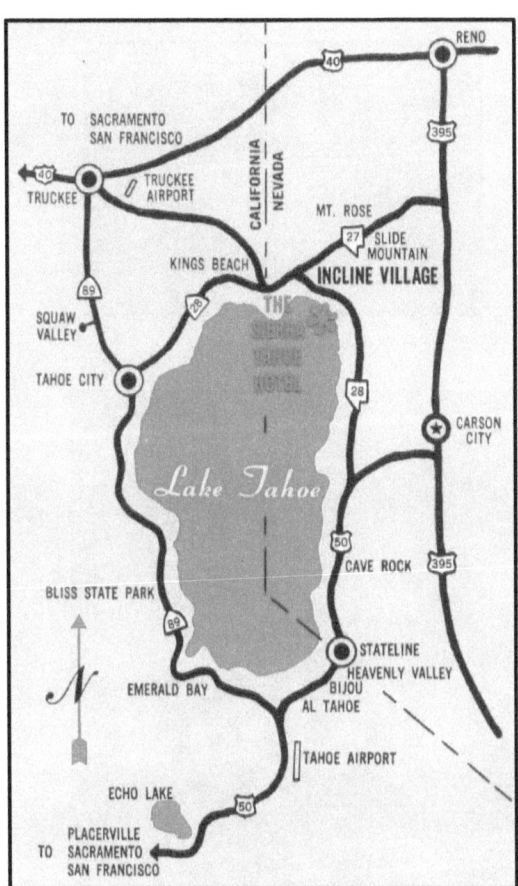

Photos of
Nathan S. Jacobson
and Camelot are
courtesy of
Beth Van Tassel's
*Wood Chips to
Game Chips*

The property's location at Lake Tahoe

Incline Village Casino gambling token

95

Nathan Jacobson

Kings Castle

Kings Castle postcard

Camelot rendering

CHAPTER 16

KINGS CASTLE (NO) WAY

1971

A nother brouhaha involving Kings Castle began in the spring when Nate Jacobson requested that Washoe County change the name of the resort's cross street to Kings Castle Way from Country Club Drive. His main hotel-casino property sat at the corner of that road and Lakeshore Boulevard (also known as State Route 28, or SR 28).

"Many millions of dollars were invested in a long existing commercial enterprise, and the damage inflicted because of the diversion of the tourist traffic created immeasurable financial damages," wrote Jacobson in a Letter to the Editor. The name change would "perhaps give some small degree of identification for the economic necessity of Kings Castle and as a courtesy for tourists seeking its location.[1]

"I have some problems finding it myself," he added.[2]

Perhaps harming Jacobson's case was his two signs alongside the Mt. Rose highway that read, "Thy Kingdom Come — Straight Ahead to Kings Castle."

One Washoe County citizen addressed them, also by Letter to the Editor:

> Who is responsible for this desecration of a Christian's most cherished possession — our Lord's Prayer? ... This letter is just to let the person responsible for the billboards know, it is deeply offensive to all who love Him.[3]

A local contingent responded to Jacobson's street name change request with outrage, contending a switch would be pandering to a business and creating a slippery slope.

Before the county commissioners were to vote, Kings Castle's attorney, Frank Petersen, argued that if customers weren't directed to the hotel-casino, the local economy therefore would suffer.

"Kings Castle pays one-fifth of tax assessments in Incline Village, and $12 million ($75 million) emanates from Kings Castle [annually] into functions of our government," he said. "How long would that [Incline Village] Golf Course sustain itself if the hotels and motels didn't sustain the economy?"[4]

With a 2-to-1 vote, the commissioners overrode the Street Naming Committee's recommendation, a rarity, and allowed the name change. All of those present voted except Chairman Roy Pagni, who deemed the issue insignificant.

"The only thing that bothered me was the people who opposed the name change were very vindictive against Kings Castle," Pagni said. "If there was something that would affect the livelihood or harm the people, I would give it serious consideration, but this is not one of those."[5]

The *Nevada State Journal* criticized Pagni for not voting and called his opting out "perplexing."[6]

"He is the commissioner from the unincorporated area," an editorial noted. "If memory serves correctly, he said, while seeking election last fall, that his incumbent opponent was not properly representing the unincorporated area — and that, if he were elected, those people would get the representation to which they were entitled."

Many Incline Village residents expressed their belief that not just Pagni but all of the commissioners continued to fail them with respect to the street name change.

"It is completely out of order. We've lost our birthright. These people of this community are 98.9 percent against it," said George Sayre, a local homeowner.[7]

Local businessman, Kirk Moon, said such a ruling in the face of heavy community opposition was what had caused the Boston Tea Party.

"It's crass commercialism," he added. "It's a flagrant abuse of representative government. A meeting should be called so the community can decide what legal or political action to take."[8]

Moon and other area property owners formed a citizen's committee, the Voice of Incline Village-Crystal Bay, to pursue getting the ruling overturned. They circulated a petition and initiated a phone campaign that primarily targeted Pagni, as he would've been the one to break a tie vote.

In imploring the Board of Commissioners to reconsider, a handful of Incline Village residents clarified their stance in a subsequent Letter to the Editor:

> We feel the issue has been clouded, and we wish to make clear the fact that this matter is not a personal vendetta against Mr. Nate Jacobson. He was within his rights in requesting this name change. That we do not agree with his reasons for so requesting is not the point. What so deeply angers us is the remaining commissioners' complete ignoral of the Planning Agency's recommendations, as well as most of the residents' wishes.[9]

Five state senators from Washoe County — Coe Swobe, Thomas Wilson, Procter Hug, Lea Harris and C. Clifton "Cliff" Young — sided with the locals. Via letter, they called the commissioners' decision shocking and asked them to revisit it.

Some Nevadans who supported the name change also made known their views. The Bakers, for instance, wrote in a Letter to the Editor:

> We are residents and property owners in Incline Village and have been a little puzzled at the resistance that some of the residents of Incline Village have displayed over the name change. ... We realize how the Kings Castle tax dollars help the economy of Washoe County (which we are part of) and are happy to have the hotel here. The roadway name change is a very small thing in comparison to what the hotel does for Washoe County residents.[10]

Similarly, Charles and Faye Zanay, owners of Faye's, Inc., the gift shop at Kings Castle, also in a Letter to the Editor, thanked the three commissioners who'd voted, for their "fair" decision.[11]

The commissioners held a hearing on a possible name change re-vote, during which they prohibited anyone but themselves from speaking; about 50 opponents and 40 proponents were there, in the room.

To his co-commissioners, Robert Rusk said:

> The time has come to consider the demands and respect the wishes of the constituents who represent the vast majority of taxpaying citizens at Incline. ... I think the democratic process flunks miserably if this request is allowed to prevail.[12]

He read a protest letter in which the author accused Jacobson of lacking spirit and not paying his bills and said she couldn't bear the thought of living on a street named in honor of such an operation.

The county commissioners voted no (3-to-2) to rescinding their previous decision, thereby reaffirming the name change. After the meeting, Rusk told the newspaper he was disappointed his peers refused to even discuss the issue, particularly when beforehand in private they'd agreed to do so.

Five days later, Jacobson gave $8,000 ($50,000) to Incline Village for an all-ages summer recreation program, the donation having been Pagni's idea. The townspeople, however, viewed it as a payoff to Pagni and/or the Board of Commissioners for approving the street name change and accused the two men of such. To end the personal attacks, Pagni recommended Jacobson withdraw the gift, which he did.

"I was amazed that several residents of the Incline community could be so malicious in making wild, unfounded accusations against community-minded citizens and public officials of high integrity," Jacobson said.[13]

By June, Country Club Drive signs, 20 in all, were replaced with Kings Castle Way ones at a cost of $9.55 apiece, or $191 in total ($1,200). Later that month, four of the new placards were vandalized, covered with blue metallic paint, the name obscured — a reflection of the locals' lingering fury over the issue.

In fact, they weren't finished fighting it. Via mail, the Voice polled residents on whether it should try to, one, reverse the road name change and, two, get Pagni recalled, indicating it would proceed according to majority opinion. Of the 3,800 property owners who'd been mailed ballots, 843 replied, per the Voice.

The results, published in the *Nevada State Journal*, revealed most respondents voted for action on both matters, 68 percent and 74 percent, respectively.

Subsequently, Pagni reminded Incline Villagers it takes more than one commissioner to pass any rule. He listed nine battles he'd pursued on their behalf in his five months on the job. The street name change "has been chastised, in my opinion, because of a personal vendetta against [Jacobson]," he added.[14]

Simultaneously, some local non-Voice members exposed the fact that the group, in its poll tally, had counted only the votes of its paying members (about 421) and disregarded the remaining roughly 50 percent of responders' answers. A Voice representative claimed the group had done that for sound reasons but said it planned to release the non-members' responses as well. It never did.

Referring to Incline Villagers, Jacobson said, "These people here belong in Nazi Germany. They're complete bigots. They're bigots on everything. They've made a few dollars, and they think they're better than anyone else. No matter who comes along, they won't accept him. You can't dislodge their ideas, and that's the nature of a bigot."[15]

The street name controversy proved to be small when compared to the one that came next.

CHAPTER 17

BUSTED, TIMES THREE

<u>1971</u>

❚❚ Judging from court action alone, the 'lavish love crackling in the air' has given way to curses," reported the *Nevada State Journal*, referring to the boast in a previous Kings Castle advertisement.[1] Indeed, during the street name change hoopla, Nate Jacobson became embroiled in a legal trifecta with Washoe County.

First, Deputy District Attorney (D.A.) Larry Struve filed a criminal suit against him for illegally running a business — the lakeside bar and restaurant — without the required county license (a misdemeanor). In a civil suit, Struve requested a temporary restraining order to halt annex operations until the mandatory license was obtained and on file.

"I'm the most surprised person in the world," Jacobson said. "This is a very drastic and uncalled for action. All of a sudden like a bolt out of the blue, we get a restraining order. There was no warning, complaint or prior notification."[2]

He asserted that Kings Castle solely used the annex as a service bar for meetings and guests staying in the beach cottages, not as a restaurant. Yet local Deputy Sheriff Jay Hughes, who wasn't staying at the resort, said he'd been served food there recently along with a roomful of people.

"It's been done, as far as we can tell, completely outside the law," Struve said. "Washoe County ordinances require a license for each separate address."[3]

The judge granted the restraining order, and Jacobson, in turn, filed to have it removed. Defying the legal directive, he kept the annex business running but did apply for the compulsory license.

Eventually, Reno Justice Judge Grant L. Bowen lifted the ban and allowed limited use of the annex, for private convention guests only. Jacobson was granted a temporary permit until the upcoming hearing with the county, when the matter was to be resolved for good.

However, six months of related court date postponements would ensue, and then further developments at Kings Castle would render the issue moot.

Second, the issue of the special use permit for the restaurant/bar annex, which had been continual and controversial since the building opened in 1964, again came under scrutiny. Jacobson allegedly had remodeled that facility without a building permit (the contractor's fault, he said).

Consequently, the Washoe County Board of Adjustment, in a public meeting, recommended the county Board of Commissioners: one, revoke the permit that had allowed operations on the lakefront; two, insist all commercial activity in the annex be curtailed immediately; and three, have Kings Castle remove all external annex-related signs. Jacobson accused the agency members of holding an illegal meeting and angrily left the room.

"If I'd any idea what I'd have to put up with [in Northern Nevada], you couldn't have brought me here with a machine gun!"

said Jacobson. "There aren't five men in the world that could do what I've done here. I gave the people of the area the finest in the world — the finest service, accommodations, food and entertainment. All I did here was make it a prettier place, a first-class place from a third-class place. I've given recreation, enjoyment, happiness and good times."[4]

Third, the county realized Jacobson reportedly hadn't filed a requisite certificate of occupancy (CO) for Kings Castle. This came to light via a letter from the office of Richard Bast, the Nevada Fire Marshal, which indicated gas supply and fire alarm system irregularities persisted at the resort.

To avoid a potential explosion there, fire officials requested the gas meter be relocated further away from the boiler room, the hydrant moved and the fire alarm system connected to the Incline Village fire station. Jacobson blamed Bast for not approving placement of the gas meters and for making unreasonable demands.

After the Baltimorean had purchased the property in 1969, the county Building Department had denied him a CO due to building code infractions, but he'd opened Kings Castle anyhow.

"This man has ignored every request by every agency," Commissioner Robert Rusk said about Jacobson. "It's incredible that a $20-million facility could open its doors and not be able to take care of some reasonable problems."[5]

The Board of Commissioners gave Jacobson 30 days to file a CO, which required Bast's approval, or face closure.

Two months later, the county would grant COs for both the hotel and annex properties because the outstanding issues supposedly were being fixed.

"Kings Castle has been subjected to extraordinary harassment [since opening], bordering on the lines of persecution," Jacobson said. "There are underlying motivations that cannot be explained by reason or justice. We do know that there have been certain individual interests that have relentlessly pursued a vicious attack against the interest of Kings Castle."[6]

That torment, Jacobson added, had included unnecessary and illegal hearings, public and private attacks, denial of due process of law and violation of constitutional rights. All of those occurred, he said, despite his cooperation with all agencies and his adherence to all regulations, and all irreparably had damaged Kings Castle financially.

Jacobson instructed his attorneys, he told the media, to sue five public figures for violating the responsibilities of their offices and for colluding to hamper and destroy Kings Castle's existing and potential business. The defendants were D.A. Robert Rose, Rusk, Nevada Senator Coe Swobe and Roy Robinette, the chairman of the Tahoe Regional Planning Agency's Citizens Advisory Committee.

No records of such a lawsuit could be found, however, meaning Jacobson never had filed it, the case file hadn't been kept or it had been archived but not locatable.

"That's fantastic," Rose responded. "An alleged criminal conspiracy is absolutely incredible."[7]

In August, Jacobson and Rusk went on a local radio show, during which each presented his version of the Kings Castle story of the three certifications.

Reno resident, Dorothy Cabbard, sided with Jacobson in a Letter to the Editor:[8]

> The entire controversy shows a clear case of selective, discriminatory railroading by county officials and Rusk's 'facts' strengthen Jacobson's charges of inefficiency.

Another Washoe County resident and businessman, Sandor Vincze, noted, also via a Letter to the Editor, that Kings Castle's payroll was enough reason, given the unemployment rate (then 5.8 percent in Washoe County versus 5.6 percent nationally) for public officials to help, rather than hinder, the resort's operations. He wrote:

> Our commissioners better initiate a policy of public relations with this as well as other businesses in Washoe County instead of running around acting like FBI agents, slapping red tags on buildings and issuing restraining orders. The last thing we need in this area is a 'tearing down' or 'harassment' of existing businesses. We need these businesses badly.[9]

Within two weeks of the radio broadcast, the county commissioners voted 3-to-2 to reinstate the special use permit, thereby allowing Jacobson to operate his lakefront restaurant and bar.

Despite all of the problems, Jacobson reiterated that he remained dedicated to making Kings Castle successful.

"I'll fight these people 'til the last breath I got," he said. "My main interest now is to make the castle highly sought by affluent people all over the world."[10]

At the suggestion of staff members, Jacobson, in a symbolic calling for a truce, threw a summer cocktail party at the resort for local residents, inviting even those who'd spoken out against him and his establishment. Many of the 50 people present seemed to have set aside their grievances, at least for the evening, and deemed the fête a thoughtful gesture.

"Whatever the result of the party, the flurry of controversy surrounding Kings Castle seems to be dying," reported the *Nevada State Journal.*[11]

That statement would prove to be more hopeful than factual.

CHAPTER 18

SHOW ME THE MONEY

<u>1971</u>

Nate Jacobson agitated the detente in October with another lawsuit, this one against the Incline Village General Improvement District (IVGID), the local provider of water, sewer, trash and recreation services to Incline Village and Crystal Bay.

He asked for a refund of the per-room recreational use taxes he'd paid in 1969 and 1970, which amounted to about $25,000 ($155,000), plus interest. He claimed he should've been exempted from paying them because his guests hadn't been able to use or even access Incline Beach due to IVGID having erected a fence between it and Kings Castle in fall 1970.

He also requested restraining orders to prevent additional liens being placed on the resort and further tax being collected. (A lien had been slapped on the hotel-casino property after Jacobson had neglected to pay the amount due earlier in 1971.)

The outcome of the lawsuit is unknown because records couldn't be located.

The hotelier also sued United Airlines (UA) for $10 million ($62 million) for excluding Kings Castle from an article about Lake Tahoe destinations in its in-flight magazine *Mainliner*. He sought $3 million for loss of past and future profits, $3 million for business reputation damage and $4 million in punitive compensation.

Mainliner editorial personnel previously had agreed to run a promotional piece in its publication to advertise Kings Castle and thereby increase travel via the airline to Northern Nevada. However, between the time a writer and photographer had visited the Incline Village resort for content and the issue went to press for March publication, several UA employees had heard unfavorable comments about the resort.

For that reason or perhaps others, the staff had included in the article some Kings Castle resort and employee photos but without any identifiers or corresponding text.

Jacobson claimed UA had conspired with unnamed individuals to remove "Kings Castle" from the article, which consequently slashed the resort's visitor counts and value. The U.S. District Court would dismiss Jacobson's antitrust and common law claims, which would prompt the plaintiff to appeal on the basis they'd been applicable.

In 1975, the U.S. Court of Appeals for the Ninth Circuit would uphold the lower court's ruling. In other words, Jacobson would lose this cause.

Also in 1971, Kings Castle and its owner found themselves the target of numerous legal actions, including the following:

• Architect Martin Stern, Jr. sued for unpaid architecture, planning and construction services he'd provided — $131,733 worth ($819,000) plus interest for Kings Castle and $90,625 ($563,000) for Kings Manor Condominiums.

This suit would wind its way through the judicial system for nine years, with Jacobson arguing he personally wasn't liable for the debt. Stern initially would win a judgement, Jacobson would appeal; the higher court would reverse the ruling and remand the case for retrial. Stern would win again the second time, and Jacobson would appeal once more.

Finally, in 1980, the Nevada Supreme Court would find Jacobson responsible for paying Stern.

• The RCA Corporation of Delaware sued for $28,767 ($179,000) in unpaid costs for Kings Castle having leased and purchased electronic radio and television equipment (which Jacobson wouldn't let the vendor retrieve) and for $4,802 on a promissory note.

The court would dismiss the case five years later, according to the Nevada Rules of Civil Procedure, because the plaintiff, RCA, would fail to take it to trial within that time frame.

In the fall, the American Broadcasting Company (ABC) subsidiary in San Francisco, KGO-TV, aired during a news segment that Kings Castle was in financial trouble and folding.

"The report is unfounded and without truth," Jacobson said, characterizing it as "malicious and beyond our understanding."[1]

Jacobson later would sue ABC and 20 unnamed people in spring 1973, claiming KGO-TV's statements were slanderous and responsible for a significant long-term drop in business, especially from Californians.

Specifically, he would cite an immediate effect of 74 room cancellations, resulting in a $4,538 deficit ($28,000), and 752 dinner theater no-shows. Jacobson would ask for damages for lost revenue — $10,000-plus ($62,400-plus) for the weekend following the telecast along with an undetermined amount for the period between October 18, 1971 and January 31, 1972.

Because the sum sought would exceed $10,000 and because the two parties were located in different states, the judge would determine the case should be moved to the U.S. District Court.

However, because additional records couldn't be found, it's unknown what happened ultimately with the suit.

After that specific KGO-TV news report in 1971, additional companies filed claims against Jacobson for unpaid bills, which had been mounting. They included:

• Hackett Enterprises, Inc. (Buddy's corporation), for $3.5 million ($22 million) in damages for breach of contract. Hackett contended Jacobson was to have paid him $132,000 ($865,000) annually for serving as a board member of A.L.W., Inc., the Kings Castle casino corporation, and was to have granted him stock for his $50,000 ($327,000) buy-in, neither of which Hackett received.

At the behest of Hackett's counsel, though, the case would be dismissed in 1976.

• Tours Unlimited, for $116,670 ($725,000) in damages and costs. It alleged Jacobson, in 1970, had agreed but had failed to pay a $100 per-person fee plus the transportation cost of flying people between New York and Lake Tahoe for a weekend junket.

The result of that case isn't known either because only partial case records could be located.

One month after the KGO-TV broadcast, Jacobson announced he was selling Kings Castle Hotel and Casino for $23 million ($143 million) to two Northern California businessmen — August Marra, 44, a Castro Valley real estate developer, and Dr. Joseph Barkett, 43, a Stockton dentist.

Marra and Barkett were to chip away at the Teamsters Pension Fund loan of $15 million in installments and give Jacobson a lump sum of around $8 million ($50 million), which he was to use to pay creditors.

Jacobson, who'd been working on that Kings Castle deal since late June (right after the annex problems had cropped up), said personal reasons had prompted him to seek a buyer because at that time, at age 56, he'd needed to slow down, quit working 18 hours a day and take a vacation.

"In another year, we could make more money, but I might be dead by then," he said.[2]

He boasted that during his so far 2.5-year reign, the resort had served tens of thousands of guests, gained a national reputation and attained pre-eminent hotel-casino status.

"I am convinced more than ever that Kings Castle will be the most successful operation in the State of Nevada," he added. "To this point, we consider it a most successful enterprise. It has done remarkably well for the short time it has been in business."[3]

Conversely, Marra and Barkett informed the Nevada Gaming Commission (NGC) that Kings Castle was in danger of closing due to its grim financial situation. Thus, the agency gave the two men permission to assume immediate control of the property when the transaction closed on November 20, pending casino licensure.

In the interim, stock would be transferred to William Farina, the current licensee and casino manager, who'd run the gambling until the NGC granted Marra and Barkett licenses.

"This is a rather unusual situation," said NGC Chairman Jack Diehl. "Whenever we are faced with an emergency situation like this, we usually have problems. I want the record to show that I am approving this with reluctance."[4]

Typically, before the NGC made the final decision to approve or deny a casino acquisition, a 90-day escrow took place, during which the NGCB members vetted the buyers for suitability as owners and the gambling license applicants, whether the purchasers and/or other individuals, as licensees. The regulators having given Barkett and Marra the green light so quickly had been unusual, wrote *Political Front* columnist Don Lynch.

"The [Nevada] Gaming Control Board [NGCB] has rarely shown such sentiment," he said. "It generally is hard-headed and deliberate about supervision of Nevada gaming."[5]

When, in mid-November, articles in regional newspapers — Reno, Nevada, and Oakland and Los Angeles, California — divulged that a financial emergency existed at Kings Castle and the plan for dealing with it was to sell the resort to Marra and Barkett, Jacobson "complained viciously" to the NGC, as documented in May 16, 1973 NGCB meeting minutes.

He inquired of the commissioners why they would issue such a press release when he hadn't agreed to it, and he asked what else they and the two buyers had been scheming behind his back.

"My attorney says, 'Don't be a damn fool. If they are buying it from you and they say they want to handle it that way, it's none of your business,'" Jacobson told the NGCB. "[But] I do not think it's bad when I protest something, beyond my control without my knowledge, somebody else has done."

This wouldn't be the last action or idea to which Jacobson would object.

CHAPTER 19

CAN IT GET WORSE?

<u>1971</u>

During a phone call to his home on Wednesday, September 1, Kings Castle keno* supervisor Raymond M. Landucci, 37, allegedly told his underling, keno manager James Martin, that he planned to cheat their employer's keno game for $12,500 ($78,000).

Martin, who'd seen Landucci manipulate the keno machines with a wire instrument previously, reported the conversation to Forrest S. Paull, the resort's vice president of security and personnel and a former police officer. Martin, who expected Landucci to call him again the next night about the scheme, requested Paull be there for it.

The following evening, Thursday, September 2, at about 7:30 p.m., Nate Jacobson informed the FBI by phone that because he'd

---

* Keno is a game of chance that's similar to bingo and lottos. "Keno" comes from the French word "quine," which translates in English to "five winning numbers." On a ticket, players choose up to 20 numbers they think will be selected from a group of 80. The winning numbers then are generated and announced and/or posted.

'felt uneasy for some time,' he'd engaged a bodyguard, Thomas J. Bruno, 32, 'a nice, clean-cut kid' who'd need to carry a gun, he said, according to agency records.

The Kings Castle owner denied any problems had precipitated the hire but noted a junketeer had threatened him in Las Vegas the previous week. 'In my business, you make a lot of enemies,' Jacobson said. 'You never know when some crackpot might try to take a shot at you.' He'd informed Sheriff Robert "Bob" Galli about Bruno the previous day, he said.

About 2.5 hours after Jacobson's FBI call, Landucci telephoned Martin and talked about perhaps revising the scam details. Paull wasn't at Martin's residence for that call, but later in the evening when Landucci rang again, he was and listened in.

According to Paull, he overheard Landucci outline this plot: Landucci would rig the machine, so it would generate certain winning numbers. When ready, he would signal to Martin and an acquaintance Norm, in the casino, by combing his hair. Next, Norm would buy a $5, five-spot ticket[†] for the winning numbers decided on in advance. Martin would blow his nose when it was safe for Norm to cash in the ticket, and Norm would do so.

Also during the overheard exchange, Martin asked Landucci if he really wanted to go forward with the plan; Landucci said he certainly did. Also, the alleged mastermind clarified a change; they now were to take the game for only $4,500 ($28,000) rather than the originally decided $12,500 so as not to look suspicious to the Internal Revenue Service.

[†] A five-spot keno ticket is one on which a player has selected five numbers. With it, the player has the chance of winning the most money in the game because a hit pays out at a much higher percentage of the total payback than any other spot-type ticket. However, with a more substantial payout, a five spot is a riskier play.

By Landucci's account, sometime after he arrived at Kings Castle that Thursday night for his shift, Paull called him to his office. There, the security head grilled him for nearly three hours, using veiled threats to get him to admit to concocting and trying to pull off a keno cheat. Eventually, Paull gave him a half-hour "to get some answers right away or Nate [Jacobson] would get them his way."[1]

While in the office with Paull, Landucci didn't admit anything because there was nothing to confess to, he claimed. He never intended to steal from the casino. His jiggering of the keno machine merely was to test Martin's honesty because he was "after my job."[2] If Martin passed, he'd be promoted; if he failed, he'd be fired. Landucci asked several times to be given a polygraph test — a routine procedure at Kings Castle — but was denied.

Paull's recollection differed slightly. He said Landucci did confess finally to the keno scheme after Paull confronted him with evidence of his phone conversation with Martin. Paull admitted to rejecting Landucci's repeated requests for a lie detector test, explaining he believed it unnecessary and Landucci's emotionality would yield inaccurate results.

The subsequent event, which all of the involved parties agreed happened, is Paull left his office. Jacobson, with Bruno in tow, entered; Paull stayed out.

"What the hell is going on?" Jacobson then asked.

"Nothing," Landucci said.[3]

Jacobson called him a liar. "Do you think you're smarter than me?"

Landucci again asked to be given a lie detector test; Jacobson refused and continued pressing him for answers.

"Jacobson was like a wild man, like he was out of his head, cussing and screaming," Landucci said.[4]

After two or three more hours of interrogation (only 20 minutes, per Jacobson), during which Landucci didn't confess, he said, Jacobson and Bruno struck him about the face and head numerous times. Bruno squeezed Landucci's neck with his hands and while doing so, lifted him off of his feet then dropped him on the couch.

Shortly after, Landucci added, Bruno removed a revolver from Paull's desk drawer and tossed it on the floor in front of Landucci. Bruno produced a pistol from somewhere, likely his person, cocked it and held it about four feet from Landucci's face.

"Pick it up," Bruno said, meaning the revolver.[5]

Landucci declined. "I definitely felt he would pull the trigger."[6]

Still aiming the pistol at Landucci's head, Bruno moved the revolver closer to Landucci. He again ordered him to grab it and instructed Jacobson to call for an ambulance.

"What do you want? I'll do whatever you want," Landucci said.[7]

Bruno reportedly told Landucci he already had one murder rap,[‡] so Landucci would best be served by keeping mum about what just had transpired.

Jacobson opened the office door, and Paull returned. The boss demanded Landucci name his accomplice. Landucci first insisted there was no one but eventually blurted Norm, a guy he said he'd met briefly in Carson City but couldn't describe physically.

Paull wrote a confession in his own words, which Landucci signed without reading, he said. In Paull and Jacobson's versions of

---

[‡] Bruno, two months earlier, had stood trial for the shooting death of 17-year-old Michael McCray in Maryland when Bruno had been the manager of Harry's Corral, a strip bar on the Block, Baltimore's red light district. Outside of Harry's, two groups of males, McCray in one, had gotten into an argument with each other. When one chased off the other, someone shot at those being pursued, hitting and killing McCray. A jury had acquitted Bruno.

events, Landucci was too nervous to write, so he dictated his confession to Paull, who jotted it down.

Then Jacobson gave Landucci the option: Stay at the hotel (presumably until Norm showed at the casino) or be turned over to the police. Landucci chose the former, thinking at the time, he said, Jacobson never would've let him leave the premises, even with law enforcement officers.

Contrarily, Jacobson recalled that Landucci was free to leave the property at any time but volunteered to hang around in a guestroom instead. Consequently, Jacobson instructed Paull to notify Landucci's wife Dawn that her husband would be delayed. (Dawn telephoned Kings Castle several times after Raymond's shift started to speak to him but was told repeatedly he was in a meeting and couldn't be disturbed.)

Jacobson then turned the matter over to the hotel-casino's security detail, letting them deal with Landucci as they saw fit and surveil the casino to intercept Norm when he showed to cash in the keno ticket.

A security guard escorted Landucci to a Kings Castle hotel room, wherein he remained locked with a guard and a disconnected telephone. An unidentified male (likely Paull) phoned and told Dawn that Raymond was working a double shift.

When Raymond didn't arrive home by 10 a.m. on Friday, September 3, Dawn became anxious, she said. When a friend of Raymond (possibly Norm) happened to call her and ask for him, she told him she was worried. He responded that he, too, had a bad feeling because when he called Kings Castle earlier, he was told Raymond wasn't seen since midnight.

Almost six hours later, at 3:45 p.m., Dawn again telephoned the hotel and threatened to show up with a sheriff and an attorney if they didn't put her through to Raymond immediately. The switchboard operator refused, and Dawn hung up. However, soon after, Jacobson's secretary called and told Dawn that Raymond was just leaving the property.

According to Landucci, at about 4 p.m. Friday, September 3, after having been sequestered for about 12 hours, he was fired and told he could depart. (Jacobson said Landucci left at noon.) On his way home, the now unemployed keno manager got into a minor traffic accident.

It was common then and for decades prior for casino owners, licensees, managers and security personnel to intimidate, threaten and even get violent with suspected cheaters, both patrons and especially employees.

"A dealer who cheats the house seriously may count on being severely beaten," wrote Wallace Turner in *Gambler's Money*. "It is widely believed around Las Vegas that a few dealers who cheated the house were murdered and their bodies buried in the desert. It matters not whether this is true; that the dealers believe it is enough."

Jacobson and Bruno, however, denied there was any involvement of guns, threats or violence in their interaction with Landucci, only some yelling and obscene name calling by Jacobson. They insisted that when Landucci left Paull's office, he wasn't cut or bleeding. Bruno said he didn't question or touch Landucci, didn't mention a murder charge and didn't even have his gun with him that night.

Jacobson said, "The substance of my conversation with Landucci was his persistent denial of intending to carry out the plan and my refusal to believe that."[8]

Because September 2 had been Bruno's first workday at Kings Castle, the FBI suspected that, at Jacobson's request, he flew in from Baltimore, where he lived, to assist with the Landucci situation. Were that the case, it would've been an ITAR-EXTORTION crime — interstate and foreign travel or transportation in aid of racketeering enterprises — however, agents never proved it.

Jacobson called Landucci's account of his, Bruno and Paull's treatment of him "a farce" and Landucci's assertion the confession was coerced, "a complete lie."[9] He, his bodyguard and security officer simply were addressing a personnel matter — a possible cheating plot against the casino, in this case — and did so within their rights, in accordance with a law passed during The Silver State's 1971 legislative session, Nevada Revised Statute 465.101. It read:

> Any gaming licensee, or his officers, employees or agents, who have probable cause for believing any person violated any provision of Nevada Revised Statute (NRS) 465.080 prohibiting cheating in gaming may detain such person in the establishment for the purpose of notifying a peace officer.

Jacobson added that fresh in his mind was a theft that had occurred 1.5 months before the Landucci incident, in which a 21 dealer and two accomplices had gotten away with stealing about $16,000 ($99,000).

Thus, the resort owner wanted to question Landucci immediately to avoid another financial loss whereas Paull's approach was to let the plan unfold and nab Landucci and his partner in the act.

Rather than have Landucci prosecuted, Jacobson believed if he could get him to cooperate, he said, he could determine who else was involved and how the machine rigging worked to avert such a cheat in the future. Because Landucci obliged, notifying the police wasn't warranted.

Events related to the supposed Landucci keno cheating scam wouldn't end that day, Friday.

CHAPTER 20

THE TROUBLESOME AFTERMATH

<u>1971</u>

Immediately following Nate Jacobson and Thomas Bruno's alleged violent attack, physical and verbal, on Raymond Landucci on September 2, 1971 and possibly into the next day to force a confession, someone from Kings Castle reported to the FBI that their boss and his bodyguard had "worked over" an employee and were holding him on the premises, FBI files showed.

That informant hadn't been Raymond Landucci, as he'd been terrified harm would befall him and/or his family regardless of what he did or didn't do, Dawn Landucci would say later. For months following the incident, Raymond kept loaded guns around the house and banned his children from opening the front door or going outside. Dawn greeted visitors to her home with a pistol in her hand. Raymond handcrafted and installed iron bars over the windows, which he locked at night. For a year, the Landuccis never went out after dark.

"In my mind, they wanted my husband dead," Dawn said, referring to Jacobson and Bruno. "My husband didn't want to worry me. He tried to tell me everything was all right. I didn't believe him because his actions showed he was so upset and afraid. He would pace the floor."[1]

Raymond also worried, she said, that if word of his supposed keno scheme got out, Nevada's gambling industry would blackball him, leaving him unable to land a job.

The day after the tipoff, two FBI agents interviewed Raymond at his home for about three hours, during which he frequently asked them to leave.

"He was upset and scared and made several comments that he thought we were not officers but instead, sent there by someone else," Agent Harold H. Newpher said. "He was very nervous. He expressed fear for his life and the safety of his family and didn't want to talk about the incident."[2]

Landucci, however, reluctantly agreed to give them a statement. Upon signing it, he commented that doing so was his "death warrant."[3] The agents instructed him not to discuss the September 2 and 3 events with anyone. They photographed bruises they noticed on his face and neck, arranged for a medical examination of Raymond and took as evidence the shirt he'd worn during the alleged ordeal.

The FBI referred the lead to the Washoe County sheriff's office for investigation. That agency then relegated it to the county district attorney's (D.A.'s) office. Anticipating a blowup from Jacobson, D.A. Robert Rose, instead of charging the two men, turned over the case to a grand jury, which subsequently issued an indictment against Jacobson and Bruno.

A week after the boss and bodyguard's alleged crimes against Landucci, an anonymous woman called the local FBI office in the late morning, "obviously hysterical," and told them the management at Kings Castle was, at gunpoint, threatening employees with killing their children if they say anything to the

D.A., a bureau report documented. 'They are bringing in guns up there,' and employees are 'scared to death. FBI, please watch them; it's terrible,' the caller said then hung up.

On November 30, three months after the alleged crimes and two weeks post indictment, local sheriff's officers apprehended Jacobson and Bruno. The charges were first and second degree kidnapping — holding someone to commit extortion and holding someone against their will, respectively — and extortion involving threats and coercion.

"[My arrest] was a despicable and unwarranted abuse of power" and harassment by D.A. Rose, Jacobson said.[4]

At Jacobson's request, relayed through his Reno attorney Frank Petersen, Rose and the Nevada Gaming Commission had agreed to delay the arrest so as not to undermine the imminent sale of Kings Castle.

Consequently, a *Reno Evening Gazette* editorial writer queried:

> Since when, we suggest our citizenry consider, is the district attorney's office supposed to participate, directly or indirectly, in how private business affairs are conducted by gamblers or anyone else? It would appear to us that if a law is broken — and we do not assert that any has been — the prosecutors have the responsibility to serve 100 percent devotion toward arrest, prosecution and conviction.[5]

Further, the writer accused Rose of putting the onus on the grand jury in this case to shield his office from criticism.

Jacobson and Bruno were released the same day on $10,000 ($62,000) bail apiece.

On local KOLO Channel 8 television, the resort owner read an Open Letter to the World, a rebuttal of the charges against him and Bruno. Near tears at times, he related his distress and humiliation at being arrested — how, for the first time in many years, he'd sobbed and how he'd have to explain his arrest to his 10-year-old grandson. He'd fought inequity, injustice and immorality all his life, he said, but now lacked the energy to keep it up.

"At this moment, I believe I don't want to even stand trial. It is a dishonor and disgrace just to face such charges," he said. "To be forced to defend such charges is tantamount to lending them dignity."[6]

Despite his proclaimed weariness, Jacobson hired a second attorney, Los Angeles-based Thomas R. Sheridan, who was known for prosecuting the 1963 Frank Sinatra, Jr. kidnapping case.[*]

After seeing Jacobson on television, one Sparks resident wrote, in a Letter to the Editor:

> I have witnessed a lot of incredible performances in Reno, but that of gambler Nate Jacobson tops them all. Here is a man who thumbed his nose at the public, put up billboards in the most gross bad taste … and allowed the most indecent shows in his showroom that I have ever seen. Now, he is appealing to the public for sympathy.[7]

Jacobson initiated a massive internal investigation to discover the source of the tip that had led to his arrest. Suspecting the leak

---

[*] Just days after Former U.S. President John F. Kennedy had been assassinated, three men had kidnapped Frank Sinatra's 19-year-old son, Frank, Jr., from Harrah's Lake Club on Lake Tahoe's South Shore, where he'd been performing. They'd demanded a $420,000 ($3.5 million) ransom. Sinatra, Sr. had paid it, and Jr. had been released, unharmed. The FBI had arrested the three suspects and had recovered most of the money.

had come from the keno department, he pulled and reviewed personnel files, ferreting out employees who might have known federal or local law enforcement officers.

He also phoned and asked Special Agent in Charge Harold Campbell, Jr. whether or not the FBI had been a party to framing him for "trumped up charges." The criminal action was a local matter, thus not in the FBI's jurisdiction, Campbell responded, according to the agency's file on Jacobson.

Campbell also made the note that "Jacobson launched into a lengthy tirade about being victimized by local authorities and possibly by federal authorities on what he termed were ridiculous and false charges."

Landucci, with the help of Reno attorney, Peter Echeverria, in mid-December, pursued a civil suit against Jacobson, Bruno, Forrest Paull and seven other Kings Castle employees.

He asked for more than $20,000 ($124,000) in compensatory and punitive damages for false imprisonment; assault and battery; conspiracy to falsely accuse him of employment misconduct and ongoing slander. He alleged that after September 2 and 3, the defendants had continued to tell and publish lies about him, causing him, his wife Dawn and two children ridicule, humiliation and anxiety.

A trial date was set for the next year.

1972

The Landuccis, in early spring, filed for bankruptcy, citing Raymond's lawsuit against Jacobson, Bruno, Paull and others as the cause.

At the time, Raymond was working as a warehouseman at Wedco, Inc., an electrical products company in Reno, and Dawn remained unemployed as a stay-at-home mom.

On their bankruptcy petition, they claimed $27,603 ($166,000) in debts (none of which was for legal fees) and $1,050 ($6,300) in assets.

As for Jacobson, his arrest would prove to be the point at which his problems increased in number and severity.

CHAPTER 21

MIRED IN CRISES

<u>1972</u>

Early in the year, Nate Jacobson's attorneys, Thomas Sheridan and Frank Petersen, began maneuvering legally, in a motion hearing, to pre-empt a trial.

One of their many tactics was requesting the names and the votes of the grand jurors who'd decided Jacobson and Bruno's case. With that data, which Jacobson had asked them to obtain, the defense counsel then could investigate each person to determine if they'd been biased against the Kings Castle head.

Deputy District Attorney (D.A.) Larry Hicks argued that Jacobson only wanted that information to subject the jurors to "violence, retaliation, intimidation and threats of bodily harm."[1]

Reno Justice Judge John Gabrielli allowed the defense to see only the voting records, not any names. They showed that all 14 of the grand jurors who'd been present (three had been absent) had voted for indictment.

Sheridan and Petersen moved for dismissal of that indictment because allegedly:

• Inadmissible evidence had been presented to the grand jury.

• Portions of testimony had been omitted from the transcript.

• Those in the D.A.'s office and on the Washoe County Board of Commissioners were prejudiced against Jacobson.

• The grand jury selection method was unconstitutional; it lent itself to bias (the commissioners and a district court judge nominated a group of people, from which jurors were selected).[*]

• Procedure hadn't been followed in that the arrest warrants had been signed November 17 but held and not used until November 30 (the day the defendants had been taken into custody).

• The grand jurors hadn't been told about Nevada Revised Statute 465.101, which, with limitations, allowed casino operators to detain suspected cheaters.

• The defendants couldn't determine which offense(s) they were charged with and had to defend against because of the word "or" in the indictment, specifically in the phrase, "confine, abduct or kidnap."

Gabrielli scheduled a continuation of the motion hearing for February.

Meanwhile, Jacobson's woes compounded.

For one, David Talisman, whose band had played as part of *Love-In* at Kings Castle, sued Jacobson for having terminated the performers' gig without giving the required prior notice and for maliciously having assaulted and battered him after he'd broached the breach of contract issue with him.

Talisman sought $17,000 ($102,400) in damages. Jacobson would file a counterclaim for $10,000 ($60,000), alleging Talisman had trespassed, made a scene and, therefore, needed escorting off of the property.

A trial would be set for 1972 but wouldn't take place then or ever. In 1977, the judge would grant the motion to dismiss the case

---

[*] In 1973, the Nevada Legislature would pass a bill that changed the process for choosing grand jurors to one of random selection.

due to a lack of activity over the previous five years, per the Nevada Rules of Civil Procedure.

Also, after four months of defaulted payments, between October 1971 and January 1972, the Teamsters Pension Fund (TPF) filed a foreclosure lien against Kings Castle, demanding Jacobson remit, within 35 days, the unpaid portion of the loan, which was $7 million ($42 million), in addition to 8 percent interest.

"[It's] just a procedural move," Jacobson said. "The sale [of Kings Castle] is expected to be forthcoming this week."[2]

Further, Nevada National Bank initiated a lawsuit against Kings Castle for $255,940 ($1.5 million) in unrepaid loans. Previously, in May 1971, Jacobson had signed a $300,000 promissory note, agreeing to pay a $100,000 installment plus 8 percent interest at the end each of July, August and September. He'd made just one payment, of only $55,000 ($331,000).

Jacobson, would, however, dispute the bank's numbers.

A trial date would be set and vacated twice, in 1972 and 1974. The bank then would request dismissal of the case without prejudice, which the judge would grant in 1975.

Additionally, Jacobsen Construction Company, Inc. took legal action against Jacobson for $164,000 ($988,000) — $84,000 in unpaid invoices and $80,000 that were past due on a promissory note.

In his counterclaim for $10,000, Jacobson would allege the plaintiff defectively constructed one of the resort's buildings by way of shoddy workmanship and inferior materials, so that it required $1 million worth of repairs.

In light of Kings Castle's financial status, the builder would agree to a $105,000 ($632,000) settlement, and the suit consequently would be dismissed.

Finally, the sale of Kings Castle fell through because the prospective buyers, Joseph Barkett and August Marra, backed out, for unclear reasons. Those, according to rumor, were problems with funds transfers from banks in Holland and England, issues resulting from the devaluation of American currency in Europe and/or difficulty obtaining capital from European banks.

The true impetus may have been Jacobson's refusal to accept one of Barkett and Marra's terms, that they assume control of the resort right away.

Did Jacobson really want out of Kings Castle? If so, why was he standing in his own way of achieving that?

CHAPTER 22

NO OTHER CHOICE

1972

H indered with Kings Castle debt and with no immediate relief in sight, Nate Jacobson shuttered the casino on February 2, nearly three years in. Nevada Gaming Control Board (NGCB) agents, present for the cease of business, revoked his gaming license and collected $7,600 ($46,000) in unpaid entertainment levies. A.L.W., Inc., however, still owed $33,800 ($203,000) in casino taxes for January.

Then Jacobson halted the rest of the resort's operations. Guests with reservations were notified. All scheduled conventions and meetings were cancelled, as was the third annual Kings Castle Snowmobile Grand Prix. Hundreds of now jobless employees received their final paycheck.

Teamsters Pension Fund (TPF) representatives took possession of the buildings and hired staff to provide security and maintenance until a solution for the Lake Tahoe establishment presented itself.

"The agony of defeat is not enviable, and Kings Castle and its management, although presently subjected to this agony, will not accept this as a final defeat and will do everything in its power to reopen in June," Jacobson said in a prepared statement.[1] "I have a job, and that's to reorganize and recapitalize or entertain the possibility of a sale."[2]

Due to the closure, owners of small Incline Village enterprises would lose up to 25 percent of their business. Local landlords who'd rented to the hotel-casino's workers would be hit hard, too. Washoe County's February jobless rate would climb from 5 percent to 6.2 percent, as Kings Castle, Ltd. and A.L.W., Inc. had employed between 500 and 700 people in the winter, about 1,400 in the summer. The county also would suffer a roughly $60,000 ($361,000) annual drop in room tax revenue.

"No question about it, the whole county is going to feel it," said Joe Coppa, county commissioner.[3]

Why did Kings Castle fail? Jacobson blamed it on financial losses of more than $5 million ($30 million) due to a myriad of uncontrollable circumstances. Among others, they included: a convention manager reporting nine months of reservations that really hadn't been booked; anti-Semitism among the Incline Village and greater communities; problems with various local officials and agencies, which resulted in negative publicity; the San Francisco television news report that the place was going under and a nationwide recession.

Those closest to Jacobson said he was "deposed by an overwhelming combination of forces, both deliberate and coincidental, that would have defeated anyone. Timing and location were both factors," reported the *Los Angeles Times*.[4]

"Jacobson's detractors are less charitable," the article went on. "They describe him as his own worst enemy, an evil-tempered tyrant who hated the community, cursed at his employees and tried to run Washoe County. They call him a genius gone sour, a man who attempted to transplant a garish segment of Las Vegas to a woodsy setting and could not abide his own bad planning."

The hotelman's character worsened after he entered the gambling business, a former NGCB member said. "Nate got swallowed up. He wasn't a gambler. He was an investor. His personality eroded from conservative businessman to a guy who would fight anyone. He turned abrasive."[5]

According to Artie Selman, Jacobson's partner in Kings Castle early on, the junkets irreversibly had damaged the resort's financial foundation and good name.[6]

Was skimming to blame, at least in part?

On February 4, 1972, Jacobson filed for bankruptcy of Kings Castle. U.S. Bankruptcy Referee Bert Goldwater, who was assigned to the case, appointed William O'Mara, attorney, to manage the resort's accounts until proceedings ended. O'Mara quantified Kings Castle's debts at $6.7 million ($40 million) and its assets at $2.5 million ($15 million). Secured[*] and unsecured[†] creditors numbered about 900.

With his Los Angeles-based bankruptcy attorney, Francis Quittner, present, Jacobson outlined to those creditors the three alternatives for Kings Castle.

One option was reorganization and recapitalization with an infusion of at least $3 million ($18 million) to fund a reopening. The second was sale of the property with the buyer assuming all liabilities. The third was a merger with another corporation. Jacobson asserted that either the TPF or he would reopen the resort in June and assured the people owed that they'd be paid.

---

[*] Secured creditors are businesses owed that have contracts regarding real property with the bankrupt party.
[†] Unsecured creditors are businesses owed for some type of merchandise or service they sold to the bankrupt party, which was consumed or disappeared.

"Anybody with claims against Kings Castle, in my opinion, will be honored," he said. "That casino is the finest of the fine. It has the best physical plant of any resort in the business, and it can be a smashing success if you will support us."[7]

Due to the Kings Castle Chapter 11 filing, a judge, in July, vacated the trial date for *Landucci v. Jacobson, Bruno, Paull, et al.* so the resort's bankruptcy case could get closed before the civil suit proceeded. However, five years later, in 1977, the suit would be dismissed for want of prosecution — failure to take certain required actions — in the intervening years.

Of Jacobson's various pending legal matters, those of a criminal nature soon would be back at the top of the list.

CHAPTER 23

DAMAGE CONTROL

1972

In early February, the hearing that had begun the previous month, resumed. Reno Justice Judge John Gabrielli denied the defense counsel's motion to quash the grand jury's charges against Nate Jacobson and Thomas Bruno but described the indictment as "clearly substantially defective in one or more particulars as objected to by the defendants."[1]

As a remedy, District Attorney (D.A.) Robert Rose's office replaced the grand jury indictment of Jacobson and Bruno with its own, thereby initiating a case in a different court, justice rather than district.

The new counts were kidnapping, coercion (both felonies) and false imprisonment (a gross misdemeanor). Those were similar but not identical to the original ones, which had been first and second degree kidnapping and extortion involving coercion and threats.

The defense attorneys began addressing the new criminal complaint against their clients. They asked the Nevada Supreme Court to order the justice court to drop the latest charges against Jacobson and Bruno. Because similar ones were pending against the men in district court, they argued, the justice court lacked jurisdiction.

The higher court, however, said no. After, Reno Justice Judge William Beemer ordered the defendants to turn themselves in in a few days.

Before that date came, though, Jacobson informed Sheriff Bob Galli he planned to not show because already he'd been hauled in on those very charges and subjecting him to fingerprinting and photographing a second time would be harassment.

In response, Deputy D.A. Larry Hicks assured Jacobson the two booking procedures wouldn't be repeated and reiterated he and Bruno better be at the sheriff's substation by noon Thursday or they'd be arrested.

Jacobson told the media that D.A. Rose and his office were persecuting him and his being charged a second time was "unwarranted," "politically motivated" and a "perversion of justice." He said, "I wish I knew what's behind all this. They've done enough damage — closed down my operation, put 1,000 people out of work. What do they want?"[2]

Come the deadline, Jacobson and Bruno weren't where Hicks had instructed them to be. The next day, Friday, they were arrested, booked and then released, with their already-paid bail still in effect.

"[The arrest] has done irreparable damage to my business operations, and I dread to think what might have happened had I not been able to post bail and afford very high legal expenses. I would have spent my time rotting in jail," said Jacobson.[3]

Reno Justice Judge Emile Gezelin eliminated one of the two indictments against Jacobson and Bruno by dismissing the one by the grand jury.

Next was the preliminary hearing, during which the prosecution attempted to establish probable cause for binding over Jacobson and Bruno for trial. From that proceeding, new information emerged.

The first revelation was that Washoe County sheriff's deputies had lawfully wiretapped Jacobson and others for 10 days in October 1971 — about 1.5 months after the alleged kidnapping of Raymond Landucci — as part of their investigation of Jacobson and Bruno related to that event.

They'd bugged the switchboard, Jacobson's private phone line and other one at Kings Castle along with Landucci's home phone (to monitor for possible threatening calls to him from Jacobson or anyone else at Kings Castle).

Officers, however, hadn't curtailed the electronic eavesdropping in time and therefore, had continued it illegally for 10 subsequent days. Over the total of 20 days, they'd amassed 49 tapes' worth of conversations.

It also came to light during the hearing that Landucci, after having lost his Kings Castle job, had lied on his unemployment insurance application about the reason for his termination. Further, he reportedly had threatened to divulge to the D.A.'s office details of the alleged beating and kidnapping if Kings Castle contradicted his false claims on that form.

Landucci said he feared that if the unemployment agency determined he'd been let go due to his own wrongdoing, he'd be blacklisted forever from casino employment in Nevada.[*]

---

[*] Nevada's Employment Security Department would require that Landucci pay back 14 weeks of unemployment compensation in the amount of $720 ($4,400) "to which he was not entitled by reason of his having made misrepresentations to obtain said benefits," a March 27, 1972 letter read.

139

It came to light, too, that the Ponderosa Hotel in Reno, a former employer of Landucci, also had fired him after a dispute with the owner, who'd suspected he and other workers had cheated at keno multiple times because the machine had gotten hit often.

In addition, during Landucci's testimony at the hearing, he admitted that at Kings Castle he'd signed out keys sometimes to the keno machine without a security guard present, against casino rules. He conceded that three or four times he'd helped a customer prepare her keno ticket and after each, had accepted a tip equal to 20 percent of her winnings, another violation.

After seven days of testimony and arguments, Gezelin ruled Jacobson and Bruno must stand trial, starting September 5.

He addressed the Nevada statute that allowed gaming operators to detain cheaters, stating it referred to customers, not employees, who were discovered trying to scam a game. The law's purpose, he said, was to give the house staff time to notify law enforcement in such cases.

Despite Gezelin's interpretation, the first legal opinion on NRS 465.101, the defendants' attorneys appealed to the state supreme court, seeking to obviate the trial because that very Nevada statute had protected them from prosecution, they argued.

Eventually, though, the higher court would agree with Gezelin.

Once the news of the pending trial spread, the community group, the Voice of Incline Village-Crystal Bay, requested the Washoe County commissioners revert all Kings Castle Way signs back to Country Club Drive because 960 of its 1,200 members supposedly desired it.

The commissioners would honor the request and have the signs replaced in August. Two months after the change, some Voice members would ask to buy the former street markers for "sentimental reasons," but their request was denied because such pieces typically got reused.[4]

At the arraignment soon after the hearing, Jacobson and Bruno pleaded not guilty.

Gezelin, in September 1972, would reschedule Jacobson and Bruno's criminal trial for June 18, 1973 to allow time for various pre-trial decisions. They included the Nevada Supreme Court's ruling on the defendants' petition for a writ of habeas corpus.

Until the trial would take place, dealing with the bankruptcy and saving Kings Castle would consume Jacobson's focus, energy and time.

CHAPTER 24

FINDING A BUYER

1972

On the bankruptcy front, Nate Jacobson remained under pressure to secure new capital for Kings Castle by June 30, or the Teamsters Pension Fund (TPF) would proceed with a foreclosure auction. He worked with another potential acquirer, whose identity remained confidential, but an agreement didn't materialize.

On the day of that early summer deadline, Jacobson unexpectedly announced in bankruptcy court he had a different set of prospective buyers lined up — a psychiatrist, Richard C. Gilmore, M.D. and his associates — as well as a gambling-licensed individual to operate the casino. Jacobson, thereby, averted the foreclosure sale.

Bankruptcy Referee Bert Goldwater gave Jacobson one week to obtain from Gilmore a $30,000 deposit ($180,000) and a signed purchase agreement, which he did.

Next, the seven potential buyers had to put $2 million ($12 million) into an escrow account in a designated Reno bank by July 25 or the TPF would sell Kings Castle the next day.

Meanwhile, the hotel-casino's creditors agreed on how Jacobson was to pay them. Unsecured creditors were to receive about 30 percent or $360,000 ($2.2 million), whichever was less, of what they were owed; secured creditors were to be paid according to negotiated settlements.

July 25 came and went, and Gilmore hadn't deposited the $2 million. Supposedly, he was having trouble getting a particular Swiss mortgage broker to confirm the money was being sent from a European bank. Goldwater gave the interested buyer a week to get it done.

Still, he didn't. That time, he claimed he couldn't procure the capital because the European financial institution would loan only to an American bank that was willing to guarantee the loan, and he couldn't find one that would. Gilmore then withdrew his purchase offer.

What had been happening with Gilmore, unbeknownst to anyone in Northern Nevada, was this. Three U.S.-based brokers had told Gilmore they had an investor — Hirkishim Dialdas, reportedly the former financial advisor to Egyptian King Farouk — with Swiss corporations and money in Barclays Bank International in Gibraltar, who'd loan Gilmore $20 million to buy Kings Castle once he wired $20,000 ($122,000) to Barclays and paid the three facilitators $10,000 apiece.

Similarly, an executive of Reno's First National Bank had received a Telex message from Barclays, noting that it would wire the $20 million to his facility once it received Gilmore's $20,000.

Gilmore had paid that amount, plus the $30,000 ($182,400) in finder's fees, but Barclays hadn't sent the money.

It turned out that no Barclays representative had messaged the Reno bank. Rather, it had been the trio of brokers who'd used

Barclays' Telex machine to perpetrate fraud.[*] The professional con men had duped Gilmore out of $50,000 ($304,000).

Due to the latest failed sale of the Kings Castle resort, two public auctions took place on August 4.

At the first, held at a Reno title office, attorneys for the TPF bid $5 million ($30 million) for the real property (primarily the buildings).

At the second, which took place on the Washoe County courthouse steps, they proffered $500,000 ($3 million) for the interior furnishings, goodwill and trade name. Some personal property was excluded from the auction and, according to Nevada law, could be sold later to a private party.

With no other bids placed, ownership of all of the facilities transferred from the Kings Castle corporations to the TPF (which already owned the underlying land).

Although Kings Castle Hotel and Casino was entirely in the TPF's hands at that point, Jacobson kept trying to find a party to purchase it. Seemingly, he desperately wanted to hang on to it.

He could; he had, for one year, the first right of refusal to purchase it, meaning he could re-acquire the resort during that period at a price that matched any other prospective buyer's offer. The TPF had granted him this right earlier in 1972, for unknown reasons.

In October, Jacobson again was negotiating a possible sale of the royal resort, asking $19 million ($115 million) for it. A group of businessmen headed by Morris Jaffe of San Antonio, Texas, a millionaire, commercial real estate developer and acquaintance of alleged Mafia figure, Carlos Marcello of New Orleans, offered to

---

[*] These swindlers had used Barclays' Telex to send more than 140 such messages to investors like Gilmore in the U.S. and Europe.

purchase the Incline Village hotel-casino and make an interim, $1 million ($6 million) good faith payment.

That fourth potential acquisition fizzled, too, but it would be the last to do so for Jacobson concerning Kings Castle.

DESPERATE FOR RESOLUTION

<u>1973</u>

Nate Jacobson plowed ahead with developing alternative arrangements for Kings Castle. His latest idea involved himself and Jud Dolan McIntosh. McIntosh, 52, was a self-made millionaire from Georgia and an executive at Lithonia Lighting, Inc., which designed, manufactured and sold fluorescent light fixtures for commercial use.

McIntosh's experience in the gambling industry, relatively recent, had been as an investor in and executive of the Caesars Palace and Circus hotel-casinos in Las Vegas. At the former, he'd been the corporate treasurer, and at the latter, he'd substituted as president for some time for Jay J. Sarno, the visionary and designer of both properties.

The structure of Jacobson's proposed arrangement with McIntosh was that the Teamsters Pension Fund (TPF) would continue to own the land, but Jacobson would purchase the hotel-casino from it and act as an absentee landlord because the Nevada Gaming Commission (NGC) wouldn't grant him another gambling license.

McIntosh would rent all of the facilities from Jacobson, paying $700,000 ($4 million) per year for the casino — which McIntosh would operate — along with 25 percent of room revenue and 5 percent of food and beverage income. Jacobson would use these monies from McIntosh to pay the creditors.

Under this new arrangement, Jacobson would retain a stake in Kings Castle, and the resort could reopen by the start of summer 1973.

Bankruptcy Referee Bert Goldwater deemed the plan both feasible and beneficial for the creditors provided the involved parties carried out the following:

One, Jacobson had to deposit $360,000 with the bankruptcy court before May 30 for payment to the unsecured creditors.

Two, those same creditors had to consent to the plan within 10 days of that payment.

Three, the NGC had to approve McIntosh as the gambling licensee and Jacobson as the resort owner.

That third requirement became problematic. At its May meeting, the Nevada Gaming Control Board (NGCB) agents grilled Jacobson about his past infractions.

One was his alleged violation of state law by issuing 7,500 shares of Kings Castle stock to himself, which was in excess of what he'd been licensed for, without first obtaining the agency's okay to do so. Further, some of the associated stock certificates illegally had been back-dated. Jacobson denied knowledge of either incident but claimed they must've been secretary and auditor mistakes.

The NGCB recommended the NGC consent to the outlined Jacobson-McIntosh arrangement provided Jacobson met a handful of its conditions. If he didn't, he would lose his standing as a suitable landlord, thereby nullifying his plan for resurrecting Kings Castle.

Among others, first, he had to agree in writing to stay off the hotel-casino premises no matter what.

Second, he had to sell his interest within 13 months of his criminal trial's end if found guilty.

Third, he had to put the rental revenue from McIntosh into escrow until the amount reached $1.5 million ($8.6 million) or until Jacobson had paid all of the unsecured claims. (This meant the gambling authorities were requiring full payment of $1.2 million to the unsecured creditors rather than the $360,000 to which the individuals owed previously had agreed).

"We're pleasantly surprised that we're going to get the full amount. These people are God," Attorney Howard McKissick, Jr., chairman of the creditors committee, said, referring to the NGC members and their collective power.[1]

Jacobson, however, resisted the terms because they were fiscally impossible, "tantamount to putting a loaded gun to my head," he said.[2] His attorney, Frank Petersen, specifically objected to the creditors getting paid in full, arguing that it violated federal bankruptcy law.

"My financial life is at stake," Jacobson added. "I'm anxious to find out whether I live or die."[3]

At the next NGC meeting, Jacobson asked the commissioners to waive or modify the triple provisos. He even proffered alternatives, but the gaming regulators remained steadfast in their adherence to the NGCB's recommendation.

Jacobson rejected the conditions and publicly declared the NGC, in demanding them, was forcing him out of Kings Castle. However, because he felt morally obligated to the resort, the banks, employees and creditors, he said, he begrudgingly presented another possibility that had the TPF's blessing.

In this new scenario, like in the last, the TPF would retain ownership of the land. Jacobson would purchase only the facilities from the TPF, which he then would sell, rather than lease, to McIntosh. McIntosh would pay Jacobson $2.5 million ($14 million) over 20 years out of either 40 percent of the net profits or 40 percent of the cash flow, whichever was less.

All relevant parties agreed to the new setup, and the deal closed!

McIntosh paid the bankruptcy court $450,000 ($2.5 million), which finally fulfilled Kings Castle's obligation to its secured creditors. With this transaction, the Georgia executive became the owner of the resort's facilities, and the TPF remained holding the land.

In a subsequent press conference, McIntosh stated that while he had no issue with Jacobson, "the more absent he is, the better. He obviously rubbed some people the wrong way. We don't want any of his problems to rub off on us."[4]

Jacobson told reporters, "I have definite emotions about it, but none of regret. I feel no remorse in leaving the area. I will not miss Washoe County whatever my endeavors may be. The county and I have been incompatible. The best thing to happen is that this thing is straightened out and put back in operation. My objective is to remove myself from the county, and I hope the county feels the same."[5]

While all appeared to have gotten resolved for Kings Castle for good, that, in short order, would prove not to be the case.

CHAPTER 26

ALLEGED MOBSTER INVOLVEMENT

<u>1973</u>

In spring 1973, preparations began for revitalizing the shut-down Kings Castle resort, keeping with the existing theme. About 600 employees were hired, many of them having been on the payroll previously. Most were from Northern Nevada, but some came from Las Vegas.

James "Jimmie" Hume, 58, was brought on as the casino host. For more than a decade, he'd been a co-owner and the host of the North Shore Club, a seasonally open, restaurant, bar and casino in neighboring Crystal Bay.

Christ "Chris" N. Karamanos, 31, was tapped for general manager, having worked most recently for four years as the executive assistant to Alex J. Shoofey, president of the Las Vegas Hilton.* He also co-owned Kyle Corporation, whose assets were Cohen and Kelly's restaurant-bar and Jet Avia, an air ambulance service and charter "for casinos to ferry high rollers and celebrities of all kinds, from the governor to [Las Vegas] Strip entertainers," wrote the authors of *The Money and the Power*.

---

* In 1972, the Las Vegas Hilton's name was changed to the International Hilton.

Before moving to Las Vegas, Karamanos had lived in Southern California, where he'd been a reserve, or volunteer, police officer for the Newport Beach Police Department and where, having studied business, he'd obtained an associate's degree from Los Angeles Valley College.

"Chris Karamanos was no random business prodigy," noted Sally Denton and Roger Morris. "The jovial, portly ex-cop had his own ties to organized crime and drug trafficking, and was also, as he would later testify secretly to Nevada officials, a sometime CIA operative, whose meteoric rise and political patronage in Las Vegas were hardly accidental."

Jud McIntosh opened Kings Castle on May 25, as scheduled. The resurrected facilities included the casino, offering 25 table games and 340 slot machines, the hotel and, for conferences and conventions, the annex. About 600 Incline Villagers attended the celebratory relaunch dinner show featuring singer and musician Tennessee Ernie Ford.

The new owner told the local media he expected the resort would need to operate for three years before consistently generating a profit and he was prepared to ride it out until then.

"If I wasn't reasonably sure of it, I wouldn't have spent all this money," he said.[1]

He announced that his approach to running the hospitality business would differ from Jacobson's and that he was working to repair Kings Castle's image. For one, he clothed Lady Godiva, who'd been displayed au naturel on the property for years. Two, he only permitted the booking of acts with family shows, such as Dinah Shore, Kenny Rogers and the First Addition, Perry Como, Glen Campbell and Diahann Carroll.

"The best thing we can do is to live out our promise for a warm, friendly operation. We feel we can do that," he added.

Several locals, however, were quick to test McIntosh's pledge. About a week later, they objected to his use of the lakeside building, even only for meetings.

They restated to the Board of Commissioners their claims of previous years and added new ones — that the area was zoned by the county for residential, not commercial, use; the closure of Kings Castle invalidated the special use permit that had allowed annex operations in the past; the Tahoe Regional Planning Agency's zoning regulations prohibited such an enterprise there; and parking, noise and dust had been problems previously.

"The residents do not want these activities to get started again," said Roy Robinette, a representative Incline Village resident. "We're not objecting to any legal operations there but do not want illegal parking and noise."[2]

The new proprietor, however, continued to host groups in the annex.

As for the casino, it was being run atypically, making one wonder why. McIntosh, as the sole gambling licensee, was legally responsible for the operation, yet Karamanos, Hume and the four shift bosses didn't answer to or defer to him regarding gaming matters.

Instead, they all took orders from a man, 51, who worked at the casino nightly, unofficially: Marty Buccieri.

"Everything came through Marty," recalled Tommy Papagna, a roulette, 21 and baccarat dealer then living in Las Vegas, who'd worked at Kings Castle's casino in 1973 and 1974, starting at age 22. "[Marty] was very stern, very matter of fact but very fair. He had a temper that could go off, but that was unusual. This guy put a lot of people to work. He was, in that respect, a great guy."[3]

This was the same Marty Buccieri who'd "worked" at this very gambling enterprise in 1966 when it'd been called the Incline

Village Casino, and it was the same Marty Buccieri who'd served prison time for allegedly framing and getting an innocent man running for office arrested, at the behest of the Cleveland Syndicate.

He reportedly was known inside the Mob as a bagman.[†] In that capacity and from years' work as a pit boss at Caesars Palace in Las Vegas, he knew many of the organized crime figures involved in that city's gambling industry.

With Buccieri seemingly in charge, Kings Castle's casino bustled, Papagna recalled, particularly due to continual junkets, nearly every weekend, many arriving via Karamanos' Jet Avia.

However, suspicious, frequently occurring activities suggested skimming was taking place, thereby decreasing the casino's bottom line. Some VIPs, such as some of the Teamsters Pension Fund executives, gambled there for free; they'd leave without signing their marker, or I.O.U.

Sometimes, when fill slips[‡] were generated, to resupply the chips or, in the case of baccarat cash, when running low at a table, all of the appropriate people would sign the form, but the chips or cash wouldn't make it to the table. In a cleanly run casino, occurrences like this were egregious and not tolerated. In a dirty operation, they were a good way to rake off the top.

At night, after Buccieri sent home the baccarat dealers, he and a shift boss closed the game themselves, free from scrutiny, as there were no cameras in the gambling club. There only was a catwalk above from which one or more persons could watch, in real time, the happenings below. The baccarat closing process, a

---

[†] A bagman is a person who collects or distributes money for racketeers.
[‡] A fill slip is the required documentation of a transaction in which a supply of chips, coins or currency is transferred from a bankroll to a table or slot machine.

ripe opportunity for stealing money, involved counting the cash that came in at the tables during the day,[§] determining whether it was a win or loss for the casino and by how much, and filling out the necessary paperwork.

A specific incident also suggests Mobsters were involved with the Lake Tahoe casino. In April, about a month before McIntosh had intended to open the resort, $500,000 in cash ($2.8 million) had been stolen from a floor safe in Buccieri's Las Vegas home. Two armed men had forced their way in, tied up all of the people there — Buccieri's wife and three children — extracted the money and left.

Buccieri supposedly was to have used this bankroll, money likely skimmed from one or more other gambling houses, to open the Kings Castle casino.

The robbery supposedly had been ordered by Anthony "Tony/The Ant" Spilotro, alleged murderous enforcer for the Chicago Outfit in Vegas and head of the Hole in the Wall Gang burglary ring there. (Attorney Oscar Goodman, on Spilotro's behalf, denied he'd had any involvement.)

Although Spilotro was aligned with the Windy City Mob, it hadn't stopped him from going rogue and allegedly committing crimes against his own people.[**]

Whose $500,000 had it been? Who'd wanted Buccieri working at Kings Castle and why, to skim for them? Had it been members of The Outfit? Is that from whom Spilotro supposedly had learned about the cash and its location?

[§] Many Nevada casinos switched to using chips instead of cash at their baccarat tables in the early 1970s, but Kings Castle wasn't one of them.

[**] Tony Spilotro and his brother, Michael, would disappear on June 14, 1986. Their severely battered bodies would be discovered buried, one atop the other, in an expansive Indiana preserve. Authorities would conclude they'd been murdered by The Outfit.

CHAPTER 27

PURSUIT OF RECOMPENSE

<u>1973</u>

In April, Nate Jacobson filed a $1 million class action suit on behalf of all of the people who'd made calls to or from Kings Castle during the 10 days the phones there had been wiretapped illegally in 1971.

Asking for $100 per day per plaintiff, he sued the local phone company and eight individuals from two Washoe County agencies. U.S. District Judge Bruce Thompson, however, would require Jacobson to limit the plaintiffs to himself and his corporation because the class action format didn't apply.

Jacobson would refile, listing 11 co-plaintiffs: Sylvia Jacobson, his wife; Sanford and Edward Jacobson, Nate and Sylvia's sons; Forrest Paull; Clyde Billman; Artie Selman; the estate of Sam Jacobson, Nate's late brother; Jacob Friedland and Richard Levy, Jacobson's Chicago-based attorneys; and Thomas Sheridan. Jacobson would seek, per plaintiff, $1 million in punitive damages and $1,000 in statutory damages.[*]

---

[*] The maximum allowable in statutory damages was the greater of either $1,000 or $100 per day.

He would sue seven parties — District Attorney (D.A.) Robert Rose, Deputy D.A. Larry Hicks, Sheriff Bob Galli, Sheriff's Chief Tom Benham, Sheriff's Captain Lorne Butner, Sheriff's Sergeant William Whitmire and the Nevada Bell Telephone Company — claiming they'd trampled the plaintiffs' rights by violating the law and disseminating information extracted from the wiretapping.

This federal criminal case would go to a jury trial in 1976, four years after Jacobson's initial lawsuit. Through testimony then, it would be revealed the taps captured confidential business calls and privileged attorney-client conversations.

Jacobson's sons would testify they made several private business calls to their father on the tapped lines during that period.

Jacobson's wife Sylvia would testify that during and before the wiretapping she telephoned "another man" from the Kings Castle premises, about which she didn't want her husband to know.[1] She'd say his discovery of those calls through the wiretap tapes led to their separation in 1972 and subsequent divorce in 1976, just four months before this wiretapping trial.

Jacobson would testify the eavesdropping was yet another barb in the ongoing poking and prodding of him by local law enforcement and Rose.

Testimony also would reveal the sheriff's office permitted the following individuals to listen to the tapes: Harold Newpher, FBI agent; Richard Crane, head of the West Coast branch of the U.S. Organized Crime Strike Force (OCSF)[†] headquartered in Los Angeles; a U.S. attorney from Crane's branch office in San Francisco; and Thomas Carrigan, a Nevada Gaming Control Board (NGCB) member.

[†] Formed in the late 1960s through a congressional effort led by Robert F. Kennedy, this group worked to root out and stop illegal racketeering.

The federal agents had listened to three intercepts, including a conversation between Jacobson and an individual who'd organized and conducted gambling junkets to Kings Castle, in which Jacobson had threatened action against a junketeer who owed the casino $2,500 ($16,000). Two calls had involved Jacobson's wagers on National Football League games.

Based on what they'd heard, the FBI and the OCSF had opened a case on Jacobson for possible ITAR-EXTORTION violations but later dropped it after an investigation.

During the wiretapping trial, Jacobson would ask the court if he could amend his lawsuit to seek compensation for actual damages.[‡] He'd assert that others' access to those taped calls had resulted in his divorce and had led to state gambling regulators compelling him to sell Kings Castle.

The judge would deny the motion, however, on the grounds that Jacobson's claims were "bizarre and extravagant."[2]

The defense would contend the extended wiretapping simply had been a mistake and unintentional.

In his ruling, Thompson would remind the parties the federal wiretap law had been written in such a way to ensure it be followed strictly.

"It's incumbent that you dot every I and cross every T," he'd say. "If you don't, you're in trouble."[3]

He'd find all of the defendants guilty of violating that law and, therefore, liable for statutory damages[§] of $1,000 per plaintiff. He'd determine Nevada Bell, Butner and Whitmire hadn't kept the wiretap going maliciously; a jury would deliver the same finding

---

[‡] Actual damages constitute compensation for financial losses resulting from a crime.

[§] Statutory damages comprise compensation for an actual violation of the law.

for Rose, Hicks, Galli and Benham. Consequently, none would have to pay punitive damages.**

The trial result would be that Washoe County and Nevada Bell together would be liable for up to $84,000 in statutory damages — $1,000 from each defendant to each plaintiff — in addition to $40,000 for reimbursement of Jacobson's legal fees.

Jacobson would tell the press he was disappointed in the jury's decision and in the fact the plaintiffs wouldn't get $1 million apiece. He would note, though, Thompson's verdict made the point he wanted established, that Washoe County law enforcement officers had disregarded the law.

One plaintiff, Benham, would say Thompson's verdict was "completely improper" and "has to be appealed" because the judgment could affect law enforcement adversely throughout the U.S.[4] Were the ruling allowed to stand, he'd add, it would "totally destroy normal workday police work."

Four months after the jury decision, Thompson would rule the defendants were jointly and severally liable, so the plaintiffs could collect only a total of $12,000 ($54,000) — $1,000 per plaintiff from the defendant group as a whole — not $84,000 ($375,000). He'd also decrease the award for Jacobson's attorney fees to $12,000 ($54,000) from $40,000 ($179,000). Every major party in the suit would appeal the decision.

In 1978, the U.S. Court of Appeals for the Ninth Circuit would let the verdict stand against Rose, Galli, Hicks and Benham but would send Nevada Bell, Butner and Whitmire back to the lower court for either a new decision or new trial(s).

The next year, that court would rule, finally putting the case to rest. It would release those three from any liability. The other four

---

** Punitive damages are monies parties found guilty must pay as punishment for their action(s).

would be required, as one, to pay the plaintiffs $12,000 total — versus the $11 million-plus ($50 million-plus) Jacobson originally had sought — plus attorney's fees, which, with interest, would total $30,000 ($133,000).

Next for Jacobson was a trial in which he wasn't in his usual plaintiff role; he was a defendant.

CHAPTER 28

INNOCENT OR GUILTY?

<u>1973</u>

After the Nevada Supreme Court had denied Nate Jacobson and Thomas Bruno's request for a habeas corpus petition, their criminal trial, *The State of Nevada v. Nathan Stanley Jacobson and Thomas Joseph Bruno*, began in June. Reno Justice Judge Grant Bowen dismissed the defense's motions for a delay, change of venue, jury sequestration and removal of District Attorney (D.A.) Robert Rose and his deputies as prosecutors.

"I know in my guts, my heart and my brain that I cannot get a fair and impartial trial in Washoe County," Jacobson said. "I'm not debating whether the prejudice against me is justified. We know it exists."[1]

Attorneys for both sides selected a jury of 10 women and 2 men.

In opening statements, Co-prosecutor Deputy D.A. Larry Hicks said the defendants were "guilty of a gross criminal over-reaction to a personnel problem and taking the law into their own hands."[2]

Defense attorney, Thomas Sheridan, said his team would establish that Raymond Landucci was an admitted liar, that he'd spoken frequently about cheating the keno game and had "concocted a preposterous story about being beaten."[3] Rose had a vendetta against Jacobson, he added, and accordingly, Rose and his office were behind this case, not Landucci.

After the court proceedings were underway, Jacobson hired friend and former Nevada Gaming Control Board member, Wayne Pearson, who then was with Nevada Research Consultants in Las Vegas, to poll Washoe County citizens about their perceptions of Jacobson.

The "Washoe County Public Opinion Survey" started with 11 questions about state and national affairs, such as, "What kind of a job is President [Richard] Nixon doing?" and "What kind of a job is Senator [Alan] Bible doing?" Five questions about Jacobson followed.

Immediate backlash occurred, with residents complaining to Rose's office. Many said the individual who'd telephoned them had misrepresented who was behind the study and why.

"Nate Jacobson is at it again — with a first — a maneuver that no one else has ever tried or probably even thought of. ... The questionnaire is extremely misleading and has the effect of making people who are sampled very angry," wrote editorialist Don Lynch.[4]

A big surprise in the trial came when the defense called Norman "Norm" Truax to the stand. This was the man Forrest Paull, the former vice president of security and personnel at Kings Castle, determined to be the Norm in Landucci's story, the name Landucci said he'd made up when pressured to give up his accomplice in the keno cheat. Paull had spent 18 months investigating who Norm could be and was certain he'd found the right person, he said.

Truax, however, wasn't in or around the courtroom. Instead, he called from a payphone, saying he wouldn't show because

Sheridan had refused to pay him $50,000 ($283,000) for his testimony. Bowen issued a bench warrant for Truax's appearance, setting bail at $50,000 ($286,000). Around midnight that night, sheriff's officers would arrest Truax, also known as "Paul Steen" and "Big Norm," at his home.

During questioning by the defense, Landucci admitted to seeing Truax enter Kings Castle once and ask for another employee but denied knowing him, meeting him at his home or planning to cheat the keno game with him. He said Truax hadn't called his wife Dawn the day Landucci allegedly had been detained at Kings Castle and denied he was supposed to have given Truax an all-clear call at 4 a.m. on September 3 so Truax could present the phony keno ticket at the casino later that morning.

The next day in court, when on the stand, Truax[*] invoked his Fifth Amendment right on every question, declaring he wouldn't testify unless he was granted full immunity. The state refused it.

Another witness, James Swiggert, who was a former Kings Castle keno employee and a distant relative of Landucci, said Landucci did know Truax, having met him in the early 1960s when Landucci had been tending bar in a place Truax had frequented. He also said a few months prior to the September 2 and 3 incidents, Landucci had asked Swiggert how to contact Truax.

On rebuttal, Landucci reiterated he'd only spotted Truax one time at Kings Castle and denied ever working in the bar where, according to Swiggert, he'd first encountered Truax.

As for other surprises, Jacobson testified at his trial, without incident, and Sheridan presented the results of the public opinion

---

[*] Previously, Norman Truax had served time in Nevada State Prison from May 1964 to July 1966 for first-degree burglary, after being caught trying to break into a Reno office building. After Jacobson and Bruno's trial, he would serve another year for burglary, for attempting to rob Spraycraft, an auto painting company in Sparks, Nevada.

sampling. Of the 1,002 eligible voters in Washoe County who'd been contacted, 906 participated. The questions asked and the response rates for each were:

Are you aware of the kidnapping case against Nathan Jacobson, former owner of Kings Castle?

Aware:	76 percent
Not aware:	15 percent
No response:	9 percent

Do you believe Nathan Jacobson is guilty as charged?

Yes:	37 percent
No:	14 percent
No response:	49 percent

Do you believe Nathan Jacobson was guilty of any other crime while he operated Kings Castle?

Yes:	22 percent
No:	19 percent
No response:	59 percent

Do you believe Nathan Jacobson is an undesirable person in the community?

Yes:	30 percent
No:	18 percent
No response:	52 percent

Do you believe Nathan Jacobson is a member of the Mafia?

Yes: 13 percent
No: 26 percent
No response: 61 percent

After five weeks of testimony, closing arguments began.

Hicks addressed the jury. "Whether or not Ray Landucci was going to participate in a keno scam makes no difference in his treatment by these defendants. These defendants are charged with what they did to Landucci, not why they did it," he said.[5]

What Jacobson and Bruno had done was unnecessary, he continued. If Jacobson and Paull[†] had believed someone was going to produce a false ticket, they should've simply required the ticket be approved by Jacobson prior to being paid. They hadn't notified the sheriff's office, and they'd seized and held Landucci without the authority of law.

Hicks explained that Jacobson's verbal attack on Landucci alone met the standard for threats and intimidation; the jury didn't even have to believe guns had been produced to terrorize Landucci. Simply the manner in which the discussion with Landucci had ensued constituted the crimes as charged.

Sheridan, on the other hand, told the jurors Landucci "will never be worthy of your belief" and asked them to acquit the defendants on all charges. "It is impossible to believe some of Mr. Landucci's testimony and not the rest and then convict beyond a reasonable doubt," he said.[6]

He asserted that no evidence existed to show the defendants had detained Landucci against his will. In fact, Landucci had

---

[†] In January 1976, Forrest Paull would take over as the chief of police for the City of Elko in Nevada.

agreed to stay, and there wasn't merit to the accusation he'd been imprisoned covertly. Further, he said, Landucci had lied about guns being produced and being beaten while questioned.

The jury began deliberating. If convicted, Jacobson and Bruno faced prison time — up to 15 years for kidnapping and up to 6 years for coercion — plus up to 1 year in county jail for false imprisonment. Were Jacobson to receive the maximum sentence and consecutive terms, he'd be in prison until at age 80, with concurrent terms, age 73.

The case was touted as the longest criminal trial to date in Washoe County's history.

After about eight hours, the jurors agreed on a decision. They found Jacobson and Bruno not guilty on all charges.

Upon hearing the verdict, Jacobson sobbed.

"What kind of victory is it?" he queried. "With 20 long months of abuse — a hollow victory."[7]

In a prepared statement, Jacobson accused Rose of pursuing a case against him "in bad faith. My punishment is almost overbearing financially, emotionally and physically. It was a tough battle I survived, but now I am scarred. There is no cure for the emotional damage." He suggested the community decide whether Rose and his staff were worthy of public office. "My opinion is they don't belong there. Vote them out."

Co-prosecutor Deputy D.A. Calvin Dunlap responded: "It's our duty to present a case when there is probable cause to believe a crime has been committed. The grand jury, two district judges and the supreme court found that there was probable cause to believe the crime was committed and the defendants committed it.

"The trial jury is always the ultimate finder of fact," he went on, "and it decided the state did not prove its case beyond a reasonable doubt. Therefore, in the opinion of the jury, the defendants are innocent."[8]

Jacobson announced he was leaving Washoe County and Nevada for good and returning to Baltimore.

He might become involved again in the gambling industry, he said, but if so, definitely elsewhere. He contended The Silver State had forced him to sell Kings Castle because of the criminal charges against him.

"This loss was the direct result of this unfounded prosecution," he said. "Several million dollars gone just to prove my innocence, and the state doesn't even say sorry. Nevada has inflicted wounds on me that will never heal. I will have no further association with Nevada."[9]

Estimating his defense cost him about $400,000 ($2.2 million), Jacobson declared he intended to work toward the passage of a Nevada law that afforded acquitted people reimbursement of their legal expenses.[‡]

"There should be a deterrent to public officials in bringing unfounded charges," he said.[10]

Despite his announcement to the contrary, Jacobson would not leave Nevada right away. He had more suing to do locally and wasn't ready yet to let go of Kings Castle.

[‡] No evidence was found that Jacobson had pursued this.

CHAPTER 29

DEALING WITH DEBTS

<u>1973</u>

In August, Bankruptcy Referee Bert Goldwater accepted and finalized the latest plan for paying off Kings Castle's unsecured creditors. As the resort owner, Jud McIntosh was to remit $360,000 ($2 million) in six monthly installments of $60,000 beginning October 1. The arrangement would achieve the Bankruptcy Act's aim and wouldn't harm the vendors, Goldwater said.

"The court is well satisfied a great deal of effort was undertaken by the parties in this case, and it was a very hard road," he added. "We are not through yet as we will have to settle the claims and the distribution of the money, but I feel we are at the top of the mountain."[1]

Yet around the same time, three months after he reopened Kings Castle, McIntosh looked to divest it, saying he wanted to concentrate on other business interests. The real reason, however, likely was because the enterprise was losing money, lots of it.

"The joint made money, but I think they took too much out of it," said Tommy Papagna, referring to the alleged skimmer(s).[2]

McIntosh negotiated a $20 million ($113 million) sale price with Allen R. Glick, 31, who was the executive vice president of the Saratoga Development Corporation, a real estate development firm in El Cajon, California. According to the agreement, Glick would own 100 percent of the operation and be chairman of the board, Chris Karamanos would serve as board president and Jimmy Hume would be vice president.

After the Teamsters Pension Fund (TPF) trustees approved the sale to Glick, the deal hinged on the Nevada Gaming Commission's (NGC's) decision.

Following the Nevada Gaming Control Board's (NGCB's) recommendation, the NGC disallowed the transaction, supposedly because of whom they'd learned Glick had been instructed to hire to operate the casino: Marty Buccieri. Due to Buccieri's prior conviction, the gaming regulators considered him "unsuitable" for a gambling license.

In hindsight, knowing that Glick would, in the same year, acquire Las Vegas' Stardust and Fremont hotel-casinos with TPF financing, as a straw owner for The Outfit, and knowing that for many ensuing years massive skimming for the underworld occurred at both properties,[*] one could speculate the Chicago Outfit and the TPF had had the same plan for Glick and Kings Castle and that the skimming, through Buccieri, already had been in motion behind McIntosh's back.

After it became known that Glick would not be acquiring Kings Castle, Chris Karamanos resigned from his position as general manager, telling the press, "We have had an outstanding summer this year, and I believe we have definitely proven that

---

[*] Eventually, authorities would discover the skimming taking place at the Stardust and Fremont. The Nevada Gaming Commission would strip Allen Glick of his gambling license and fine his firm, Argent Corporation, $500,000.

Kings Castle can be an important part of the overall hotel and casino business in Nevada and particularly be of great significance to the economy of north Lake Tahoe."[3]

Why did Karamanos[†] quit? Was he no longer needed because the business had turned around? Did he leave because the sale to Glick had fallen through, and he'd been there only to help facilitate it and/or Buccieri's involvement with the casino pre and post Glick's acquisition? Did he leave to pursue other work? Or was it maybe for an entirely different reason?

McIntosh chose, and the NGC allowed, Kings Castle's casino host Jimmie Hume to replace Karamanos as the resort's general manager and to assume McIntosh's own position of president.

In a financial bind after the failed sale, McIntosh reorganized the Northern Nevada business to stem its cash outflow and ensure it could keep operating. The enterprise, however, continued to hemorrhage cash, most likely from the alleged skimming going on, which McIntosh presumably didn't know about. These circumstances set off a spate of staff member resignations.

Another person who was focused on generating revenue at the time was Nate Jacobson, who still was in Nevada. He sued another party, this time the Tahoe Regional Planning Agency (TRPA), charging it with inverse condemnation — the unintentional taking of private property for public benefit — of the Kings Castle lake frontage. This was about the sixth lawsuit brought by Jacobson since he'd acquired the Incline Village hotel-casino in 1969, excluding countersuits.

He claimed an ordinance the TRPA had passed in February 1972 had dedicated the property to the public, without compensating Jacobson for doing so, thereby making it unusable

---

[†] Chris Karamanos would take his own life at age 47 in a Mesquite, Nevada motel room by overdosing on Xanax in 1989.

for Kings Castle guests to enjoy. The change, he added, had devalued the resort and, therefore, had resulted in a several million-dollar loss when Jacobson had sold it. He asked that TRPA's zoning action be declared unconstitutional and he be compensated for the financial shortfall.

In January 1975, U.S. District Judge Bruce Thompson would dismiss the case because Jacobson failed to state a claim upon which relief could be granted. Value loss alone wasn't sufficient to establish an unconstitutional usurping of private property. Further, Thompson said, monetary relief wasn't possible because the TRPA lacked eminent domain power.

Jacobson would amend his complaint to ask for declaratory and injunctive relief, yet Thompson would dismiss this action, too. This was because Jacobson, no longer the current landowner, lacked standing for such a request. Also, he'd filed for bankruptcy before the TRPA had passed the 1972 ordinance, so his interest in the affected property had been assigned elsewhere.

Jacobson would appeal.

In August 1977, the U.S. Court of Appeals for the Ninth Circuit would agree with Thompson that because the TRPA lacked condemnation authority, there couldn't be compensation for an inverse condemnation. However, the question lingered of whether Jacobson might be entitled to some money for lost profits or other compensable harm.

As such, the jurists would vacate Thompson's dismissal of Jacobson's complaint and would remand it "for a determination whether, in fact, Jacobson has retained a cause of action upon which his suit can be based and for further proceedings in light of this opinion," the decision would read.

Upon the request for the Ninth Circuit appeals court to re-hear Jacobson's case, which it would deny in December 1977, the judges would determine that Jacobson did not prove a cause of action and, therefore, Thompson properly had dismissed the case on a lack of standing basis.

The U.S. Supreme Court would weigh in, too, instructing the lower court to establish whether the TRPA had violated Jacobson's constitutional due process.

Finally, in 1979, Thompson would rule the TRPA hadn't done so and, consequently, Jacobson wasn't entitled to damages. It would be yet another legal loss for Jacobson.

While that case progressed through the judicial system, Jacobson concocted a plan by which he possibly could regain his grip on Kings Castle, particularly the casino, the revenue generator.

Under his new scheme, he would hold a second deed of trust on the property, and in the event Jud McIntosh defaulted on his payments to the TPF, Jacobson could step in, assume payments and again own the property.

His one obstacle was getting the state's gambling officials to approve.

They didn't. Instead, behind closed doors, they unanimously agreed they did not want Jacobson again involved with any Nevada casino ... ever.

At 1973's end, McIntosh's Kings Castle remained open, barely hanging on, and business during the early winter was slow. Though that was typical for North Lake Tahoe hotel-casinos then, this time it presaged an ominous near future.

CHAPTER 30

ANOTHER ROUGH PATCH

<u>1974</u>

Excitement erupted at Kings Castle in mid-January when Moonstone Films of Hollywood, California began shooting the movie *Lady Cocoa*[*] there. Featuring singer-dancer Lola Folana, Gene Washington of the San Francisco 49ers and Joe Green of the Pittsburgh Steelers, the mystery-comedy climaxed with a snowmobile-versus-car chase through the hotel lobby, in and around the casino and, finally, into the swimming pool.

Behind the scenes at the resort, though, the situation was much more serious, in fact dire. Jud McIntosh lacked the $200,000 ($1 million) needed for payroll, so the Teamsters Pension Fund (TPF) covered the difference despite recently having infused the operation with $400,000 ($2 million).

McIntosh should've paid off the unsecured creditors by then but hadn't dispensed any funds toward that obligation. He didn't want to sink any more money into Kings Castle, he said, especially for gambling taxes, and hinted at again trying to sell the resort.

---

[*] The movie also was known as *Pop Goes the Weasel*.

During the two weeks of cinematic filming, McIntosh shut down the casino.

"What we heard is that he didn't even know what was going on," Tommy Papagna said, referring to the supposed skimming. "When he found out,[†] he closed the place."[1]

McIntosh kept open the hotel, the Kings Table restaurant and bar, beauty salon, health spa, stock brokerage, dress and gift shops. The Royal Box business was to restart soon, with gourmet Cantonese food and a piano bar for entertainment. Movies again were to be shown in the Camelot theater beginning March 15.

"We're aware of the fact they have been having some meetings with respect to certain economic aspects of their operation," Nevada Gaming Commission Chairman Peter Echeverria acknowledged regarding Kings Castle's management. "We're never happy to see economic problems with any of our licensees. It doesn't make us happy."[2]

To avoid lengthy foreclosure proceedings, McIntosh turned over to the TPF the Kings Castle deed and stepped out of the resort operations in February.

As a result, the onus of paying the unsecured creditors reverted back to Nate Jacobson. The only way he could clear that debt through the Kings Castle corporation was with proceeds from selling the hotel-casino. Accordingly, the bankruptcy court allotted him 30 days to find a buyer.

Jacobson was confident he could get it done, he said, but requested double the time. Bankruptcy Referee Bert Goldwater granted it but required that Jacobson cover all Kings Castle expenses — insurance, taxes and upkeep — that would accrue

---

[†] Not all fronts initially knew they were being used by Mobsters and for what purpose.

during those 60 days, an amount the TPF tallied at about $50,000 ($255,000) per month.

Jacobson, though, disputed the pension fund's figure and balked at paying it. He argued that the costs were the TPF trustees' responsibility because they hadn't considered any of the prospective buyers he'd introduced to them.

The TPF's attorney countered that the fund would consider any seemingly financially responsible person with a concrete plan but that no one Jacobson had presented had been legitimate.

Consequently, Goldwater rescinded the month-long extension, leaving Jacobson only 30 days to effect a sale, and mandated he cover the resort's expenses for that shorter period.

During that time, the Kings Castle operations continued to run except the already-closed gambling. However, the hospitality components of the enterprise, even combined, didn't generate anywhere close to the revenue the gambling house had, which had been significant. A 1973 survey of 16 Nevada hotel-casinos showed that 71 percent of their revenue came from their gaming business.

Likely due to the curtailed cash flow from gambling at Kings Castle, the TPF's trustees sought to secure, as soon as possible, a lessee to run the casino or a purchaser of the entire hotel-casino enterprise.

Attorney William O'Mara, the bankruptcy comptroller assigned to the Kings Castle case, successfully petitioned to have all of the resort's personal property — slot and adding machines, cash registers, television sets, sound systems, some food and beverage items, etc. — transferred to him so he could sell it and, with the revenue, pay off the unsecured creditors. In agreement, Goldwater ordered a judicial lien on the merchandise.

The TPF offered to buy that personal property for $360,000 ($2 million), the amount the creditors had agreed to, two years earlier, as payment in full.

Jacobson, though, who had no say in the matter, had his attorneys try to stop the sale of the personal property. That went nowhere. O'Mara asked the creditors' committee members if they'd accept the TPF's purchase proposal, and they did.

At the subsequent bankruptcy hearing, in March, Jacobson announced he found a buyer for Kings Castle. As such, he asked Goldwater to delay the sale of the resort's personal property, but the bankruptcy referee didn't have the power to do so.

Thus, O'Mara sold the items to the TPF and with that income, paid the unsecured creditors, finally eliminating that debt. (They received about one-third of the $1.2 million reimbursement that Nevada's gambling regulators, in their May 1973 discussions with Jacobson, had tried to make him pay.)

Jacobson would appeal the transaction, arguing that Goldwater's lien on the personal property unfairly excluded major secured creditors (ones whom McIntosh already had paid in accordance with previously negotiated settlements) from potentially getting any money out of it.

U.S. District Judge Bruce Thompson would dismiss the case.

As for Jacobson's alleged buyer of the resort, either that person or entity never had existed or had changed their mind, as nothing developed in that regard.

With Kings Castle then entirely owned by the TPF, Jacobson sued McIntosh and the pension fund, claiming that the parties had conveyed the resort to the TPF without fair consideration of other options and that they owed him $1.3 million ($6.6 million) for the personal property.

In 1976, Reno Justice Judge Grant Bowen would grant a summary judgment in favor of the defendants, prompting Jacobson to appeal.

In the following year, the Nevada Supreme Court would rule that because Jacobson and McIntosh had had an undisclosed agreement in place when ownership of Kings Castle had reverted to the TPF, the defendants hadn't perpetrated any fraud and Jacobson hadn't been hurt by the transaction. As such, the judges would dismiss the case with prejudice, meaning it couldn't be refiled.

After all that had happened with Kings Castle, Jacobson seemingly would be obsessed with it still.

CHAPTER 31

VARIOUS FINALITIES

<u>1975</u>

In early 1975, the Teamsters Pension Fund (TPF) was keeping Kings Castle running as it had been for the past year, sans casino, and was seeking a buyer.

Fund trustees reached out to the Hyatt Hotels Corporation, a hotel operator that it previously had lent money to and that was in good standing with the TPF. In those past transactions, the Hyatt had procured a TPF loan for its Palo Alto, California hotel, and the Hyatt's subsidiary, Elsinore Corporation, had obtained a TPF loan for its Four Queens Hotel and Casino in Las Vegas.

"The Teamsters say, knowing the Hyatt background and all, 'Hey, we've got a property on the North Shore, Incline Village at Lake Tahoe, that we want to do something with. We'll give it to you. We'll assign a $20 million value to it [$94 million] and only charge you 6 percent, and none of that will be payable until sometime in the future. And if you need fix-up money, we'll help you with that. Please just take a shot that will clean us up again,'" Jeanne Hood explained in the oral history, *Whatever Will Help! A Woman's Rise to the Top in the Gaming Industry*. At the time of this TPF plea, Hood's husband David was the regional president of

Nevada Hyatt operations; Jeanne would assume that position after his passing.

Hyatt agreed to the proposal but with one caveat. If the Northern Nevada hotel-casino wasn't successful within a certain period of time, the TPF would reimburse Hyatt for any money the corporation had invested in it.

"[Hyatt] was not going to be a loser here in any way, shape or form, but they would give it a shot," Hood added.

The two parties consummated the agreement. In late January, with the blessing of the state's gaming authorities, the publicly traded Hyatt announced its acquisition of Kings Castle from the TPF for $19.25 million ($90 million).

"Gentlemen, I am delighted, as I told you outside, that you are going up there and taking over Kings Castle. ... You are going to have a great success out there. ... It will be nice to see that place lighted up," Nevada Gaming Commission (NGC) Chairman Peter Echeverria told Hyatt representatives at the NGC's April 24, 1975 meeting.

In the complex deal, Hyatt agreed to spend $2.5 million ($12 million) to remodel and refurbish the resort. The TPF agreed to purchase a $30 million debenture ($140 million) — a debt instrument that isn't secured by physical assets or collateral — in Elsinore, with a mortgage on the Four Queens as security. Hyatt agreed to guarantee the first $5 million ($23.4 million) in principal payments.

Nate Jacobson responded to the sale announcement by suing members of the NGC and the Nevada Gaming Control Board for damages of $7 million ($33 million).

He asserted they'd trampled his civil rights when they'd denied him a gambling license to reopen Kings Castle as the landlord. He claimed the money was due him as he'd been licensed previously and had had a bankruptcy court-approved plan in place to satisfy the hotel-casino's debt.

In August of 1975, U.S. District Judge Bruce Thompson would dismiss Jacobson's suit due to several inherent defects. He would say Jacobson could refile, which he would do.

Three months later, Thompson would determine "not one scintilla" of evidence existed to support the notion that state gaming agencies violated Jacobson's right or acted without a "reasonable belief in the propriety of their actions."[1] Had the regulators acted in bad faith, he would say, Jacobson might've had grounds for damages.

Thompson, in a landmark interpretation of Nevada law, would add that people don't have the right to be granted a gambling license and, accordingly, gaming authorities may issue them at their discretion.

Jacobson would appeal.

Five years later, the U.S. Court of Appeals for the Ninth Circuit would affirm Thompson's ruling, agreeing that Jacobson had no protectable interest in a new gaming license because his original one had expired and his position had become just like any other first-time applicant. The judges would dismiss the case.

Fifteen years after Pacific Bridge Company & Associates had created The Sierra Tahoe, Hyatt's Elsinore, on May 1, 1975, took it over and renamed it Hyatt Lake Tahoe.

"Now that Hyatt has bought Kings Castle, the hotel will hopefully look a little more appropriate to the Tahoe scene," said columnist Robin Orr.[2]

That, in fact, was Hyatt/Elsinore's first order of business. It got busy transforming the "flagrantly garish" property, as columnist Bill Fiset described it — remodeling and harmonizing the interior and exterior with the natural surroundings and reorienting the property toward families.[3]

That meant discarding the remaining Kings Castle décor, including the naked Lady Godiva statue. The corporation auctioned off all of those pieces in a benefit for the North Lake Tahoe Historical Society.

"Hyatt, through extensive renovation, completely eradicated any semblance to the former castle and its occupant," wrote author Bethel Holmes Van Tassel in *Wood Chips to Game Chips*.

Eleven days after the Hyatt Lake Tahoe launch, four people exiting their car in Caesars Palace's parking lot in Las Vegas noticed a man slumped over the wheel in the adjacent vehicle. The group notified the resort's security detail, members of which hurried to the scene, at around 9 p.m.

They discovered that the person in question was Marty Buccieri, that he was deceased and that he'd been shot several times in the back of the head.

Buccieri's violent argument with Allen Glick a week earlier is what allegedly had led to his execution on Monday, May 13.

At one of Glick's Sin City properties, Buccieri had confronted the casino magnate and demanded he pay him $30,000 to $50,000 ($140,000 to $234,000) and/or give him an executive level position at Argent Corporation as compensation for having introduced Glick to the TPF individuals who'd helped facilitate Glick's purchase of the Stardust in 1974, for one.

The murder victim also had claimed to have paved the way with the TPF for Glick to acquire Kings Castle.

"Buccieri had been pissed at Glick for years," Beecher Avants told Nicholas Pileggi, the author of *Casino: Love and Honor in Las Vegas*. Avants had been the lieutenant and commander of the Las

Vegas Metro Police Department's robbery and homicide division then.

"Buccieri told anyone who listened that he first got Glick the pension fund loans and then Glick aced him out. Here was Glick owning four casinos, three hotels, jet airplanes, houses all over the place while Marty's standing on his feet in the pit at Caesars for an eight-hour shift."

When Glick refused to comply, Buccieri allegedly grew irate and violent and threatened him. (What Buccieri reportedly did to Glick varied among the newspapers: he put his hands around Glick's throat, he pushed Glick, he grabbed Glick's lapels, he hit Glick.) Whatever happened, security guards supposedly came to Glick's rescue.

"Marty Buccieri was killed because he posed a threat to Glick, and Glick was the Mob's front man. A threat to Glick was seen as a threat to the bosses and the skim," Pileggi wrote.

Local detectives and FBI agents believed that The Outfit's Tony Spilotro had arranged the hit on Buccieri on orders from above. However, ultimately, neither Spilotro nor the shooter(s), who hadn't been identified at least publicly, was charged for the slaying.

A month after Buccieri's murder, in Northern Nevada, Hyatt/Elsinore threw a grand opening party for its new Lake Tahoe resort on the weekend of June 27 to 29.

The celebration began Friday night with a pre-opening reception in the newly named Crystal Forest Theatre for locals. The following dinner, which featured an open bar and buffet, lasted five hours and was attended by more than 1,500 guests.

A morning hot air balloon race, in which Senators John Tunney (Calif.) and Edward "Ted" Kennedy (Mass.) participated with their 13-year-old sons, kicked off Saturday's festivities. (Tunney was a friend of Jay Pritzker, brother of the late Don Pritzker who'd created the Hyatt hotel chain; Kennedy didn't have ties to the corporation.) Tours on Lake Tahoe aboard the M.S. Dixie paddle wheeler filled the afternoon. A gala called the Steamer Ball marked the finale on Sunday night.

Throughout the weekend, visitors gambled in the casino, which housed 300 slot machines and 17 table games. The success of the launch accurately foretold the Hyatt Lake Tahoe's future.[*]

In the following month, July, with the resort sale complete and all priority and unsecured creditors paid, Bankruptcy Referee Bert Goldwater closed the Kings Castle bankruptcy case.

1976

Nate Jacobson received the last installment of his multimillion payout from the sale of Caesars Palace. Before he agreed to this final settlement, however, he allegedly insisted the casino waive his gambling markers, or debt, which amounted to several hundred thousand dollars, FBI records indicated.

Subsequently, despite all of his troubles with Kings Castle, Jacobson strove to develop another grand hotel-casino and in 1976, started to scout a location for it. Based on information that the European country, Spain, likely would legalize gambling soon, Jacobson moved there and lobbied to build a $60 million ($284 million) megaresort in Costa del Sol.

Government officials would approve such an industry in 1977 but would refuse Jacobson a gambling license because they suspected he was a Mobster or, at a minimum, had underworld ties.

---

[*] Now the Hyatt Regency Lake Tahoe Resort, Spa and Casino, it continues to thrive. An outside company runs the gambling there.

Jacobson would give up on Spain and move back to the U.S., specifically Florida.

Because New Jersey had authorized gaming in 1976, Jacobson next would envision, for Atlantic City, a sizable hotel-casino also with a royalty theme. He'd name it Camelot, defined in the Merriam-Webster dictionary as "the site of King Arthur's palace and court" and "a time, place or atmosphere of idyllic happiness."

He would convince those in power at American Midland, Inc.,[†] a holding company with interests in hotels, drugstores and nursing homes, of the benefits of owning such an entity. The corporation, therefore, would add an internal real estate division called Camelot, Inc. and appoint Jacobson as its president. Their purpose would be to develop Jacobson's Camelot resort.

In 1980, Camelot, Inc. would purchase 8.2 acres of property in Atlantic City for the proposed 24-story hotel, 60,000-square-foot casino and numerous amenities. Compared to Kings Castle, Camelot was to boast a hotel with four times as many floors and a casino with seven times the area.

The same year, Jacobson would entertain the idea of partnering with Wayne Newton to purchase the troubled Aladdin hotel-casino in Las Vegas, but nothing would come of it (possibly because Jacobson couldn't get a Nevada gambling license).

Meanwhile, Jacobson would continue trying to secure the $200 million ($617 million) needed to build Camelot.

However, after six years of various futile attempts, including a failed deal with South African investors, the task would prove near, if not wholly, impossible.

[†] American Midland, Inc. was the result of a merger between American Leisure Corporation of Atlantic City, New Jersey, a hotel and casino concern, and Midland Resources, Inc. of Fort Lee, New Jersey, a holding company with interests in hotels, real estate, coal mining and oilfield services.

As such, the American Midland executives would want to scale back the project, but Jacobson wouldn't, and in 1985, he'd resign from his position at the company "by mutual agreement."[4]

Finally, in 1985, at age 70, Jacobson[‡] would end his nearly decade-long pursuit of Camelot.[§] It never would be built.

[‡] Nate Jacobson would pass away on July 27, 1987 in North Miami.
[§] Coincidentally, today, a handful of hotels named Camelot exist — in the Philippines, Thailand, Greece and the U.S., but none is tied to American Midland.

A.L.W., Inc.: founded by Arthur Wood, corporate owner of the Incline Village Casino and later, the Kings Castle casino

American Midland, Inc.: New Jersey-based holding company, with interests in hotels, drugstores and nursing homes, which hired Nathan Jacobson to build the Camelot hotel-casino in Atlantic City

Argent Corporation: Allen R. Glick's gaming corporation

Barkett, Joseph: Stockton, California dentist who, with August Marra, pursued buying Kings Castle in 1971 but didn't

Bast, Richard: Nevada fire marshal

Beemer, William: Reno Justice judge

Benham, Tom: Washoe County sheriff's chief

Berrum, Lou: Washoe County zoning board chairman

Billman, Clyde: Kings Castle public relations director

Boise Cascade Corporation: acquirer of the Crystal Bay Development Company in 1968

Bonanza: Las Vegas hotel-casino acquired by Nathan Jacobson and Levin-Townsend Computer Corporation in 1969

Bowen, Grant L.: Reno Justice judge who presided over the 1973 Jacobson-Bruno criminal case

Broudy, Mr. Sherrill: Santa Barbara, California-based architect who, with William Swigert and Jack Ferguson as Pacific Bridge Company & Associates, envisioned, developed and owned The Sierra Tahoe from construction in 1963 to 2/65

Bruno, Thomas J.: Nathan Jacobson's bodyguard at Kings Castle

Buccieri, Edward "Marty" A.: ex-convict; alleged Mob bagman; unofficial worker at the Incline Village Casino in 1966 and Kings Castle in 1973 and 1974; Caesars Palace pit boss; murder victim

Butner, Lorne: Washoe County sheriff's captain

Caesars Forum: casino in Las Vegas' Caesars Palace

Caesars Palace: hotel-casino on the Las Vegas Strip, which debuted in August 1966

Callister, Charles Warren: California-based architect who designed The Sierra Tahoe buildings

Cal-Neva Lodge: hotel-casino on Lake Tahoe's North Shore, purchased by Nathan Jacobson, Jay Sarno and two others from Frank Sinatra in 1967 then sold to Sierra Development Company, owners of the Reno Club Cal Neva, in 1968

Camelot, Inc.: corporate division formed by American Midland, Inc. for the development of Camelot in Atlantic City

Campbell, Jr., Harold: FBI special agent in charge

Carrigan, Thomas: Nevada Gaming Control Board member

Central States, Southeast, Southwest Areas Pension Fund of the International Brotherhood of Teamsters (TPF): founded by James Hoffa and administered by eight trustees, fund containing employer contributions for retirement, disability and death benefits; financier of The Sierra Tahoe (under Harold Riel and Roy Lewis' ownership starting in 2/65 and Calvin Kovens' ownership starting in 12/65), Caesars Palace, Kings Castle and the Hyatt Lake Tahoe

Coppa, Joe: Washoe County Board of Commissioners member

Crane, Richard: West Coast Organized Crime Strike Force head

Crystal Bay: census-designated place in Washoe County on Lake Tahoe's North Shore, adjacent to Incline Village

Crystal Bay Development Company (CBDC): Incline Village-based real estate development company that purchased 9,000 Incline Village acres from Nevada Lake Tahoe Investment Company in 1960

Desert Palace, Inc.: first corporate owner of Las Vegas' Caesars Palace

Dickerson, George M.: Nevada Gaming Commission chairman in 1967 and 1968; brother of Harvey Dickerson, Nevada attorney general, 1/63–1/71

Diehl, Jack: Nevada Gaming Commission chairman, 1968–1973

Dunlap, Calvin R.: Washoe County deputy district attorney who, with Robert Rose and Larry Hicks, co-prosecuted the 1973 Jacobson-Bruno criminal case

Echeverria, Peter: Raymond Landucci's attorney for his 1971 suit against Nathan Jacobson; Nevada Gaming Commission chairman, 1973–1977

Elsinore Corporation: Hyatt Hotels Corporation's subsidiary

Farella, Frank: Pacific Bridge Company's California-based attorney

Farina, William: Kings Castle casino manager, 1971–1974

Ferguson, Jack: Lake Tahoe businessman who, with William Swigert and Sherrill Broudy as Pacific Bridge Company & Associates, envisioned, developed and owned The Sierra Tahoe from construction in 1963 to 2/65

Fresnay, Michael: designer of Kings Castle's staff costumes

Gabrielli, John E.: Reno Justice judge

Galli, Robert "Bob": Washoe County sheriff, 1971–1982

Gatterdam, Clayton P.: Incline Village Casino stickman caught cheating at craps using misspot dice

Gezelin, Emile: Reno Justice judge

Gilmore, Richard C.: psychiatrist who negotiated to purchase Kings Castle in 1972 but didn't

Glick, Allen R.: El Cajon, California's Saratoga Development Corporation executive vice president, who tried to acquire Kings Castle in 1973; owner of Argent Corporation; front for the Chicago Outfit

Goldwater, Bert: bankruptcy referee assigned to the Kings Castle case

Guinan, James: Washoe District judge

Hancock, Newell F.: Reno accountant who proposed to buy Incline Village Casino in 1/68 but changed his mind

Hannifin, Philip: Nevada Gaming Control Board chairman, 1971–1977

Hicks, Larry R.: Washoe County deputy district attorney who, with Robert Rose and Calvin Dunlap, co-prosecuted the 1973 Jacobson-Bruno criminal case

Hoffa, Jr., James "Jimmy" Riddle: president of the International Brotherhood of Teamsters, 1958–1971; convicted in 1963 of jury tampering, convicted in 1964 of mail/loan fraud with Calvin Kovens

Hotchkiss, James W.: Nevada Gaming Commission member

Hughes, Jay: Washoe County deputy sheriff

Hume, James "Jimmie": Kings Castle casino host in 1973; co-owner and casino host of Crystal Bay's North Shore Club previously

Hyatt Hotels Corporation: acquirer of Kings Castle in 1975

Incline: a timber source in the 1800s for nearby mines; Incline Village today

Incline Village: township on Lake Tahoe's North Shore whose development began in the 1960s

Incline Village Casino: formerly part of The Sierra Tahoe; leased and operated by Arthur Wood, 1966–5/68

Incline Village General Improvement District (IVGID): agency providing utilities and recreation services to Incline Village and Crystal Bay

Jacobson, Edward: one of Nathan Jacobson's two sons

Jacobson, Morris: one of Nathan Jacobson's two brothers

Jacobson, Nathan "Nate" S.: Insurance brokerage owner in Baltimore, Maryland; Caesars palace co-owner, president and casino operator, 1966–1969; Lake Tahoe's Cal-Neva Lodge co-owner with Jay Sarno in 1967; Las Vegas' Bonanza hotel-casino co-owner with Levin-Townsend Computer Corporation in 1969; Kings Castle owner/operator, 1969–1973

Jacobson, Samuel: one of Nathan Jacobson's two brothers

Jacobson, Sanford: one of Nathan Jacobson's two sons

Jacobson, Sylvia: Nathan Jacobson's wife until their divorce in 1976

Jaffe, Morris: San Antonio, Texas millionaire and commercial real estate developer who offered to acquire Kings Castle in 1972 but didn't

Johnson, Frank: Nevada Gaming Control Board chairman, 1967–1971

Karamanos, Christ "Chris" N.: Kings Castle general manager in 1973; co-owner of Kyle Corporation, parent company of Jet Avia; suicide victim

Kings Castle: Nathan Jacobson's renovated version of the Lake Tahoe Hotel and Incline Village Casino, formerly The Sierra Tahoe, opened in 1970, sold in 1975

Kings Castle, Ltd.: corporate owner of the Kings Castle hotel

Kings Manor Condominiums: Nathan Jacobson's proposed lakefront condominium complex nixed by the Washoe County Board of Commissioners

Kovens, Calvin: Florida-based construction contractor/developer; The Sierra Tahoe owner, 12/65–5/69; Irvin Kovens' brother; Alvin Kroll's brother-in-law

Kovens, Irvin S.: Baltimore, Maryland businessman and fundraiser; Caesars Palace and Kings Castle investor; Calvin Kovens' brother; Alvin Kroll's brother-in-law

Kroll, Alvin B.: owner of Florida-based Home Appliance Inc.; The Sierra Tahoe operator, 7/65–1/66; Calvin and Irvin Kovens' brother-in-law

Lake Tahoe Hotel: new name of The Sierra Tahoe hotel only, as of 1966

Landucci, Dawn: Raymond Landucci's wife

Landucci, Raymond M.: Kings Castle keno supervisor

Lassoff, Benjamin "Benny": Incline Village Casino bartender and co-gambling licensee with Arthur Wood in 1967

Laxalt, Paul D.: Republican Nevada governor, 1/67–1/71

Levin, Howard S.: Levin-Townsend Computer Corporation president/CEO who, with Nathan Jacobson, co-owned Las Vegas' Bonanza hotel-casino in 1969

Levin-Townsend Computer Corporation: publicly traded, computer leasing and real estate investment firm co-owned by Howard S. Levin and James E. Townsend

Lewis, Roy G.: The Sierra Tahoe co-owner, with Harold K. Riel, 2/65–1/66

Lum's, Inc.: nationwide family restaurant chain that purchased Caesars Palace for $58 million in 1968

Marra, August: Castro Valley, California real estate developer who, with Joseph Barkett, expressed interested in buying Kings Castle in 1971 but didn't

Martin, James: Kings Castle keno manager

McIntosh, Jud D.: George-based Lithonia Lighting, Inc. executive; Caesars Palace investor and corporate treasurer; Las Vegas' Circus interim president; Kings Castle owner, 5/73–2/74

McKissick, Jr., Howard: Kings Castle creditors committee chairman

McKissick, Sr., Howard: Washoe County Board of Commissioners member

Murtha, Francis J.: Teamsters Pension Fund executive secretary

Nevada Gaming Commission (NGC): successor to the Nevada Tax Commission, the state gambling regulatory agency created in 1959, then primarily involved with the issuing of gambling licenses

Nevada Gaming Control Board (NGCB): founded in 1955, the state gambling regulatory agency that oversaw administration, investigation and enforcement of gambling and state laws; it made recommendations, based on its findings, to the Nevada Gaming Commission

Nevada Lake Tahoe Investment Company (NLTIC): conglomerate of Oklahoma, Hawaii and Kansas businessmen who purchased 9,000 acres of undeveloped Lake Tahoe property from George Whittell, Jr. in 1959

Newpher, Harold H.: FBI agent

Olsen, Edward "Ed" A.: Nevada Gaming Control Board chairman, 1961–1966

O'Mara, William: bankruptcy attorney assigned to the Kings Castle case

Pacific Bridge Company (PBC): Alameda, California commercial construction company noted for the bridges it constructed in the Western U.S., including the Bay and Golden Gate

Pacific Bridge Company & Associates (PBC&A): partnership between William Swigert, Sherrill Broudy and Jack Ferguson that envisioned, developed, owned and operated The Sierra Tahoe, 1963–2/65

Pagni, Roy: Washoe County Board of Commissioners chairman

Papagna, Tommy: Kings Castle roulette, baccarat and 21 dealer, 1973–1974

Park Lake Enterprises: Frank Sinatra's gaming corporation that owned the Cal-Neva Lodge

Parsons, Stanley: Incline Village Casino manager

Paull, Forrest S.: Kings Castle vice president of personnel and security

Pearson, Wayne: Nevada Gaming Control Board member

Peccole, Robert "Bob" J.: Incline Village Casino owner, 1968–1969

Petersen, Frank R.: Reno-based attorney for Nathan Jacobson and Kings Castle

Picard, Pamela: Eastern Airlines flight attendant who had a brief relationship with Nathan Jacobson in 1972

Piper, Richard "Dick": first Kings Castle casino manager

Polando, John: Kings Castle publicist

Quittner, Francis F.: Nathan Jacobson's bankruptcy attorney

Renaud, Line: French singer/actress; Kings Castle entertainment director

Riel, Harold K.: The Sierra Tahoe co-owner, with Roy Lewis, 2/65–1/66

Roosevelt, Elliott: Norman Tyrone's business partner in the mortgage banking firm Financial Services International (formerly Elliott Roosevelt International Bank and Trust, Ltd.); son of former U.S. President and First Lady, Franklin D. and Eleanor Roosevelt

Rose, Robert: Washoe County district attorney who, with Larry Hicks and Calvin Dunlap, co-prosecuted the 1973 Jacobson-Bruno criminal case

Rusk, Robert: Washoe County Board of Commissioners member

Sahara-Tahoe: hotel-casino on Lake Tahoe's South Shore often confused with The Sierra Tahoe on the North Shore

Sandy, Don: San Francisco, California-based architect with Sandy and Hedley; creator of the final blueprints for The Sierra Tahoe

Sarno, Jay J.: Caesars Palace visionary, designer and managing operator

Sawyer, Frank "Grant" G.: Democratic Nevada governor, 1/59–1/67

Selman, Arthur "Artie": Kings Castle co-owner, partner to Nathan Jacobson and vice president of food and beverage

Sheridan, Thomas R.: Los Angeles, California-based attorney for Nathan Jacobson

Sierra Development Company: Reno Club Cal Neva owners who purchased the Cal-Neva Lodge in Crystal Bay in 1968

Spilotro, Anthony "Tony/The Ant": Chicago Outfit enforcer in Las Vegas; Hole in the Wall Gang burglary ring leader; murder victim

Stern, Jr., Martin: Beverly Hills, California-based architect who designed Kings Castle and Kings Manor Condominiums

Struve, Larry: Washoe County deputy district attorney

Swigert, Jr., William "Bill" G.: Pacific Bridge Company president who, with Sherrill Broudy and Jack Ferguson as Pacific Bridge Company & Associates, envisioned, developed and owned The Sierra Tahoe hotel from construction in 1963 to 2/65

Swobe, Coe: Republican Nevada senator, 11/66–11/74

Tahoe Forum: never-built, $15 million, 40-acre recreational/cultural community envisioned in 1961 for the property on which The Sierra Tahoe was built

Tahoe Regional Planning Agency (TRPA): bistate (Nevada and California) agency charged with developing and maintaining development standards for the Lake Tahoe region

The Sierra Tahoe: hotel, lakeshore bungalows and pavilion in Incline Village on Lake Tahoe's North Shore, envisioned, funded, developed and owned by Pacific Bridge Company & Associates, 1963–2/65

Thompson, Bruce R.: U.S. District judge

Tiller, Harold B.: Crystal Bay Development Company executive vice president; certified public accountant

Truax, Norman "Norm": Raymond Landucci's alleged co-conspirator in the supposed Kings Castle keno cheat

Tyrone, Norman B.: Southern California financier who presented the TPF loan to The Sierra Tahoe owners; owner of the International Mortgage and Statistical Corporation of the Bahamas; partner with Elliott Roosevelt in the mortgage banking firm Financial Services International (formerly Elliott Roosevelt International Bank and Trust, Ltd.)

Valenzuela, Mario: freelance artist who created the Tahoe Forum renderings

Voice of Incline Village-Crystal Bay: citizen's committee that protested the street name change to Kings Castle Way from Country Club Drive

Washoe County: Northern Nevada county in which Incline Village and Crystal Bay, on Lake Tahoe's North Shore, are located

Washoe County Board of Adjustment: county's zoning board that made recommendations to the Washoe County Board of Commissioners regarding approval or denial of construction permit applications

Washoe County Board of Commissioners: body of five elected individuals charged with managing the county

Whitmire, William: Washoe County sheriff's sergeant

Whittell, Jr., George: wealthy industrialist who owned 40,000 North Lake Tahoe acres and sold 9,000 of them to the Nevada Lake Tahoe Investment Company in 1959

Wood, Arthur "Art" L.: certified public accountant; Nevada Lake Tahoe Investment Company investor; Crystal Bay Development Company founder; major developer of Incline Village; Incline Village Casino owner and operator, 1966–5/68

NOTES

CHAPTER 1: DIP INTO THE UNDERWORLD

[1] *Nevada State Journal,* "Teamster Fund Trial Starts on Tahoe Loan," Jan. 26, 1971.
[2] Interview of William G. Swigert, Jr., June 24, 2010.
[3] *Oakland Tribune,* "$200,000 Fee on Loan for Teamsters," June 5, 1970.
[4] Ibid.
[5] Brandt, Charles. *I Heard You Paint Houses: Frank "The Irishman" Sheeran & Closing the Case on Jimmy Hoffa,* Hanover, N.H.: Steerforth Press, 2005. Ebook.
[6] Interview of William G. Swigert, Jr., June 24, 2010.
[7] *Oakland Tribune,* "$200,000 Fee on Loan for Teamsters," June 5, 1970.

CHAPTER 2: HAIR-BRAINED SCHEME

[1] *Reno Evening Gazette,* "Whittell Sells Land at Tahoe for $5 Million," Sept. 9, 1959.
[2] Interview of Sherrill Broudy, Oct. 31, 2009.
[3] Ibid.

CHAPTER 3: SEEKING ELUSIVE MONEY

[1] Interview of William G. Swigert, Jr., June 24, 2010.
[2] Ibid.
[3] Ibid.
[4] Ibid.
[5] Interview of Sherrill Broudy, Oct. 31, 2009.

CHAPTER 4: CHANGE OF HANDS

[1] Interview of Sherrill Broudy, Oct. 31, 2009.
[2] *Nevada State Journal,* "Signs Point to North Shore Boom," June, 22, 1960.
[3] Lahey, Edwin. *Chicago Daily News,* "Las Vegas Smells of Underworld," April 7, 1966.
[4] Ibid.
[5] Interview of Sherrill Broudy, Oct. 31, 2009.

CHAPTER 5: TO THE RESCUE?

[1] *Oakland Tribune,* "$200,000 Fee on Loan for Teamsters," June 5, 1970.
[2] Interview of Sherrill Broudy, Oct. 31, 2009.
[3] Interview of William G. Swigert, Jr., June 24, 2010.
[4] Interview of Sherrill Broudy, Oct. 31, 2009.

CHAPTER 6: A FRESH START

[1] *Los Angeles Times,* "The Nation," March 16, 1966.

[2] *Los Angeles Times*, "A Traveler's Diary," Oct. 15, 1967.

CHAPTER 7: CATCHING THE CASINO BUG

[1] *Nevada State Journal*, "Jacobson Says Goodbye," Nov. 12, 1971.
[2] Church, Foster. *Nevada State Journal*, "Jacobson—He Sensed the Village Antagonism," July 23, 1971.
[3] *The Daily Mail* (Md.), "Irvin Kovens: 'Golden Touch' Nets Influence, Money and Friends," Sept. 22, 1971.
[4] *Los Angeles Times*, "Give My Regards to…Vegas?" July 18, 1999.
[5] *Naugatuck News*, "My New York," Aug. 31, 1966.

CHAPTER 8: MORE GAMBLING DRAMA

[1] *Nevada State Journal*, "Burglars Bind, Gag Janitor," May 20, 1966.
[2] *Reno Evening Gazette*, Other Editors—"Firm Action is Essential," Nov. 3, 1967.
[3] *Nevada State Journal*, "Wood Wants to Sell Closed Down Casino," Dec. 5, 1967.

CHAPTER 9: A TENTACLED REACH

[1] Church, Foster. *Nevada State Journal*, "Jacobson—He Sensed the Village Antagonism," July 23, 1971.
[2] Interview of Arthur Selman, April 12, 2016.
[3] Interview of Pamela Picard, June 2015.
[4] Church, Foster, *Nevada State Journal*, "Jacobson—He Sensed the Village Antagonism," July 23, 1971.
[5] *The Post-Standard* (Syracuse), "Lyons Den," Sept. 27, 1967.

CHAPTER 10: WANTING STABILITY

[1] *Reno Evening Gazette*, "Hancock Drops Tahoe Casino License Bid," Jan. 10, 1968.
[2] *Reno Evening Gazette*, "Wood Granted One More Year on Tahoe Permit," April 25, 1968.
[3] *Reno Evening Gazette*, "Wood to Ask Again for Permit Extension," April 23, 1968.
[4] *Oakland Tribune*, "Sierra Ski Resorts Aim to Attract Europeans," July 14, 1968.
[5] *Oakland Tribune*, "$200,000 Fee on Loan for Teamsters," June 5, 1970.
[6] Interview of William G. Swigert, Jr., June 24, 2010.

CHAPTER 11: WHEELING AND DEALING

[1] Interview of Arthur Selman, April 12, 2016.
[2] *Los Angeles Times*, "Resort Opened on Tahoe North Shore," July 4, 1970.
[3] *The Times* (San Mateo), Advertisement for Kings Castle, July 2, 1969.

CHAPTER 12: ONE-TWO PUNCH

[1] *Nevada State Journal*, "Small Business Chief Faces House Quiz; Case of the 'Stolen' Highway at Tahoe," July 18, 1970.
[2] Church, Foster. *Nevada State Journal*, "Jacobson—He Sensed the Village Antagonism," July 23, 1971.
[3] *Nevada State Journal*, "Relocation Work Pushed at Incline," April 25, 1969.
[4] *Nevada State Journal*, "Tahoe Protected," Feb. 19, 1970.
[5] *Nevada State Journal*, "Incline High-Rise 'Delayed,'" Feb. 4, 1970.
[6] *Reno Evening Gazette*, "Judge Rejects County Bid to Dismiss Suit," May 29, 1970.
[7] *Nevada State Journal*, "Jacobson to Appeal Condominium Decision," Aug. 10, 1970.
[8] *Oakland Tribune*, "Court Fight Over Tahoe High-Rise," Aug. 16, 1970.

CHAPTER 13: ASSUMING THE THRONE

[1] Interview of Arthur Selman, April 12, 2016.
[2] *Moberly Monitor-Index and Evening Democrat* (Mo.), "Lake Tahoe Debut Was No Laugh-In for Miss Graves," Sept. 5, 1970.
[3] *The Cedar Rapids Gazette*, "Along Broadway," July 10, 1970.
[4] *Oakland Tribune*, "Night Sounds," July 3, 1970.
[5] Interview of Arthur Selman, April 12, 2016.
[6] *Los Angeles Times*, "Resort Opened on Tahoe North Shore," July 4, 1970.
[7] *Oakland Tribune*, "$200,000 Fee on Loan for Teamsters," June 5, 1970.
[8] *Oakland Tribune*, "Night Sounds," July 3, 1970.

CHAPTER 14: BETTING ON BUSINESS

[1] *Star-News* (Pasadena), "Hollywood Hotline," July 13, 1970.
[2] *Billboard*, "Kings Castle Making Bid for Vegas' Silver Circuit Gold," July 18, 1970.
[3] *Nevada State Journal*, Advertisement for Kings Castle, July 30, 1970.
[4] *Los Angeles Times*, "Resort Opened on Tahoe North Shore," July 4, 1970.

CHAPTER 15: FROM JEWELS TO JUNKETS

[1] *Nevada State Journal*, "Postscripts," Dec. 22, 1970.
[2] *Nevada State Journal*, "Snowmobile Grand Prix at Incline," Nov. 8, 1969.
[3] *Nevada State Journal*, "Tahoe Snowmobile Races to Offer Broad Contrast," Dec. 16, 1969.
[4] *Independent* (Long Beach), "Tennis at Tahoe Now Winter Sport," Aug. 31, 1971.
[5] *Nevada State Journal*, "Casino Show Rooms Close Doors; Weather, Repairs are Reason," Dec. 10, 1971.
[6] *Reno Evening Gazette*, "Reno-Tahoe Tourism Booms With Holiday," Feb. 15, 1971.
[7] *The News* (Van Nuys), "Fans Can Chop Rickles," June 24, 1971.
[8] *Daily Times* (Pa.), "Senator's Speechwriter Fouls Him Up With S.O.B.," July 22, 1971.

CHAPTER 16: KINGS CASTLE (NO) WAY

[1] *Reno Evening Gazette*, "Kings Castle's Jacobson Disagrees With Editorial on Public Relations," April 10, 1971.
[2] *Reno Evening Gazette*, "Kings Castle Way Approved, Reconsideration Asked," April 6, 1971.
[3] *Nevada State Journal*, Letters to the Editor—"Offensive Sign," July 6, 1971.
[4] Ibid.
[5] *Reno Evening Gazette*, "Kings Castle Way Approved, Reconsideration Asked," April 6, 1971.
[6] *Nevada State Journal*, Editorials—"Changing a Street Name at Incline, Lake Tahoe," April 14, 1971.
[7] Ibid.
[8] Ibid.
[9] *Nevada State Journal*, Letters to the Editor—"The Name Change," April 10, 1971.
[10] *Reno Evening Gazette*, Letters to the Editor—"Helps County," April 15, 1971.
[11] *Reno Evening Gazette*, Letters to the Editor—"Fair Decision," April 7, 1971.
[12] *Nevada State Journal*, "Kings Castle Way Name Confirmed," April 16, 1971.
[13] *Nevada State Journal*, "Proposed Incline Village Recreation Plans Appear Doomed," April 30, 1971.
[14] *Nevada State Journal*, "Selective Counting Charged in North Lake Tahoe Poll," July 3, 1971.
[15] Church, Foster. *Nevada State Journal*, "Jacobson—He Sensed the Village Antagonism," July 23, 1971.

CHAPTER 17: BUSTED, TIMES THREE

[1] Church, Foster. *Nevada State Journal*, "Jacobson—He Sensed the Village Antagonism," July 23, 1971.
[2] *Nevada State Journal*, "Kings Castle Closure Threatened by County," July 16, 1971.
[3] *Nevada State Journal*, "Kings Castle, County Argue Over Licenses," June 17, 1971.
[4] Church, Foster. *Nevada State Journal*, "Jacobson—He Sensed the Village Antagonism," July 23, 1971.
[5] *Nevada State Journal*, "Kings Castle Closure Threatened by County," July 16, 1971.
[6] *Nevada State Journal*, "Board Suggests Pulling Kings Castle Annex Permit," July 21, 1971.
[7] *Reno Evening Gazette*, "Kings Castle Question: Who's in Control in Nevada?" July 21, 1971.
[8] *Nevada State Journal*, Letters to the Editor—"Castle's Troubles," Aug. 7, 1971.
[9] *Reno Evening Gazette*, Letters to the Editor—"County Harassment," Aug. 14, 1971.
[10] Church, Foster. *Nevada State Journal*, "Jacobson—He Sensed the Village Antagonism," July 23, 1971.
[11] *Nevada State Journal*, "Kings Castle Truce:...And Love Verily Cracked Again...," Sept. 1, 1971.

CHAPTER 18: SHOW ME THE MONEY

[1] *Reno Evening Gazette*, "Jacobson Files Suit Against ABC," March 28, 1973.
[2] *Nevada State Journal*, "Jacobson Says Goodbye: 'I'm Weary,'" Nov. 12, 1971.
[3] *Reno Evening Gazette*, "Kings Castle Sale Near," Nov. 3, 1971.
[4] *Reno Evening Gazette*, "Stock Transfer Approved for Kings Castle," Nov. 19, 1971.
[5] *Nevada State Journal*, Political Front—"Why the Fast Kings Castle Transfer?" Dec. 12, 1971.

CHAPTER 19: CAN IT GET WORSE?

[1] *Nevada State Journal*, "Key Jacobson Case Figure Tells Story," March 21, 1972.
[2] *Reno Evening Gazette*, "Jacobson Attorney Calls Landucci 'An Admitted Liar, A Strange Liar,'" March 24, 1972.
[3] Ibid.
[4] *Nevada State Journal*, "Ex-Kings Castle Boss Claims Gun Forced False Confession," June 22, 1973.
[5] Ibid.
[6] *Nevada State Journal*, "Kings Castle Keno 'Scam' Idea Explained by Landucci," March 22, 1972.
[7] *Reno Evening Gazette*, "Ordeal Described by Key Witness," June 22, 1973.
[8] *Nevada State Journal*, "A 'Nasty, Distasteful Scene': Kidnapping Denied by Jacobson," July 17, 1973.
[9] *Nevada State Journal*, "Allegations of Beating, Gun Play Said 'Inconsistent With Reality,'" Dec. 29, 1971.

CHAPTER 20: THE TROUBLESOME AFTERMATH

[1] *Reno Evening Gazette*, "Landucci's Wife Tells of Weeks of Family Terror," July 9, 1973.
[2] *Nevada State Journal*, "Informant: FBI Tipster Remains Unknown at Jacobson Trial," July 11, 1973.
[3] Ibid.
[4] *Nevada State Journal*, "Developer Arrested at Tahoe," Dec. 1, 1971.
[5] *Reno Evening Gazette*, Editorials—"Poor Performance," Dec. 2, 1971.
[6] *Reno Evening Gazette*, "Jacobson Writes 'An Open Letter to World,'" Dec. 6, 1971.
[7] *Reno Evening Gazette*, Editorials—"Poor Performance," Dec. 2, 1971.

CHAPTER 21: MIRED IN CRISES

[1] *Reno Evening Gazette*, "Jacobson, Bruno Request Look at Grand Jury Vote," Jan. 4, 1972.
[2] *Reno Evening Gazette*, "Jacobson Calls Note Foreclosure by Teamsters 'Procedural Move,'" Jan. 25, 1972.

CHAPTER 22: NO OTHER CHOICE

[1] *Reno Evening Gazette*, "Jacobson Closing Kings Castle," Feb. 2, 1972.
[2] *Reno Evening Gazette*, "Opening a Hotel Was Easy, But Closing It, Well...," Feb. 3, 1972.
[3] *Reno Evening Gazette*, "Advance Warning—Shirts Stopped Coming," Feb. 4, 1972.
[4] *Los Angeles Times*, "How Tahoe Monarch Lost a Kingdom," Oct. 8, 1972.
[5] Ibid.
[6] Interview of Arthur Selman, April 12, 2016.
[7] *Reno Evening Gazette*, "Reopening Seen For Kings Castle," Feb. 18, 1972.

CHAPTER 23: DAMAGE CONTROL

[1] *Nevada State Journal*, "Motion Denied to Quash Kidnaping [sic] Indictment," Feb. 5, 1972.
[2] *Reno Evening Gazette*, "Jacobson Motion Attacks Charges," March 2, 1972.
[3] *Nevada State Journal*, "D.A. Seeks Dismissal of Duplicate Indictments Against Jacobson, Bruno," March 10, 1972.
[4] *Nevada State Journal*, "Kings Castle Way Draws 'Sentiment,'" Oct. 5, 1972.

CHAPTER 25: FINDING A BUYER

[1] *Nevada State Journal*, "Kings Castle Due to Reopen," May 17, 1973.
[2] *Nevada State Journal*, "Jacobson to Sell Castle Interest," May 25, 1973.
[3] *Nevada State Journal*, "Jacobson Balks at Rules for Kings Castle License," May 23, 1973.
[4] *Nevada State Journal*, "No Regrets: Kings Castle Owner Can't Leave Too Soon," May 3, 1973.
[5] Ibid.

CHAPTER 26: ALLEGED MOBSTER INVOLVEMENT

[1] *Nevada State Journal*, "No Regrets: Kings Castle Owner Can't Leave Too Soon," May 3, 1973.
[2] *Nevada State Journal*, "Group Claims Kings Castle Zone Violation," June 6, 1973.
[3] Interview of Tommy Papagna, March 2, 2018.

CHAPTER 27: PURSUIT OF RECOMPENSE

[1] *Nevada State Journal*, "FBI Agent's Testimony Blocked in Wiretap Trial of State Lawmen," July 9, 1976.
[2] *Nevada State Journal*, "Obscene Calls," July 8, 1976.
[3] *Nevada State Journal*, "'Charge Your Boss,'" July 14, 1976.
[4] *Nevada State Journal*, "Wiretap Verdict Views Mixed," July 17, 1976.

CHAPTER 28: INNOCENT OR GUILTY?

[1] *Nevada State Journal*, "Jacobson Has 'Gut' Feeling on Fair Trial," June 21, 1973.
[2] *Nevada State Journal*, "Ex-Kings Castle Boss Claims Gun Forced False Confession," June 22, 1973.
[3] Ibid.
[4] *Nevada State Journal*, "Political Front—In Nevada," June 24, 1973.
[5] *Reno Evening Gazette*, "Jacobson, Bruno Penalty Possibilities Given Jury," July 19, 1973.
[6] *Nevada State Journal*, "Jury Deliberates Kidnaping [sic] Case," July 20, 1973.
[7] *Nevada State Journal*, "'Hollow Victory' for Acquitted Nate Jacobson," July 21, 1973.
[8] Ibid.
[9] *Reno Evening Gazette*, "Jacobson Loses Gaming Interest," Aug. 24, 1973.
[10] *Nevada State Journal*, "'Hollow Victory' for Acquitted Nate Jacobson," July 21, 1973.

CHAPTER 29: DEALING WITH DEBTS

[1] *Reno Evening Gazette*, "Jacobson's Kings Castle Creditor Plan Approved," Aug. 29, 1973.
[2] Interview of Tommy Papagna, March 2, 2018.
[3] *Reno Evening Gazette*, "Kings Castle Executive Plans to Leave," Sept. 29, 1973.

CHAPTER 30: ANOTHER ROUGH PATCH

[1] Interview of Tommy Papagna, March 2, 2018.
[2] *Reno Evening Gazette*, "Castle's Gaming Closed," Jan. 28, 1974.

CHAPTER 31: VARIOUS FINALITIES

[1] *Reno Evening Gazette*, "Judge Dismisses Gaming Suit," Dec. 23, 1977.
[2] *Oakland Tribune*, "The Social Circle," April 6, 1975.
[3] *Oakland Tribune*, Bill Fiset's column, July 6, 1975.
[4] *The Wall Street Journal*, "American Midland's Jacobson Quits Unit," April 9, 1985.

SOURCES

CHAPTER 1: DIP INTO THE UNDERWORLD

Brandt, Charles. *'I Heard You Paint Houses': Frank 'The Irishman' Sheeran and the Inside Story of the Mafia, the Teamsters, and the Last Ride of Jimmy Hoffa.* Hanover, N.H.: Steerforth Press, 2005. Ebook.
Interview of William G. Swigert, Jr., June 24, 2010.
Nevada State Journal, "Sierra Tahoe Hotel Opens Next Friday," May 24, 1964, 37.
Nevada State Journal, "Teamster Fund Trial Starts on Tahoe Loan," Jan. 26, 1971, 8.
Nevada State Journal, "Teamster Loan Letter Recalled in Reno Trial," Jan. 27, 1971, 12.
Oakland Tribune, "$200,000 Fee on Loan for Teamsters," June 5, 1970, 1, 16.
Oakland Tribune, "Broker Quizzed on Teamster Loan," Jan. 26, 1971, 32.
Reno Evening Gazette, "Businessman Found Guilty in Perjury Case," Jan. 29, 1971, 15.
Reno Evening Gazette, "Lake Tahoe's Newest Resort Hotel Opens," May 29, 1964, 10.
Sifakis, Carl. *The Mafia Encyclopedia*, 3rd ed. New York, N.Y.: Facts on File Inc., 2005. Print.
Turner, Wallace. *Gambler's Money*. Boston, Mass.: Signet Books, 1966, 197-198. Print.

CHAPTER 2: HAIR-BRAINED SCHEME

Interview of Sherrill Broudy, Oct. 31, 2009.
Interview of William G. Swigert, Jr., June 24, 2010.
Nevada State Journal, "$25 Million Tahoe Land Transaction Disclosed," June 4, 1960, 22.
Nevada State Journal, "$30 Million Hotel, Resort Center Set at Incline Village," May 28, 1961, 2.
Nevada State Journal, "Lake Casino Hits Snag," Nov. 17, 1960, 8.
Nevada State Journal, "New Station Slated at Tahoe," May 14, 1961, 26.
Nevada State Journal, "Signs Point to North Shore Boom," June 22, 1960, 8.
Oakland Tribune, "Old Alameda Firm Switches to Unique New Ventures," June 9, 1963, C1, C4.
Reno Evening Gazette, "$25 Million Real Estate Deal at Lake," June 4, 1960, 11.
Reno Evening Gazette, "Incline Village Co-founder Tiller Resigns," Oct. 3, 1968, 10.
Reno Evening Gazette, "Whittell Sells Land at Tahoe for $5 Million," Sept. 9, 1959, 11.
Straka, Thomas J. *Forest History Today*, "Timber for the Comstock," Spring/Fall 2007.
The Daily Oklahoman, "Sooner, Kansas Investors Will Sell 19 Movie Houses," July 3, 1959.
Wolf, Donald E. *Big Dams and Other Dreams: The Six Companies Story*. Norman: University of Oklahoma Press, 1996. Print.

CHAPTER 3: SEEKING ELUSIVE MONEY

Brandt, Charles. *'I Heard You Paint Houses': Frank 'The Irishman' Sheeran and the Inside Story of the Mafia, the Teamsters, and the Last Ride of Jimmy Hoffa.* Hanover, NH: Steerforth Press, 2005. Ebook.
Interview of Sherrill Broudy, Oct. 31, 2009.

Interview of William G. Swigert, Jr., June 24, 2010.

Kennedy, Robert F. *The Enemy Within*. New York: Harper & Row, 1960. Print.

Leader-Times (Pa.), "Hoffa Most Active Man During Own Fraud Trial," June 29, 1964, 7.

Los Angeles Times, "Ailing Teamster Fund Faces Dose of Intensive Care," Oct. 2, 1977, F1, F8.

Nevada State Journal, "New Hotel Sets Opening Date," April 10, 1964, 2.

Nevada State Journal, "Sierra Tahoe Hotel Opens Next Friday," May 24, 1964, 37.

News Tribune (Fort Pierce), "Shopping Center Developer Faces Fine, Prison Term," Sept. 24, 1967, 3.

Oakland Tribune, "Broker Denies He Sought $200,000," Jan. 28, 1971, 20.

Release of Easement, Washoe County, Nev., March 23, 1964.

Reno Evening Gazette, "48-Unit Motel Boosts Value of Construction," March 3, 1964, 9.

Reno Evening Gazette, "Light Industry Zoning Granted on Northeast Reno Land," March 18, 1964, 36.

Reno Evening Gazette, "Permit Given for First Unit," May 29, 1963, 5.

The New York Times, "Hoffa Convicted on Use of Funds," July 27, 1964, 1.

The New York Times, "Hoffa Given 5 Years and Fined in Fraud," Aug. 18, 1964, 1.

The Sierra Tahoe (brochure), 1964. Print.

Times-News (N.C.), "Hoffa's Prison Term Lengthened," Sept. 23, 1967.

Tri-City Herald (Wash.), "Teamster Chief Faces 20-Year Prison Term," July 27, 1964.

Turner, Wallace. *Gambler's Money*. Boston, Mass.: Signet Books, 1966, 197-198. Print.

CHAPTER 4: CHANGE OF HANDS

Deed; Deed of Trust and Chattel Mortgage, Washoe County, Nev., Feb. 23, 1965.

Economic Impact Series, "Taxation on Tourism in Nevada: A Brief History," vol. 3, no. 1, January 2011.

"Fortune 500: 1961," money.cnn.com.

Independent Star-News (Long Beach), "New Tahoe Resort Under Way," Feb. 28, 1965.

Kennedy, Robert F. *The New York Times*, "Robert Kennedy Defines the Menace," Oct. 13, 1963, 224.

Lahey, Edwin. *Chicago Daily News*, "Las Vegas Smells of Underworld," April 7, 1966.

Lease Agreement, Washoe County, Nev., Feb. 23, 1965.

Nevada Gaming Commission Meeting Minutes, May 18, 1965.

Nevada Gaming Control Board Meeting Minutes, Dec. 10, 1964; May 6, 1965; May 17, 1965.

Nevada State Journal, "Californians Ask Gaming Licenses," March 28, 1965.

Nevada State Journal, "Casino at Lake Wins Approval of Board," Feb. 11, 1965.

Nevada State Journal, "Los Angeles Trio Buys Washoe County Hostelry," March 3, 1965.

Nevada State Journal, "Nevada Looks Ahead," Jan. 27, 1966, 33.

Nevada State Journal, "Signs Point to North Shore Boom," June 22, 1960, 8.

Oakland Tribune, "$200,000 Fee on Loan for Teamsters," June 5, 1970, 1, 16.

Reno Evening Gazette, "Light Industry Zoning Granted on Northeast Reno Land," March 18, 1964, 36.

Reno Evening Gazette, "Sierra Tahoe Hotel Sold; Expansion Due," Feb. 27, 1965, 9.

Reno Evening Gazette, "Summons to Answer Complaint," Dec. 10, 17, 24, 31, 1965.

Subordination Agreement, Washoe County, Nev., Feb. 24, 1965.

The Salt Lake Tribune, "Underworld Smell Reeks in Las Vegas," April 7, 1966, A19.

The Valley News (Van Nuys), "Complete Valley Department of Mercedes-Benz Firm," June 28, 1959, 18-A.

Turner, Wallace. *Gambler's Money*. Boston, Mass.: Signet Books, 1966, 9, 28-30. Print.

CHAPTER 5: TO THE RESCUE?

Deed; Deed of Trust and Chattel Mortgage; Deed of Trust Modification Agreement, Washoe County, Nev., Dec. 23, 1965.

Interview of Sherrill Broudy, Oct. 31, 2009.

Interview of William G. Swigert, Jr., June 24, 2010.

Los Angeles Times, "Man in Hoffa Case Buys Nevada Hotel," Jan. 14, 1966, 65.

Los Angeles Times, "West Side News in Brief," Dec. 22, 1966, WS1.

Nevada Gaming Commission Meeting Minutes, Oct. 26, 1965.

Nevada Gaming Control Board Meeting Minutes, Oct. 14, 1965; Oct. 25, 1965.

Nevada State Journal, "Floridian Seeks Stock in Hotel," Sept. 9, 1965, 13.

Nevada State Journal, "Incline Village Financing Issue Causes Disagreement," July 14, 1966, 1.

Nevada State Journal, "Miami Beach Man With Fraud Record Buys Sierra Tahoe," Jan. 12, 1966, 14.

Nevada State Journal, "Nevada Looks Ahead," Jan. 27, 1966, 33.

News Tribune (Fla.), "Shopping Center Developer Faces Fine, Prison Term," Sept. 24, 1967, 3.

Oakland Tribune, "$200,000 Fee on Loan for Teamsters," June 5, 1970, 1, 16.

Ogden Standard-Examiner, "Hoffa Figure Buys Big Resort Hotel," Jan. 13, 1966, 15A.

Reno Evening Gazette, "Fraud Figure is Hotel Buyer," Jan. 12, 1966, 23.

Reno Evening Gazette, "Miami Beach Man Gets Approval for Tahoe Gambling," Oct. 27, 1965, 12.

Termination of Lease Agreement and Release; Quitclaim Deed, Washoe County, Nev., Nov. 30, 1965.

The Post-Register (Idaho), "Grand Jury Indicts Hoffa, 7 Aides for Loan Fraud," June 4, 1963, 1.

CHAPTER 6: A FRESH START

Grant, Bargain and Sale Deed; Deed of Trust and Chattel Mortgage, Washoe County, Nev., April 14, 1966.

Los Angeles Times, "A Traveler's Diary," Oct. 15, 1967, P8.

Los Angeles Times, "The Nation," March 16, 1966, 2.

Los Angeles Times, "The Spectator," Aug. 11, 1966, D1.

Nevada Gaming Commission Meeting Minutes, April 19, 1966.

Nevada Gaming Control Board Meeting Minutes, March 3, 1966; April 7, 1966; June 9, 1966; Aug. 4, 1966.

Nevada State Journal, "Gaming Permit Lost by Sierra Tahoe," March 16, 1966, 1.

Nevada State Journal, "Tahoe Residents Protest Gambling Near Lake Shore," April 19, 1966, 1.

Nevada State Journal, "Wood Wins Shoreline Gaming OK," April 20, 1966, 1.

Reno Evening Gazette, "Gaming Bids Under Study by State," April 8, 1966, 18.

CHAPTER 7: CATCHING THE CASINO BUG

Billboard, "Las Vegas Profile—Major Riddle," Aug. 27, 1966, LV-38.

Billboard, "Las Vegas Profile—Nathan S. Jacobson," Aug. 27, 1966, LV-44.

Church, Foster. *Nevada State Journal*, "Jacobson—He Sensed the Village Antagonism," July 23, 1971, 14.

Earley, Pete. *Super Casino: Inside the New Las Vegas*. New York: Bantam Books, 2000, 53, 60. Print.

Eau Claire Leader-Telegram, "Mandel Broke, 'Starts Over,'" Oct. 8, 1977.

Las Vegas Sun, "Nationwide 'Awe' for Caesar," Aug. 7, 1966, A39.

Los Angeles Times, "Casino Chief Again Denies Crime Tie-In," Aug. 18, 1966, 31.

Los Angeles Times, "Give My Regards to…Vegas?" July 18, 1999.

Los Angeles Times, "Reno and Lake Tahoe Casino Heads Testify," Aug. 17, 1966, A8.

Naugatuck News, "My New York," Aug. 31, 1966, 6.

Nevada Gaming Commission Meeting Minutes, May 18, 1966.

Nevada Gaming Control Board Meeting Minutes, May 1966.

Nevada State Journal, "51 Investors Get Licenses for Caesars Palace," May 19, 1966, 14.

Nevada State Journal, "Jacobson Says Goodbye," Nov. 12, 1971, Entertainment 1.

Nevada State Journal, "Resort Hotel Opens on Las Vegas Strip," Aug. 7, 1966, 34.

Nevada State Journal, "Skimming Probe Makes Progress," Aug. 19, 1966, 1, 3.

Schwartz, David G. *Grandissimo: The First Emperor of Las Vegas: How Jay Sarno Won a Casino Empire, Lost It, and Inspired Modern Las Vegas*. Winchester Books, 2013. Ebook.

The Daily Mail (Md.), "Irvin Kovens: 'Golden Touch' Nets Influence, Money and Friends," Sept. 22, 1971, 5.

Wilson, Jane. *Los Angeles Times*, "A Double Roman Holiday," June 18, 1967, A39.

CHAPTER 8: MORE GAMBLING DRAMA

FBI File on Benjamin Lassoff, Sept. 9, 1960.

Great Bend Daily Tribune (Kan.), "13 Men Indicted on Phone Charges," June 27, 1961.

Los Angeles Times, "Race-Betting Network Cracked; U.S. Indicts 13," June 28, 1961.

Mansfield News-Journal, "9 Acquitted of Gambling," March 13, 1963.

Neff, James. *Mobbed Up: Jackie Presser's High-Wire Life in the Teamsters, the Mafia, and the FBI*, Open Road Media: 1989. Online.

Nevada Gaming Control Board Meeting Minutes, Feb. 15, 1967; March 20, 1967; April 1, 1967.

Nevada State Journal, "Bar Manager Asks Investment," Jan. 27, 1967, 18.

Nevada State Journal, "Burglars Bind, Gag Janitor," May 20, 1966, 16.

Nevada State Journal, "Reno Accountant Hancock Seeks Incline Casino," Jan. 3, 1968, 17.

Nevada State Journal, "Suit Challenges Gaming Chairman," Jan. 10, 1968, 1.

Nevada State Journal, "Wood Surprised at Commission Refusing Incline Casino Bid," Oct. 27, 1967.

Nevada State Journal, "Wood Wants to Sell Closed Down Casino," Dec. 5, 1967.

Reno Evening Gazette, "Incline Casino Asks State to Allow it to Operate," Oct. 20, 1967.

Reno Evening Gazette, Other Editors—"Firm Action is Essential," Nov. 3, 1967, 4.

Reno Evening Gazette, "State Closes Incline Casino," Oct. 16, 1967.

Reno Evening Gazette, "Wood: State is Unfair in Casino Suspension," Nov. 28, 1967.

State Gaming Control Board v. A.L.W. Inc., et al., Nov. 17, 1967.

The Marion Star, "Federal Trial of 6 Continues at Covington," June 11, 1962, 11.

The Marion Star, "Rights Case is Given to Jury at Covington," June 22, 1962, 8.

The Middletown Journal, "2 Convicted, 4 Cleared in Newport Conspiracy," Aug. 7, 1963, 28.

The New York Times, "Six in Newport, Ky., Charged With Plot for a False Arrest," Oct. 28, 1961, 22.

The Times (San Mateo), "Casino Owner is Suspended for One Year," Nov. 28, 1967, 3.

The Times Recorder (Zanesville), "Conviction Upheld by U.S. Court," July 9, 1966, 5.

The Times Recorder (Zanesville), "2 Men Enter Prison After Long Delay," March 12, 1967, 10.

United States of America, Appellee, v. Charles E. Lester and Edward Anthony Buccieri, Appellants, 363 F.2d 68, July 8, 1966.

CHAPTER 9: HIS TENTACLED REACH

Church, Foster. *Nevada State Journal*, "Jacobson—He Sensed the Village Antagonism," July 23, 1971, 14.

Deed, Washoe County, Nev., Nov. 15, 1968.

Interview of Arthur Selman, April 12, 2016.

Interview of Pamela Picard, June 2015.

Los Angeles Times, "Ex-Casino Executive Carl Cohen; Noted for Punching Frank Sinatra," Dec. 30, 1986, articles.latimes.com.

Nevada Gaming Commission Meeting Minutes, Oct. 26, 1967; Nov. 16, 1967; Nov. 27, 1967; Dec. 28, 1967.

Nevada Gaming Control Board Meeting Minutes, Nov. 13, 1967; Dec. 19, 1967.

Nevada State Journal, "An Open Letter to the Washoe County Commissioners," Nov. 7, 1968, 22.

Nevada State Journal, "Cal Neva Hotel Opening Draws Throngs to North Shore Hostelry," June 24, 1969, 6.

Nevada State Journal, "Tahoe High-Rise Wins County Board Approval," Nov. 7, 1968, 1.

Reno Evening Gazette, "Cal-Neva Lodge Asks Permit for Building," Oct. 2, 1968.

Reno Evening Gazette, "High Rise Hotel at North Tahoe Approved by Board of Adjustment," Oct. 3, 1968.

Schwartz, David G. *Grandissimo: The First Emperor of Las Vegas: How Jay Sarno Won a Casino Empire, Lost It, and Inspired Modern Las Vegas*. Winchester Books, 2013. Ebook.

The New York Times, "Mob-Casino Inquiry Ordered in Nevada," Nov. 28, 1967, 95.

The New York Times, "Sinatra, in Brawl, Loses Two Teeth in Las Vegas Hotel," Sept. 13, 1967, 49.

The Post-Standard (N.Y.), "Lyons Den," Sept. 27, 1967, 26.

CHAPTER 10: WANTING STABILITY

Economic Impact Series, "Taxation on Tourism in Nevada: A Brief History," vol. 3, no. 1, January 2011.

Holmes Van Tassel, Bethel. *Wood Chips to Game Chips: Casinos and People at North Lake Tahoe*. Sacramento: TCH, 1999, 42. Print.

Interview of William G. Swigert, Jr., June 24, 2010.

Los Angeles Times, "Ailing Teamster Fund Faces Dose of Intensive Care," Oct. 2, 1977, F1.

Los Angeles Times, "Ex-Commissioner Gets 6 Months in Beverly Ridge Case," Jan. 23, 1973, 3.

Nevada Gaming Commission Meeting Minutes, May 28, 1968.

Nevada Gaming Control Board Meeting Minutes, May 22, 1968; June 19, 1968.

Nevada State Journal, "Businessman Faces Trial on False Testimony Charge," Sept. 16, 1970, 26.

Nevada State Journal, "Hancock Drops Incline Casino Purchase Plans," Jan. 10, 1968.

Nevada State Journal, "Las Vegan Peccole Asks Incline Casino License," May 22, 1968.

Nevada State Journal, "Miami Broker Ridicules Teamster Link Charges," Jan. 28, 1971, 16.

Nevada State Journal, "Reno Accountant Hancock Seeks Incline Casino," Jan. 3, 1968, 17.

Nevada State Journal, "Tahoe Club Relocation Planned," Jan. 4, 1968, 18.

Nevada State Journal, "Tahoe Hotel Loan Probe Brings Warrant," July 16, 1970, 22.

Nevada State Journal, "Teamster Loan Letter Recalled in Reno Trial," Jan. 27, 1971, 12.

Nevada State Journal, "New Chamber Project," Dec. 11, 1966, 58.

Nevada State Journal, "Tyrone Fined $4,000," Feb. 27, 1971, 14.

Oakland Tribune, "$200,000 Fee on Loan for Teamsters," June 5, 1970, 1, 16.

Oakland Tribune, "Broker Denies He Sought $200,000," Jan. 26, 1971, 20.

Oakland Tribune, "Broker Quizzed on Teamster Loan," Jan. 26, 1971, 32E.

Oakland Tribune, "Mortgage Broker Indicted," July 13, 1970, 1F, 12F.

Oakland Tribune, "Pension Fund Probe is Sought," Sept. 22, 1969, 1, 4.

Oakland Tribune, "Sierra Ski Resorts Aim to Attract Europeans," July 14, 1968, 4-C.

Oakland Tribune, "Teamster Fund Trial Starts on Tahoe Loan," Jan. 26, 1971, 8.

Reno Evening Gazette, "Businessman Found Guilty in Perjury Case," Jan. 29, 1971, 15.

Reno Evening Gazette, "Businessman Pleads Innocent to Indictment Charging Perjury," Sept. 15, 1970, 18.

Reno Evening Gazette, "Hancock Drops Tahoe Casino License Bid," Jan. 10, 1968.

Reno Evening Gazette, "Lassoff Drops Challenge Suit, Case Dismissed," Nov. 25, 1968.

Reno Evening Gazette, "Wood Granted One More Year on Tahoe Permit," April 25, 1968.

Reno Evening Gazette, "Wood to Ask Again for Permit Extension," April 23, 1968, 7.

United States of America v. Norman Tyrone, 451 F.2d 16, Nov. 5, 1971; Dec. 29, 1971.

CHAPTER 11: WHEELING AND DEALING

Albuquerque Journal, "Bobby Baker Denied Parole," Dec. 21, 1971, C-6.

Earley, Pete. *Super Casino: Inside the New Las Vegas*. New York: Bantam Books, 2000, 66. Print.

Faiss, Robert, Faiss, D. and Gregory R. Gemignani. Center for Gaming Research's *Occasional Paper Series,* "Nevada Gaming Statutes: Their Evolution and History," no. 10. September 2011, 5-6.

Grant, Bargain and Sale Deed, Washoe County, Nev., May 1, 1969.

Interview of Arthur Selman, April 12, 2016.

Las Vegas Sun, "Caesars Palace Purchased by Lums," Oct. 1, 1969.

Los Angeles Times, "Bonanza Casino Permit Threatened by Dispute," Aug. 22, 1969, C12.

Los Angeles Times, "Burt Bacharach Opens Tahoe Run," March 28, 1970, C8.

Los Angeles Times, "Colson and Rebozo Linked to Scheme to Parole Hoffa Aide," June 27, 1973, A1.

Los Angeles Times, "Group Agrees to Buy Vegas' Bonanza Hotel," March 13, 1969, E15.

Los Angeles Times, "Jacobson Will Keep Post at Bonanza in Settlement of Feud," Aug. 26, 1969, C8.

Los Angeles Times, "Levin-Townsend Announced Plans to Develop Three Resorts in the West," April 4, 1969, F11.

Los Angeles Times, "Levin-Townsend Buys Bonanza Hotel, Casino," March 14, 1969, F14.

Los Angeles Times, "National News," Aug. 1, 1969, C11.

Los Angeles Times, "Resort Opened on Tahoe North Shore," July 4, 1970, A5.

Nevada Gaming Commission Meeting Minutes, May 22, 1969; June 26, 1969; Sept. 16, 1969.

Nevada Gaming Control Board Meeting Minutes, May 14, 1969; June 16, 1969; July 11, 1969; Aug. 13, 1969; Aug. 21, 1969; Sept. 10, 1969; October 1969.

Nevada State Journal, "Bonanza Officials Warned to Settle Dispute," Aug. 22, 1969, 19.

Nevada State Journal, "Carpenters 'Build' Rock, Soul, Jazz Music in Kings Castle Lounge," June 13, 1970, Entertainment 12.

Nevada State Journal, "Incline Casino Licensed," June 19, 1969, 8.

Nevada State Journal, "Kings Castle Approved for Winter Casino," Oct. 10, 1969.

Nevada State Journal, "Kings Castle Granted Use Permit Extension," Oct. 17, 1969.

Nevada State Journal, "Riot Control Ordinance Adopted," April 26, 1969, 6.

Nevada State Journal, "Tahoe's Newest Resort Hotel Opens Doors," July 2, 1969.

Oakland Tribune, "Lake Tahoe Hotel Sold; 7-Story Addition Planned," March 30, 1969, 6-C.

Schwartz, David G. *Grandissimo: The First Emperor of Las Vegas: How Jay Sarno Won a Casino Empire, Lost It, and Inspired Modern Las Vegas*. Winchester Books, 2013. Ebook.

The New York Times, "Hoffa Given 5 Years and Fined in Fraud," Aug. 18, 1964, 1.

The New York Times, "Tenneco Plans Bid to Increase Stake in Case Company," Sept. 4, 1969, 65.

The Times (San Mateo), Advertisement for Kings Castle, July 2, 1969, 12.

CHAPTER 12: ONE-TWO PUNCH

Church, Foster. *Nevada State Journal*, "Jacobson—He Sensed the Village Antagonism," July 23, 1971, 14.

Nevada Gaming Control Board Meeting Minutes, June 19, 1970; Nov, 19, 1970.

Nevada State Journal, "Condominium Denial Appealed by Kings Castle," Feb. 6, 1970, 7.

Nevada State Journal, "High Court Upholds Tahoe Ruling," Oct. 31, 1972, 7.

Nevada State Journal, "Incline High-Rise 'Delayed,'" Feb. 4, 1970, 10.

Nevada State Journal, "Jacobson to Appeal Condominium Decision," Aug. 10, 1970, 8.

Nevada State Journal, "Kings Castle Plans Incline Apartments," Jan. 30, 1970, 18.

Nevada State Journal, Letters to the Editor—"Tahoe Protected," Feb. 19, 1970.

Nevada State Journal, "Relocation Work Pushed at Incline," April 25, 1969.

Nevada State Journal, "Small Business Chief Faces House Quiz; Case of the 'Stolen' Highway at Tahoe," July 18, 1970, 4.
Oakland Tribune, "Court Fight Over Tahoe High-Rise," Aug. 16, 1970, 16.
Reno Evening Gazette, "Brief Backs Gabrielli Decision on Planners," June 2, 1971, 8.
Reno Evening Gazette, "Commissioners Deny Promise to Jacobson," Nov. 6, 1970.
Reno Evening Gazette, "County Board Has Hearing in Court," May 28, 1970, 23.
Reno Evening Gazette, "Judge Rejects County Bid to Dismiss Suit," May 29, 1970, 8.
San Antonio Express, Postcard—"Snow Bunny," Nov. 24, 1970, 8-A.
"State Motor Vehicle Registrations, by Years, 1900-1995," fhwa.dot.gov.

CHAPTER 13: ASSUMING THE THRONE

Interview of Arthur Selman, April 12, 2016.
Los Angeles Times, "Little Towns Rise on Tahoe's Shore," Nov. 29, 1970, J3.
Los Angeles Times, "Resort Opened on Tahoe North Shore," July 4, 1970, A5.
Moberly Monitor-Index and Evening Democrat (Mo.), "Lake Tahoe Debut Was No Laugh-In for Miss Graves," Sept. 5, 1970, 10.
Nevada Gaming Commission Meeting Minutes, June 19, 1970.
Nevada Gaming Control Board Meeting Minutes, June 19, 1970.
Nevada State Journal, "Celebrities Help Open Kings Castle," July 2, 1970.
Nevada State Journal, "Grand Opening Planned at Kings Castle," June 7, 1970, 27.
Nevada State Journal, "Uniforms Go Mod-Medieval at Castle," July 7, 1970.
Oakland Tribune, "$200,000 Fee on Loan for Teamsters," June 5, 1970, 1, 16.
Oakland Tribune, "Night Sounds," July 3, 1970, 39.
Reno Evening Gazette, "Kings Castle Plans Opening Wednesday," June 30, 1970, 13.
The Cedar Rapids Gazette, "Along Broadway," July 10, 1970, 14.

CHAPTER 14: BETTING ON BUSINESS

Billboard, "Kings Castle Making Bid for Vegas' Silver Circuit Gold," July 18, 1970, 26, 55.
Interview of Arthur Selman, April 12, 2016.
Interview of Pamela Picard, June 2015.
Los Angeles Times, "Joe Frazier Taking a New Count," May 3, 1971.
Los Angeles Times, "Resort Opened on Tahoe North Shore," July 4, 1970, A5.
Nevada Gaming Commission Meeting Minutes, Nov. 19, 1970; Dec. 17, 1970; April 22, 1971.
Nevada Gaming Control Board Meeting Minutes, Oct. 4, 1970; Nov. 12, 1970; Dec. 9, 1970; April 14, 1971; June 16, 1971; Sept. 15, 1971.
Nevada State Journal, Advertisement for Kings Castle, June 30, 1970, 4.
Nevada State Journal, Advertisement for Kings Castle—Connie Stevens, Nov. 21, 1970, Entertainment 12.
Nevada State Journal, Advertisement for Kings Castle—Don Rickles, Jan. 31, 1971, 27.
Nevada State Journal, Advertisement for Kings Castle—Woody Allen; Phyllis McGuire, Sept. 23, 1970.
Nevada State Journal, "Billings/Clubs/North Shore," July 10, 1970, Entertainment 2.
Nevada State Journal, "Grand Opening Planned at Kings Castle," June 7, 1970, 27.

Nevada State Journal, "Hear & Now, Platters, Flesh Share Kings Castle Marquee," Nov. 6, 1970, Entertainment.

Nevada State Journal, "Incline Has 4,200 Residents; $35 Million in Building Going," Dec. 17, 1969, 9.

Nevada State Journal, "Kings Castle Landlord Applications Approved," Nov. 20, 1970, 8.

Nevada State Journal, "State Gaming Commission Accepts Recommendations," Dec. 22, 1970, 27.

Oakland Tribune, "Night Sounds," July 3, 1970, 39.

Reno Evening Gazette, Advertisement for Kings Castle—Phyllis Diller; Della Reese; Woody Allen; Johnny Mathis, Dec. 23, 1970, 12.

Reno Evening Gazette, Advertisement for Kings Castle Ski-Casino Tahoe, Nov. 11, 1970, 17.

Reno Evening Gazette, "Entertainers to Own Part of Kings Castle," May 28, 1970, 11.

Star-News (Pasadena), "Hollywood Hotline," July 13, 1970, 6.

CHAPTER 15: FROM JEWELS TO JUNKETS

Daily Times (Pa.), "Senator's Speechwriter Fouls Him Up With S.O.B.," July 22, 1971, 7.

Daily Times (Pa.), "You See Needles in This Show," June 23, 1971, 33.

FBI File on Nathan S. Jacobson.

Independent (Long Beach), "Tennis at Tahoe Now Winter Sport," Aug. 31, 1971, C-5.

Interview of Arthur Selman, April 12, 2016.

Los Angeles Times, "Little Towns Rise on Tahoe's Shore," Nov. 29, 1970, J3.

Los Angeles Times, "'Love-In' Musical Set at Kings Castle," June 25, 1971, E9.

Nevada State Journal, Advertisement for Cassius Clay v. Oscar Bonavena, Dec. 7, 1970, 13.

Nevada State Journal, Advertisement for Kings Castle—Jose Feliciano, July 17, 1971, 13.

Nevada State Journal, Advertisement for Kings Castle—Paul Anka, Aug. 7, 1971, 9.

Nevada State Journal, Advertisement for Kings Castle—Robert Goulet, July 10, 1971, 9.

Nevada State Journal, Advertisement for Kings Castle—Tony Bennett; Pearl Bailey, Aug. 28, 1971, 9.

Nevada State Journal, "Bubble in Trouble at Castle," April 11, 1971, 12.

Nevada State Journal, "Casino Show Rooms Close Doors; Weather, Repairs Are Reasons," Dec. 10, 1971, Entertainment 1-2.

Nevada State Journal, "Celebrity-Packed Field in Snowmobile Classic," Feb. 22, 1970, 47.

Nevada State Journal, "Convention Announced," Aug. 29, 1971, 20.

Nevada State Journal, "Creative Convention Sales High," July 4, 1971, 25.

Nevada State Journal, "Don Rickles 'Greets' Patrons in Kings Castle," Feb. 12, 1971, Entertainment 8.

Nevada State Journal, "Incline Village Date 'Firmed' for Joe Frazier," March 11, 1971, 25.

Nevada State Journal, "Kings Castle Prepares to Host World's Richest Snowmobile Race," Feb. 23, 1971, 11.

Nevada State Journal, "Kings Castle Site of 1972 Attorney Meet," July 1, 1971, 37.

Nevada State Journal, "Lake Residents Complain About Snowmobile Run," Jan. 16, 1970, 6.

Nevada State Journal, "Postscripts," Dec. 22, 1970, 5.
Nevada State Journal, "Proposed Snowmobile Event Land Use Request Rejected," Nov. 13, 1970, 22.
Nevada State Journal, "Sandbag Golf Festivities Begin Today," Aug. 4, 1971, 14.
Nevada State Journal, "Snowmobile Grand Prix at Incline," Nov. 8, 1969, 16.
Nevada State Journal, "Snowmobile Race Runs Start," Feb. 28, 1970, 1.
Nevada State Journal, "Tahoe Snowmobile Races to Offer Broad Contrast," Dec. 16, 1969, 22.
Nevada State Journal, "Unique Net Courts Slated at Tahoe," Dec. 8, 1970, 11.
Nevada State Journal, "Woman Titlist Enters Tahoe Race," Jan. 23, 1970, 24.
Reno Evening Gazette, Advertisement for Cassius Clay v. Jerry Quarry, Oct. 26, 1970, 15.
Reno Evening Gazette, Advertisement for Joe Frazier v. Bob Foster, Nov. 18, 1970, 30.
Reno Evening Gazette, Advertisement for Kings Castle—Joan Rivers; Lou Rawls, Aug. 11, 1971.
Reno Evening Gazette, Advertisement for Kings Castle—Sergio Mendes; Brasil '66, May 25, 1971, 15.
Reno Evening Gazette, Advertisement for Kings Castle—The 5th Dimension, Jan. 13, 1971, 31.
Reno Evening Gazette, "Kings Castle Hosts Tourney," Dec. 2, 1971.
Reno Evening Gazette, "North Tahoe 11th Snow Ball Dec. 17 Event," Nov. 4, 1971.
Reno Evening Gazette, "Reno-Tahoe Tourism Booms With Holiday," Feb. 15, 1971, 1.
Reno Evening Gazette, "Sports Mags Praise Castle," Jan. 7, 1972, Entertainment.
Reno Evening Gazette, "'The Excitement is Unbelievable'—Miss World-U.S.A. From Illinois," Oct. 5, 1970, 7.
The News (Van Nuys), "Fans Can Chop Rickles," June 24, 1971.

CHAPTER 16: KINGS CASTLE (NO) WAY

Church, Foster. *Nevada State Journal*, "Jacobson—He Sensed the Village Antagonism," July 23, 1971, 14.
Nevada State Journal, "County Officials Split on Incline Road Name Fight," April 9, 1971, 14.
Nevada State Journal, Editorials—"Changing a Street Name at Incline, Lake Tahoe," April 14, 1971.
Nevada State Journal, Editorials—"Street Gets a New Name Despite Voter Protest," April 17, 1971.
Nevada State Journal, "Incline Residents Blast County Action," April 6, 1971, 1-2.
Nevada State Journal, "Incline Street Name Change Hearing Slated," March 31, 1971, 10.
Nevada State Journal, "Kings Castle Owner Loses First Round in Attempt to Change Street Name," April 2, 1971, 12.
Nevada State Journal, "Kings Castle Way Name Confirmed," April 16, 1971, 16.
Nevada State Journal, Letters to the Editor—"Offensive Sign," July 6, 1971, 15.
Nevada State Journal, Letters to the Editor—"The Name Change," April 10, 1971.
Nevada State Journal, "North Tahoe Poll Shows Residents Are Dissatisfied," July 2, 1971, 17.
Nevada State Journal, "Pagni Answers Incline Critics," July 3, 1971, 14.

Nevada State Journal, "Proposed Incline Village Recreation Plans Appear Doomed," April 30, 1971, 21.

Nevada State Journal, "Selective Counting Charged in North Lake Tahoe Poll," July 3, 1971, 5.

Nevada State Journal, "Senators Ask Rehearing on Street Name Change," April 7, 1971, 18.

Nevada State Journal, "Street Name Changed to Oblige Kings Castle," April 6, 1971, 1-2.

Reno Evening Gazette, "Incline Poll Questions Get Early 'Yes' Votes," June 30, 1971, 29.

Reno Evening Gazette, "Incline Village Residents Oppose Street Name," April 16, 1971, 17.

Reno Evening Gazette, "Kings Castle's Jacobson Disagrees With Editorial on Public Relations," April 10, 1971, 7.

Reno Evening Gazette, "Kings Castle Way Approved, Reconsideration Asked," April 6, 1971, 1.

Reno Evening Gazette, Letters to the Editor—"Commends Decision," April 12, 1971, 4.

Reno Evening Gazette, Letters to the Editor—"Fair Decision," April 7, 1971, 4.

Reno Evening Gazette, Letters to the Editor—"Helps County," April 15, 1971, 4.

Reno Evening Gazette, "New Hearing Set on Renaming of County Street at Lake Tahoe," April 9, 1971, 24.

Reno Evening Gazette, "Street Signs Paint Sprayed," June 16, 1971, 19.

CHAPTER 17: BUSTED, TIMES THREE

Church, Foster. *Nevada State Journal*, "Jacobson—He Sensed the Village Antagonism," July 23, 1971, 14.

County of Washoe v. Kings Castle Limited Partnership, 270367, July 16, 1971.

Nevada State Journal, Advertisement for K-NEV-FM, Aug. 7, 1971, 10.

Nevada State Journal, "Board Suggests Pulling Kings Castle Annex Permit," July 21, 1971, 14.

Nevada State Journal, "Jacobson Contests Closure," June 19, 1971, 10.

Nevada State Journal, "Jacobson Wins Respite in Effort to Run Annex," June 23, 1971, 22.

Nevada State Journal, "Kings Castle Beach to Continue Temporary Permit Until Hearing," July 8, 1971, 34.

Nevada State Journal, "Kings Castle Closure Threatened by County," July 16, 1971, 14,

Nevada State Journal, "Kings Castle, County Argue Over Licenses," June 17, 1971, 22.

Nevada State Journal, "Kings Castle Court Ruling Due Today," June 22, 1971, 10.

Nevada State Journal, "Kings Castle Hotel, Annex Issued Occupancy Papers," Aug. 6, 1971, 19.

Nevada State Journal, "Kings Castle Truce:...And Love Verily Cracked Again...," Sept. 1, 1971.

Nevada State Journal, "Kings Castle Wins County Permit Approval," Aug. 17, 1971, 3.

Nevada State Journal, "Legal Battle Promised by Kings Castle Owner," July 21, 1971, 1.

Nevada State Journal, Letters to the Editor—"Castle's Troubles," Aug. 7, 1971.

Reno Evening Gazette, "Kings Castle Annex Closed," June 17, 1971, 2.

Reno Evening Gazette, "Kings Castle Question: Who's in Control in Nevada?" July 21, 1971, 1-2.

Reno Evening Gazette, "Kings Castle Restraining Order Dropped," June 22, 1971, 1-2.

Reno Evening Gazette, Letters to the Editor—"County Harassment," Aug. 14, 1971.
Reno Evening Gazette, "Step by Step on the Path of Kings Castle Controversy," July 22, 1971.

CHAPTER 18: SHOW ME THE MONEY

Agreement of Purchase and Sale, Nov. 1, 1971.
A.L.W., Inc. v. UAL, Inc., CV-S-71-1606.
A.L.W., Inc. v. United Air Lines, Inc., 510 F.2d 52, Jan. 20, 1975, leagle.com.
Church, Foster. *Nevada State Journal*, "Jacobson—He Sensed the Village Antagonism," July 23, 1971, 14.
Hackett Enterprises, Inc. v. A.L.W., Inc., CV-S-71-1721, November 1971.
Jacobson v. Stern, 605 P.2d 198, Jan. 16, 1980; March 4, 1980.
Martin Stern, Jr. v. A.L.W., et al., 268395, March 1970.
Martin Stern, Jr. v. Nathan Jacobson, No. 7234, March 26, 1974.
Nathan Jacobson, A.L.W., Inc. v. ABC Co., Inc., et al., 285342, March 27, 1973.
Nevada Gaming Commission Meeting Minutes, May 24, 1973.
Nevada Gaming Control Board Meeting Minutes, May 16, 1973.
Nevada State Journal, "Disputed Fence at Incline May Lead to Court Action," Jan. 31, 1971, 34.
Nevada State Journal, "Jacobson Calls Report False, 'Shocking,'" Oct. 17, 1971.
Nevada State Journal, "Jacobson Complaint Lavish," May 1, 1971.
Nevada State Journal, "Jacobson Disputes Suit Figures," Feb. 2, 1972.
Nevada State Journal, "Jacobson Says Goodbye: 'I'm Weary,'" Nov. 12, 1971, Entertainment 1.
Nevada State Journal, "Jacobson's Kings Castle Sale Completion Expected," Jan. 26, 1972, 10.
Nevada State Journal, "Kings Castle Suit Names Bay Area Radio Station," March 29, 1973.
Nevada State Journal, Political Front—"Why the Fast Kings Castle Transfer?" Dec. 12, 1971.
Oakland Tribune, "Kings Castle to Close Tomorrow," Feb. 2, 1972, 24.
R.C.A. Corporation v. A.L.W., et al., 268852, April 6, 1971.
Reno Evening Gazette, "Board Recommends Castle Stock Transfer to Casino Manager," Nov. 18, 1971, 23.
Reno Evening Gazette, "Hackett Names Kings Castle in Lawsuit," Nov. 19, 1971, 2.
Reno Evening Gazette, "Jacobson Closing Kings Castle," Feb. 2, 1972, 1-2.
Reno Evening Gazette, "Jacobson Files Suit Against ABC," March 28, 1973, 17.
Reno Evening Gazette, "Kings Castle, Jacobson Named in Court Suit," March 20, 1971, 9.
Reno Evening Gazette, "Kings Castle, Jacobson Sued in Washoe Court," April 7, 1971, 2.
Reno Evening Gazette, "Kings Castle Owner Ponders Next Move," Feb. 3, 1972.
Reno Evening Gazette, "Kings Castle Sale Near," Nov. 3, 1971, 1.
Reno Evening Gazette, "Kings Castle Sale Near Completion," Dec. 1, 1971, 2.
Reno Evening Gazette, "Kings Castle Sues Airline Over Magazine," April 13, 1971, 14.
Reno Evening Gazette, "Kings Castle Suit Against Airline Dismissed," Dec. 24, 1971, 22.
Reno Evening Gazette, "Stock Transfer Approved for Kings Castle," Nov. 19, 1971, 6.
Reno Evening Gazette, "Washoe Files Answer to Kings Castle Suit," Nov. 11, 1971, 19.
The Daily Review (Hayward), "C.V. Man Buying Tahoe Casino," Nov. 18, 1971, 14.

The Daily Review (Hayward), "Tahoe Casino Sale Not Completed," Jan. 19, 1972, 4.
The Fresno Bee, "$23 Million Deal Fails; King's [sic] Castle Will Close," Feb. 3, 1972, A16.
Tours Unlimited v. A.L.W., Inc., et al., 275308, Jan. 20, 1972.

CHAPTER 19: CAN IT GET WORSE?

FBI File on Nathan S. Jacobson.
Nevada National Bank v. Nathan Jacobson, et al., 275547, Jan. 31, 1972.
Nevada State Journal, "Allegations of Beating, Gun Play Said 'Inconsistent With Reality,'" Dec. 29, 1971, 12.
Nevada State Journal, "A 'Nasty, Distasteful Scene': Kidnapping Denied by Jacobson," July 17, 1973, 1.
Nevada State Journal, "Ex-Kings Castle Boss Claims Gun Forced False Confession," June 22, 1973, 14.
Nevada State Journal, "Former Guard Testifies Landucci Cried," June 29, 1973, 12.
Nevada State Journal, "Jacobson, Bruno Must Stand Trial," March 29, 1972, 1-2.
Nevada State Journal, "Jacobson Describes Personal Humiliation," Dec. 6, 1971, 10.
Nevada State Journal, "Key Jacobson Case Figure Tells Story," March 21, 1972, 1-2.
Nevada State Journal, "Kidnaping [sic] Denied by Jacobson," July 17, 1973, 12.
Nevada State Journal, "Kings Castle Keno 'Scam' Idea Explained by Landucci," March 22, 1972, 14.
Nevada State Journal, "Police Officials Weren't Called," July 3, 1973, 8.
Nevada State Journal, "What Happened to Landucci in the Back Room Sept. 2?" March 24, 1972, 16.
Reno Evening Gazette, "Jacobson Attorney Calls Landucci 'An Admitted Liar, A Strange Liar,'" March 24, 1972, 13.
Reno Evening Gazette, "Keno Manager Testifies 'Confession' Was Forced," March 21, 1972, 13.
Reno Evening Gazette, "Landucci Changes His Version of Kings Castle Keno Incident," June 26, 1973.
Reno Evening Gazette, "'Mr. Jacobson Didn't Care to Lose Any More Money,'" July 2, 1973, 15.
Reno Evening Gazette, "Ordeal Described by Key Witness," June 22, 1973.
The Baltimore Sun, Maryland Briefs—"Bruno Acquitted in Shooting," July 10, 1971, 3.
The Baltimore Sun, "Witness is Indicted for Perjury," Aug. 25, 1971, 16.
Turner, Wallace. *Gambler's Money*. Boston, Mass.: Signet Books, 1966, 27. Print.

CHAPTER 20: THE TROUBLESOME AFTERMATH

Landucci Bankruptcy Files, BK-R-72-149; BK-R-72-150, March-November 1972.
Nevada State Journal, "Developer Arrested at Tahoe," Dec. 1, 1971, 1-2.
Nevada State Journal, "Informant: FBI Tipster Remains Unknown at Jacobson Trial," July 11, 1973, 18.
Nevada State Journal, "Jacobson Says Grand Jury Claims Faulty," Dec. 15, 1971, 16.
Nevada State Journal, "Jury Vote Unanimous for Jacobson Indictment," Jan. 16, 1972, 12.
Nevada State Journal, Letters to the Editor—"'Tops Them All,'" Dec. 11, 1971.

Nevada State Journal, "Nate Jacobson Accused of Kidnaping [sic], Extortion," Dec. 1. 1971, 1.

Reno Evening Gazette, "Casino Figure Fires Lawsuit at Jacobson," Dec. 14, 1971, 1-2.

Reno Evening Gazette, Editorials—"Poor Performance," Dec. 2, 1971, 4.

Reno Evening Gazette, "Jacobson, Bruno Ask Dismissal of Indictment," Jan. 11, 1972, 9.

Reno Evening Gazette, "Jacobson, Bruno Hearing Postponed," Jan. 7, 1972, 26.

Reno Evening Gazette, "Jacobson Writes 'An Open Letter to World,'" Dec. 6, 1971, 13.

Reno Evening Gazette, "Landucci is Judged Bankrupt," March 23, 1972, 21.

Reno Evening Gazette, "Landucci's Wife Tells of Weeks of Family Terror," July 9, 1973, 13.

Reno Evening Gazette, "More Testimony on Cheater Trap," March 23, 1972.

Reno Evening Gazette, "State Reveals Jacobson Kidnap Case Testimony," Dec. 28, 1971, 1-2.

Reno Evening Gazette, "Washoe Jury Indicts Jacobson on Kidnaping [sic], Extortion Charges," Dec. 1, 1971, 1-2.

Reno Evening Gazette, "Washoe Prosecutors Biased—Jacobson," Jan. 21, 1972, 13.

Reno Evening Gazette, "Witness Claims Discussing 'Taking the (Keno) Game,'" March 23, 1972, 21.

CHAPTER 21: MIRED IN CRISES

David Talisman v. Nathan Jacobson, et al., 275308, Jan. 20, 1972.

Famous Cases and Criminals, "Frank Sinatra, Jr., Kidnapping," fbi.gov.

Jacobsen Construction Co., Inc., v. Kings Castle, et al., 275565, February 1972.

Nevada Gaming Control Board Meeting Minutes, May 16, 1973.

Raymond Landucci v. Nathan Jacobson, et al., 274502, Dec. 10, 1971.

Reno Evening Gazette, "Another Suit for Jacobson, Kings Castle," Feb. 2, 1972, 28.

Reno Evening Gazette, "Bandleader Files Action," Jan. 24, 1972, 13.

Reno Evening Gazette, "Bank Files Suit Against Jacobson," Feb. 1, 1972, 20.

Reno Evening Gazette, "Jacobson, Bruno Request Look at Grand Jury Vote," Jan. 4, 1972, 11.

Reno Evening Gazette, "Jacobson Calls Note Foreclosure by Teamsters 'Procedural Move,'" Jan. 25, 1972, 1.

Reno Evening Gazette, "Jacobson Jury Voting Records Given to Lawyer," Jan. 14, 1972, 26.

Reno Evening Gazette, "The Grand Jury: Is the Secrecy Cloak Necessary?" May 12, 1973, 13.

The Daily Review (Hayward), "Tahoe Casino Sale Not Completed," Jan. 19, 1972, 4.

CHAPTER 22: NO OTHER CHOICE

A.L.W., Inc. (dba Kings Castle) Bankruptcy Files, BK-R-72-47; BK-R-95-96, February 1972-September 1975.

Interview of Arthur Selman, April 12, 2016.

Los Angeles Times, "How Tahoe Monarch Lost a Kingdom," Oct. 8, 1972, B1.

Nevada State Journal, "Hundreds Jobless as Kings Castle Operation Stops," Feb. 3, 1972, 1-2.

Nevada State Journal, "Jacobson Fumes at Legal Morass," March 2, 1972, 12.

Nevada State Journal, "Kings Castle Petitions for Bankruptcy," Feb. 5, 1972, 8.

Nevada State Journal, "Teamsters Custodians of Castle," Feb. 3, 1972, 1.

Nevada State Journal, "Washoe's Red Ink Budget?" Oct. 31, 1972, 22.

Press-Telegram (Long Beach), "Tahoe Hotel Halts Wagers, Will Close," Feb. 2, 1972, B-7.

Reno Evening Gazette, "Advance Warning—Shirts Stopped Coming," Feb. 4, 1972, 1-2.

Reno Evening Gazette, "Jacobson Closing Kings Castle," Feb. 2, 1972, 1-2.

Reno Evening Gazette, "Kings Castle Files Petition for Bankruptcy," Feb. 5, 1972, 2.

Reno Evening Gazette, "Nevada's Jobless Rate Rises," March 18, 1972, 2.

Reno Evening Gazette, "Opening a Hotel Was Easy, But Closing It, Well...," Feb. 3, 1972, 1-2.

Reno Evening Gazette, "Reopening Seen for Kings Castle," Feb. 18, 1972, 1-2.

The Fresno Bee, "$23 Million Deal Fails; King's [sic] Castle Will Close," Feb. 3, 1972, A16.

The New York Times, "Casino in Nevada Closes; World Money Crisis Cited," Feb. 6, 1972, 57.

CHAPTER 23: DAMAGE CONTROL

Nevada State Journal, "Ask Name Change," July 2, 1972.

Nevada State Journal, "County Board Wants Poll of Road Name," April 7, 1972.

Nevada State Journal, "Court Studies Jacobson's Petition Plea," April 12, 1973, 9.

Nevada State Journal, "D.A. Seeks Dismissal of Duplicate Indictments Against Jacobson, Bruno," March 10, 1972, 14.

Nevada State Journal, "Jacobson, Bruno Appeal Dismissed," July 20, 1972, 28.

Nevada State Journal, "Jacobson Case Court Hearing Ends Abruptly," March 15, 1972, 1-2.

Nevada State Journal, "Jacobson Charged Again," Feb. 19, 1972, 10.

Nevada State Journal, "Judge Hears Arguments on Jacobson Motion," Aug. 12, 1972, 12.

Nevada State Journal, "Kings Castle Way Draws 'Sentiment,'" Oct. 5, 1972, 22.

Nevada State Journal, "Motion Denied to Quash Kidnaping [sic] Indictment," Feb. 5, 1972, 8.

Nevada State Journal, "'Voice' Asks Kings Castle Way Change," April 4, 1972.

Reno Evening Gazette, "Incline Residents Want Street Name Change, Park," June 6, 1972.

Reno Evening Gazette, "Jacobson-Bruno Hearing Begins," March 14, 1972, 20.

Reno Evening Gazette, "Jacobson, Bruno Kidnap, Coercion Trial Delayed," Sept. 1, 1972, 11.

Reno Evening Gazette, "Jacobson, Bruno Must Stand Trial," March 29, 1972, 19.

Reno Evening Gazette, "Jacobson, Bruno Named in Complaint," Feb. 18, 1972, 1.

Reno Evening Gazette, "Jacobson, Bruno Plead Not Guilty, Trial Date Set," April 14, 1972.

Reno Evening Gazette, "Jacobson, Bruno Request Change of Venue," May 22, 1972, 8.

Reno Evening Gazette, "Jacobson Loses Round in Court," March 10, 1972, 13.

Reno Evening Gazette, "Jacobson Motion Attacks Charges," March 2, 1972, 15.

Reno Evening Gazette, "Judge Denies Jacobson Bail Request," Feb. 29, 1972, 9.

Reno Evening Gazette, "Kings Castle Kidnap Case Figures Arrested," March 4, 1972, 2.

Reno Evening Gazette, "Landucci Relates Threat, Lever to Obtain Benefits," March 22, 1972, 13.

Reno Evening Gazette, "More Testimony on Cheater Trap," March 23, 1972.
Reno Evening Gazette, "Now It's Country Club Drive Again," Aug. 7, 1972.
Reno Evening Gazette, "Street Naming Committee Favors Country Club Drive," July 15, 1972.
Reno Evening Gazette, "Wire Taps Cited at Kings Castle," March 17, 1972, 1-2.
The State of Nevada v. Nathan Stanley Jacobson and Thomas Joseph Bruno, 31775, Feb. 18, 1972.

CHAPTER 24: FINDING A BUYER

Amarillo Globe-Times, "Texas Millionaire Seeking to Buy Casino in Nevada," Oct. 26, 1972, 11.
Nevada State Journal, "Check From Purchaser Prevents Kings Castle Foreclosure Sale," July 8, 1972, 10.
Nevada State Journal, "Kings Castle Put on Auction Block," Aug. 3, 1972, 1.
Nevada State Journal, "Tangled Web of International High Finance," July 31, 1979.
Nevada State Journal, "Teamsters Union Buys Kings Castle," Aug. 4, 1972, 1-2.
Reno Evening Gazette, "Jacobson Expects to Avert Hotel Sale," June 28, 1972, 19.
Reno Evening Gazette, "Jacobson Gets Week to Sell Kings Castle," June 30, 1972, 1-2.
Reno Evening Gazette, "Kings Castle Creditors' Hearing Slated," March 29, 1973, 5.
Reno Evening Gazette, "Kings Castle Creditors Must Agree," March 29, 1972, 3.
Reno Evening Gazette, "Kings Castle Reopening Plan Offered," Feb. 28, 1973, 1-2.
Reno Evening Gazette, "Kings Castle Sale Reported," May 23, 1972, 1.

CHAPTER 25: DESPERATE FOR RESOLUTION

Nevada Gaming Control Board Meeting Minutes, May 16, 1973.
Nevada State Journal, "Final Confirmation of Kings Castle Plan Hinges on Deposit, State Gaming License," April 18, 1973, 12.
Nevada State Journal, "Jacobson Balks at Rules for Kings Castle License," May 23, 1973, 16.
Nevada State Journal, "Jacobson to Sell Castle Interest," May 25, 1973, 1-2.
Nevada State Journal, "Kings Castle Due to Reopen," May 17, 1973, 1-2.
Nevada State Journal, "Kings Castle Re-Opening Plan Offered," April 5, 1973, 5.
Reno Evening Gazette, "Jacobson Agrees to Sell Kings Castle Operation," May 25, 1973.
Reno Evening Gazette, "Jacobson Fails to Modify Castle Rules," May 22, 1973, 17.
Reno Evening Gazette, "Jacobson Loses Gaming Interest," Aug. 24, 1973, 12.
Reno Evening Gazette, "Jacobson's Kings Castle Credit Plan Approved," Aug. 29, 1973, 13.
Reno Evening Gazette, "Kings Castle Operation Approved With Conditions," May 17, 1973, 14.
Reno Evening Gazette, "Kings Castle Reopening Plan Offered," Feb. 28, 1973, 1-2.

CHAPTER 26: ALLEGED MOBSTER INVOLVEMENT

Denton, Sally and Roger Morris. *The Money and The Power: The Making of Las Vegas and Its Hold on America*. New York: Vintage, March 2002. Print.

Gibson, Steve. *The Independent* (Long Beach), "Dope, Explosives in Newport Raid," Feb. 6, 1966.

Holmes Van Tassel, Bethel. *Wood Chips to Game Chips: Casinos and People at North Lake Tahoe.* Sacramento: TCH, 1999. Print.

Interview of Tommy Papagna, March 2, 2018.

Las Vegas Strip History, lvstriphistory.com/ie/hilton70.html.

Las Vegas Sun, "Karamanos Replaces Thompson," Nov. 10, 1976.

Nevada Gaming Commission Meeting Minutes, May 24, 1973.

Nevada Gaming Control Board Meeting Minutes, May 16, 1973.

Nevada State Journal, "Burglars Bind, Gag Janitor," May 20, 1966, 16.

Nevada State Journal, "Group Claims Kings Castle Zone Violation," June 6, 1973, 24.

Nevada State Journal, "No Regrets: Kings Castle Owner Can't Leave Too Soon," May 3, 1973, 20.

Oakland Tribune, "Night Sounds," May 8, 1973, 46.

Reno Evening Gazette, "Kings Castle Sale Talks Announced," Aug. 30, 1973, 21.

Reno Evening Gazette, "May 25 Opening of Kings Castle Planned," May 1, 1973, 11.

The Marion Star, "Mafia Ledger Authenticity Questioned," Aug. 18, 1978.

The Middletown Journal, "2 Convicted, 4 Cleared in Newport Conspiracy," Aug. 7, 1963, 28.

The Palm Beach Post, "Denono's Ledger," Aug. 17, 1978, 13.

CHAPTER 27: PURSUIT OF RECOMPENSE

Divorce Record, Nathan and Sylvia Jacobson, Certificate No. 014030, March 30, 1976.

FBI File on Nathan S. Jacobson.

Jacobson v. Rose, 592 F.2d 515, March 21, 1976; Nov. 29, 1978.

Nathan S. Jacobson, et al. v. Bell Telephone Co. of Nevada, et al., 592 F.2d 515, Nov. 29, 1978.

Nevada State Journal, "A New Twist," July 10, 1976, 14.

Nevada State Journal, "'Charge Your Boss,'" July 14, 1976, 18.

Nevada State Journal, "Class Action: U.S. Judge Rules on Kings Castle Wiretapping Suit," April 12, 1973, 18.

Nevada State Journal, "FBI Agent's Testimony Blocked in Wiretap Trial of State Lawmen," July 9, 1976, 12.

Nevada State Journal, "Nevada Bell Dismissed From Wiretap Case," Aug. 1, 1979.

Nevada State Journal, "Nevada Lawmen Ordered to Pay Damages," July 15, 1976, 1-2.

Nevada State Journal, "Nevada's Lawmen in Court," July 7, 1976, 16.

Nevada State Journal, "Obscene Calls," July 8, 1976, 16.

Nevada State Journal, "Wire Tap Case Headed Toward Trial," June 26, 1976, 18.

Nevada State Journal, "Wiretap Verdict Views Mixed," July 17, 1976.

Reno Evening Gazette, "Ahlswede: Hicks in Wiretapping," April 30, 1974.

Reno Evening Gazette, "Illegal Wire Taps Claimed Against County Officials," May 17, 1972, 13.

Reno Evening Gazette, "Jacobson Loses Wire Tap Suit," April 12, 1973.

Reno Evening Gazette, "Officials Tell of Threats, Obscenity From Jacobson," July 8, 1976.

Reno Evening Gazette, "Rose Violated Wiretap Rules, Defense Claims," June 27, 1973.

Reno Evening Gazette, "Wiretap Case: Nobody Happy," July 16, 1976.

CHAPTER 28: INNOCENT OR GUILTY?

Nathan Stanley Jacobson and Thomas Joseph Bruno v. The State of Nevada, No. 7113, 510 P.2d 856, May 30, 1973; June 13, 1973.

Nevada Gaming Control Board Meeting Minutes, May 16, 1973.

Nevada State Journal, "Court Receives Jacobson Poll," July 17, 1973, 12.

Nevada State Journal, "Elko Selects Police Chief," Oct. 26, 1975, 6.

Nevada State Journal, "Ex-Kings Castle Boss Claims Gun Forced False Confession," June 22, 1973, 14.

Nevada State Journal, "Former Gaming Agent: Incident at Hotel Worried Castle Official," July 7, 1973, 14.

Nevada State Journal, "Four Inmates Granted Parole," May 11, 1966, 12.

Nevada State Journal, "'Hollow Victory' for Acquitted Nate Jacobson," July 21, 1973, 1-2.

Nevada State Journal, "Jacobson Faces Criminal Trial—Supreme Court," May 31, 1973, 1-2.

Nevada State Journal, "Jacobson Has 'Gut' Feeling on Fair Trial," June 21, 1973, 1-2.

Nevada State Journal, "Jacobson Loses Trial Delay Bid," June 7, 1973, 12.

Nevada State Journal, "Jacobson Polls Area to Find His Own Image," June 23, 1973, 1-2.

Nevada State Journal, "Jacobson Trial," June 27, 1973, 18.

Nevada State Journal, "Jury Deliberates Kidnaping [sic] Case," July 20, 1973, 2.

Nevada State Journal, "Jury Picked in Jacobson, Bruno Trial," June 20, 1973, 16.

Nevada State Journal, "Kidnaping [sic] Denied by Jacobson," July 17, 1973, 12.

Nevada State Journal, "No Hatred," June 23, 1973, 14.

Nevada State Journal, "Political Front—In Nevada," June 24, 1973.

Nevada State Journal, "Rebuttal: Earlier Jacobson Trial Witnesses Back on Stand," July 18, 1973.

Nevada State Journal, "Selection of Jacobson Jury Starts," June 18, 1973, 12.

Nevada State Journal, "She Thought They Wanted Husband Dead," July 10, 1973, 12.

Nevada State Journal, "Supreme Court Denies Trial Delay Bid," June 14, 1973, 2.

Nevada State Journal, "Try, Try Again: State Opens Fourth Trial in Sparks Burglary Case," June 10, 1976, 8.

Nevada State Journal, "Witness Sought in Jacobson Trial," July 13, 1973, 14.

Reno Evening Gazette, "Both Sides Rest Cases in Jacobson, Bruno Trial," July 18, 1973, 13.

Reno Evening Gazette, "Hannifin: Gaming Board Decisions Not Whims," July 21, 1973, 1-2.

Reno Evening Gazette, "Jacobson, Bruno Penalty Possibilities Given Jury," July 19, 1973, 21.

Reno Evening Gazette, "Jacobson: Didn't Believe Witch-Burning Still Existed," July 17, 1973, 13.

Reno Evening Gazette, "Jacobson Mystery Witness Found," July 13, 1973, 17.

Reno Evening Gazette, "Jacobson's 'Bodyguard' Testifies After Four Weeks," July 14, 1973, 2.

Reno Evening Gazette, "Jacobson Takes Stand in Kidnap Case Trial," July 16, 1973, 13.

Reno Evening Gazette, "Jacobson Trial Cost Him 'Small Fortune,'" July 25, 1973, 1-2.

Reno Evening Gazette, "Jacobson 'Very Appreciative' of Jury Verdict," July 20, 1973, 1-2.

Reno Evening Gazette, "Jacobson Wiretap Ruled Out," Sept. 15, 1972, 13.

Reno Evening Gazette, "Keno Writer Claims Landucci Plotted Cheat," July 10, 1973, 15.
Reno Evening Gazette, "Police, Deputies Team to Trap Burglary Suspect," April 4, 1964, 7.
Reno Evening Gazette, "Raggio, Echeverria, Others Sued for $50 Million," June 18, 1977, 13.

CHAPTER 29: DEALING WITH DEBTS

Hevener, Phil. *Las Vegas Sun*, "State Fines Argent Corp.; Revokes Game License," Aug. 24, 1979.
Interview of Tommy Papagna, March 2, 2018.
Los Angeles Times, "Mafia Target?: Dark Threat Clouds Life of Opulence," Sept. 13, 1973, B1.
Nathan Jacobson v. Tahoe Regional Planning Agency, 566 F.2d 1353, Aug. 5, 1977.
Nevada State Journal, "$20 Million Bid for Kings Castle," Sept. 13, 1973, 24,
Nevada State Journal, "Californian Asks to Buy Kings Castle," Sept. 12, 1973, 5.
Nevada State Journal, "Center Stage," Oct. 12, 1973, Entertainment.
Nevada State Journal, "Former Kings Castle Boss Names Tahoe Group in Suit," Oct. 17, 1973.
Nevada State Journal, "Gaming Board Rejects Jacobson Contract Plan," Aug. 25, 1973, 10.
Nevada State Journal, "Landmark: 'Immunity' Ruling Sends Ripples Across Tahoe," Aug. 9, 1977, 1-2.
Nevada State Journal, "No Money for Casino Condemnation," Aug. 16, 1979.
Pileggi, Nicholas. *Casino: Love and Honor in Las Vegas*. New York: Pocket Books, June 2011. Print.
Reno Evening Gazette, "Jacobson Bankruptcy Plan Heard," Aug. 28, 1973, 13.
Reno Evening Gazette, "Jacobson Loses Gaming Interest," Aug. 24, 1973, 12.
Reno Evening Gazette, "Jacobson's Kings Castle Creditor Plan Approved," Aug. 29, 1973, 13.
Reno Evening Gazette, "Kings Castle Cuts Power Use 50 Per Cent [sic]," Nov. 24, 1973.
Reno Evening Gazette, "Kings Castle Executive Plans to Leave," Sept. 29, 1973.
Reno Evening Gazette, "Kings Castle Sale Talks Announced," Aug. 30, 1973.
Reno Evening Gazette, "Landmark Decision Pondered at Tahoe," Aug. 9, 1977.
Reno Evening Gazette, "Tahoe Suits Rejected," Jan. 11, 1975, 7.
Reno Gazette-Journal, "Regent Committed Suicide, Officials Say," June 15, 1989.
The Times (San Mateo), "Tahoe Lawsuits Dismissed," Jan. 11, 1975, 10.

CHAPTER 30: ANOTHER ROUGH PATCH

Interview of Tommy Papagna, March 2, 2018.
Nevada State Journal, "Casino Property Put in Hands of Creditors' Agent," Feb. 1, 1974.
Nevada State Journal, "'Castle' for Sale at Tahoe," Feb. 20, 1974, 16.
Nevada State Journal, "Gambling's Come a Long Way in Nevada," March 14, 1974.
Nevada State Journal, "Kings Castle Closes Casino; Sale Hinted," Jan. 29, 1974.
Nevada State Journal, "Kings Castle Might Go Back to Teamsters," Jan. 29, 1974.
Nevada State Journal, "Tahoe Suit Dismissed," Nov. 5, 1977, 14.
News-Chronicle (Vallejo), "Incline Village Owner to Sell," Feb. 20, 1974, 8.
Oakland Tribune, Bill Fiset's column, Jan. 11, 1974.

Reno Evening Gazette, "Bid Lost to Delay Personal Property Sale," March 19, 1974.
Reno Evening Gazette, "Castle's Gaming Closed," Jan. 28, 1974.
Reno Evening Gazette, "Castle Stays Open," Feb. 1, 1974.
Reno Evening Gazette, "Jacobson Appeal Dismissed," July 27, 1974.
Reno Evening Gazette, "Kings Castle Offers All Hotel Services," March 5, 1974.
Reno Evening Gazette, "Teamsters Ruling Upheld," May 3, 1977.
Vallejo Times-Herald, It's Rich—"Scenic Setting," Jan. 18, 1974, 1-2.

CHAPTER 31: VARIOUS FINALITIES

A.L.W., Inc. (dba Kings Castle) Bankruptcy Files, BK-R-72-47; BK-R-95-96, February 1972-September 1975.
Elsinore Shore Associates Bankruptcy, 91 B.R. 238, March 24, 1988.
FBI File on Nathan S. Jacobson.
Holmes Van Tassel, Bethel. *Wood Chips to Game Chips: Casinos and People at North Lake Tahoe*. Sacramento: TCH, 1999. Print.
Hood, Jeanne. *Whatever Will Help!: A Woman's Rise to the Top in the Gaming Industry*, University of Nevada Oral History Program, 83-85.
Jacobson v. Hannifin, 627 F.2d 177, May 13, 1980; Sept. 5, 1980.
Las Vegas Sun, "Glick Denies Link With Mob, Murder," Nov. 25, 1975.
Los Angeles Times, "Kings Castle Hotel Sold," Feb. 2, 1975, K9.
Los Angeles Times, "Mafia Target?: Dark Threat Clouds Life of Opulence," March 26, 1984.
Los Angeles Times, "Spain Lets The Chips Fall," Feb. 12, 1978, 82.
Merriam-Webster, "Camelot," merriam-webster.com.
Nevada Gaming Commission Meeting Minutes, April 24, 1975; May 22, 1975.
Nevada Gaming Control Board Records, April 16, 1975; May 14, 1975.
Nevada State Journal, "Aladdin Deal Fails," Aug. 12, 1980.
Nevada State Journal, "Appeals Court Rules in State's Favor," Sept. 18, 1980.
Nevada State Journal, "Details of $155 Million Hotel-Casino Unveiled," July 17, 1980.
Nevada State Journal, "Hyatt Lake Tahoe Hotel," May 25, 1975.
Nevada State Journal, "Hyatt Makes Move for Kings Castle," Feb. 28, 1975, 19.
Nevada State Journal, "Jacobson Enters Aladdin Picture," July 31, 1980.
Nevada State Journal, "Judge Rejects Jacobson Suit on Gaming License," Aug. 23, 1975, 14.
Oakland Tribune, Bill Fiset's column, July 6, 1975.
Oakland Tribune, "Neil Sedaka Makes Lake Tahoe Debut," June 29, 1975, 23E.
Oakland Tribune, "The Social Circle," April 6, 1975, 41; June 27, 1975.
Pileggi, Nicholas, *Casino: Love and Honor in Las Vegas*. New York: Pocket Books, June 2011.
Reno Evening Gazette, "Details of $155 Million Hotel-Casino Unveiled," July 17, 1980.
Reno Evening Gazette, "Hyatt Buys Kings Castle," Jan. 27, 1975, 1.
Reno Evening Gazette, "Judge Dismisses Gaming Suit," Dec. 23, 1977, 24.
Reno Evening Gazette, "List Hails Gaming Ruling," Dec. 24, 1977, 21.
Reno Evening Gazette, "Saudis Finance Jersey Casino," Oct. 6, 1980.
Reno Evening Gazette, "Senators Take Balloon Ride at Tahoe," June 28, 1975, 11.
Reno Gazette-Journal, "Ex-Incline Casino Operator Part of Merger Deal," Jan. 5, 1984.
The Baltimore Sun, "In Memoriam—Jacobson," July 29, 1987, 43.
The Desert Sun, "Casino Boss Killed," May 13, 1975.

The Miami Herald, "Miami Area Deaths," July 30, 1987, 4D.

The New York Times, "American Leisure Forms New Unit," July 29, 1982, D4.

The New York Times, "Costa del Sol's Tourism Hopes Are Riding on Legalized Gambling," April 13, 1977, 2.

The New York Times, "Midland Resources," March 13, 1984.

The New York Times, "South Africans Drop Casino Plans," June 16, 1983, B2.

The Times (San Mateo), "Las Vegas Casino Boss Shot," May 13, 1975.

The Wall Street Journal, "American Midland's Jacobson Quits Unit," April 9, 1985, Eastern Edition, 1.

OTHER SOURCES

Fuller, Harvey J. *Index of Nevada Gambling Establishments, 1931-1981*. Minden, Nev.: The Coin Company, 2008. Print.

Gaming.nv.gov.

Kling, Dwayne. *The Rise of the Biggest Little City: An Encyclopedic History of Reno Gaming, 1931-1981*. Reno: University of Nevada Press, 2000. Print.

Nevada Revised Statutes, Chapter 463—Licensing and Control of Gaming, leg.state.nv.us.

235

237

239

Doresa Banning is a 20-year freelance journalist in Reno, Nevada and an author who writes about gambling history and true crime.

In her *It Really Happened!* blog, she tells casino-related stories of the past with an emphasis on Nevada, and she hosts the website, gambling-history.com.

Doresa's next project, *The Ends*, is slated for publication in 2020. It's the compelling, true story of two young lovebirds' spate of felonious crimes in 1947 and their legal journey and life afterward.

In her free time, albeit limited, Doresa loves to read, solve crossword puzzles (in pencil), jog, root for the (really San Diego) Chargers and watch crime shows.

For more information about her, visit doresabanning.com. Feel free to connect with her there, at db@doresabanning.com or through Facebook or LinkedIn.